a new
HOPE

ROBYN CARR

a new HOPE

MIRA®

Car

MIRA

Recycling programs
for this product may
not exist in your area.

ISBN-13: 978-0-7783-1736-4

A New Hope

For questions and comments about the quality of this book, please contact us at CustomerService@Harlequin.com.

www.MIRABooks.com

Printed in U.S.A.

First printing: July 2015
10 9 8 7 6 5 4 3 2 1

a new
HOPE

CHAPTER ONE

The Basque really know how to get married, Ginger Dysart thought. She hadn't attended the wedding ceremony and she'd had doubts about attending this reception, given all the sadness she'd suffered over the past year. Her own marriage had barely begun when it ended in divorce. But she was so glad she'd come to the reception. It was an ethnic extravaganza—the Basque food, the music, the dancing. The bride and groom, Scott and Peyton Grant, had whirled around the dance floor a couple of times, then parted so Scott could dance with his mother and Peyton could dance with her father. And then there was a series of handsome dark-haired men who claimed the bride—brothers, cousins, uncles.

Paco Lacoumette presided over the party with all the aplomb of a king and was clearly in his element. The couples dancing would cease and the Basque men in their traditional dress of white with red vests and caps would take the floor and put on a show to the wild applause of the guests. Then more couples dancing. Even Ginger was dragged from her chair and pulled out to dance, despite her efforts to decline. She danced with men she knew—Cooper, Spencer, Mac, Scott—and men she didn't know, those good-looking, dark Lacoumette relatives. At one point she spied Troy, Grace's boyfriend, who must have just arrived. Grace, Ginger's boss and owner of the flower shop in Thunder Point, thought Troy wasn't going to make it and had been so disappointed, yet there he was, twirling Grace around with almost professional skill. And judging by the glowing look on Grace's face, she was completely thrilled!

Wine flowed, food was constantly replenished, dancing and laughter filled the night. Ginger felt pretty for the first time in so long. She wore a new dress, cut to her slim figure. She'd lost a lot of weight in the past several months; men were looking at her in a way they hadn't before, and she actually enjoyed the feel of their eyes on her. Those lusty, dark-haired Basque men did nothing to conceal their appreciative gazes.

The whole atmosphere was magical—teenagers were dancing or dashing about the grounds and orchard, sneaking behind trees for stolen kisses, children were riding on the shoulders of fathers, grandfathers and uncles, women were clapping in time to the music, laughing, singing, gossiping. Peyton and Scott were in much demand on the dance floor and in between songs many toasts were made. There were far too many Lacoumettes to remember all their names, but they made her feel welcome and appreciated, thanking her repeatedly for helping Grace bring the wedding flowers.

There was one darkly handsome man she'd noticed right away because he was the only one who seemed sulky and unhappy, and he was the one approaching her now as she stood beside her table. He had the swarthy good looks and fierce eyes of a pirate or maybe a serial killer. And with such precision timing, he had singled her out while everyone else from her table was dancing.

"Hey, pretty lady," he said with a smile that was off-kilter. His words were slurred. That would at least partially account for the half-mast eyes and pouting expression—he was obviously drunk. Well, this happened at weddings with great regularity, especially weddings where the wine flowed so liberally.

"Time for a dance!" he said.

"Thank you, but I'm going to sit this one out," she replied.

"Hmm," he said, stroking his chin. "Then we should go straight to the hayloft!"

She was appalled. But she remained composed and confident. "I'm sitting that out, as well."

"No, come with me," he said. "You and me—let's do this." And then he reached for her. And grabbed her right breast.

She shrieked, shoved him away. His feet got tangled, he fell backward over a chair and went down, hitting his head on the way. And there he lay, motionless and unconscious.

"Help," she said. Then louder. *"Help!"*

She got far more attention than she wanted or expected. And of course, there were the questions. *What happened? Are you hurt? Did he pass out? Is he dead?*

"He grabbed at me," she said, waving a hand over the area of her breast without pointing or saying it. "I shoved him away and he fell and... I think he might've hit his head on the table."

There he lay in a heap, on his back, his legs twisted awkwardly.

In just seconds Peyton and Scott were there, Scott crouching and lifting the man's eyelids, looking at his pupils. "Well, they're equal, but damn...they're big. Does he take anything?" he asked his bride.

"Yes, wine," Peyton said. "He killed a full skin before the dancing."

Then Paco was pushing his way through the crowd, looking down. "I knew it would come to this," he said. "There was no slowing him down."

"I think we should call 911, get a head CT, make sure he didn't crack his skull," Scott said.

"His head is made of wood," Paco said. "It would serve him right to be carried out of his sister's wedding on one of those backboard things and spend the night in a hospital." Paco reached for the ice bucket on the table. Everyone scooted back immediately, as if they knew what was coming. Peyton pulled Scott away while Paco took a bottle of white wine out of the bucket, put it on the table and doused the man with the ice water.

He sputtered and coughed and sat up.

"See what I'm telling you? Wood. George! Sal! Mikie! Get Matthew from your sister's wedding! Hide his keys!" The men moved into action immediately. Paco looked at Ginger and said, "There's always one. I apologize." Then he took in the gathering crowd and clapped. "I think it's time I dance with my wife!"

Grace arrived, pushing her way through the crowd. "Ginger! Is everything all right?"

"I'm not sure," she said, looking as the men were leaving—three of them walking steadily and one weaving dangerously.

"My brother, Matt," Peyton said. "He has issues. Divorce issues. He was divorced a little over a year ago but it appears he's still very bitter. Weddings don't seem to bring out the best in him. He didn't hurt you, did he?"

"He didn't quite connect," Ginger said. "I was about to say good-night anyway. I'm going back to my folks' house in Portland for the night."

"I might kill Matt," Peyton said.

"Just enjoy the rest of your party," Ginger said. "No harm done. To me, anyway. God, I hope I didn't hurt him."

"You heard my father—his head is made of wood."

"I'll call you in the morning," Grace said. "Troy had some car trouble on the way up here and we'll have to see where that stands in the morning and figure out how we're all getting home. I've got the van, you take your father's car back to him."

Ginger turned to Peyton. "It was a wonderful reception. You look ravishing. And I was just thinking, the Basque people really know how to get married."

Ginger's parents, Dick and Sue, had waited up. That was definite evidence as to how concerned they were about her—they stayed up past ten when their usual bedtime was before nine. And when she walked in the front door, looking perfectly alive, they both stood from their recliners. They looked at her expectantly.

"Did you have a good time?" Sue asked hesitantly.

"I had a lovely time," she said. "The flowers were beautiful, the wedding party was gorgeous and the party was like something out of a fairy tale. You wouldn't believe the fun of Basque dancing and music! And the food? Oh, my God, the food was just amazing. And I'm exhausted—I'm going straight to bed."

"Are you…comfortable in your room, Ginger?" Sue asked.

"Yes, of course. And thank you for making it so nice for me."

She kissed them both on their cheeks and went upstairs. Upstairs to the large bedroom and small adjacent nursery that had been renovated especially for her when she'd come home to her parents', pregnant and alone; to the room where she had cared for her little son for the four short months of his life.

Ginger had been staying with her father's cousin Ray Anne in Thunder Point for the last month. It was through Ray Anne that she'd gotten the job in Grace's flower shop, a job that was really saving her life, hour by hour. Before she came back to Portland with Grace for this wedding and weekend visit, Ray Anne had called Sue and asked her to pack up all those baby things that Ginger had been looking at since his death over nine months ago. The crib and mobile had been taken down, the clothes removed from the drawers, boxed up and stored, the necessary accoutrements like the car seat, bouncy chair, baby bean bag, bath items and changing table were all gone. She didn't think her parents had given them away, but they were out of sight. Probably stored in the attic or garage. There was only one framed picture of Ginger and Josh that she found in the top drawer.

She took it out, put it on the bedside table and changed into her pajamas.

When her father had suggested, rather emotionally, that Ginger go to Thunder Point and stay with Ray Anne for at least a few weeks, she had not wanted any part of it. But it was plain to see her parents needed a break from her grief. Now she was so glad she had gone. When she was in Thunder Point, she at least had the illusion of getting on with her life. She had a new, improved appearance, at Ray Anne's insistence. She had that lovely little job in the flower shop. She had slept well and had an appetite again. Oh, she'd longed for little Josh, like always. But she was marching on.

She crawled into the bed at her parents' house, turned the picture of herself and her baby toward her, left the light on so she could see it and sobbed.

Troy Headly had missed the Lacoumette-Grant wedding ceremony and barely made it to the reception. His Jeep had broken down by the side of the road and AAA had to send a tow truck. At least the tow-truck driver had been willing to drop him off at the Lacoumette farm where the festivities were held, but it left him and Grace with her flower-delivery van to drive to a hotel in Portland. They left the valet to park the flower van so they could check in. The day was not going the way he'd hoped it would.

He had proposed, however. In the pear grove at the farm while the revelers had partied under a big tent beside the grove. And Grace had said yes.

When he finally had her alone in the hotel room, he kissed her senseless. "Do you really like the ring, Gracie? Because we could go together to the jeweler and get a better one..."

"You're not taking my ring!" she said emphatically. She placed it on her finger. "You picked it out yourself and I love it! I love you! I couldn't wear it tonight and draw attention to myself like that—it's Peyton's day. But the second we get home, I'm going to be showing everyone." Then she was the one who grew serious. "Are you sure about this, Troy? Because you didn't want a wife so soon..."

He laughed and whirled her around and swept her onto the bed. He pulled off her pumps and ran a hand up her thigh. "I didn't want children so soon, either, but guess what? We're starting right now." He covered her flat belly with his big hand. "We're going to have to get better at this birth-control thing or we'll end up with twenty."

"I don't think there's time for twenty," she said.

"Gracie," he said, his hand roaming, his voice a little breathless. "Is this a garter belt?"

She shrugged. "I think you bring out the slutty underwear in me."

"Oh, honey, you plan to drug me with sex and get at least ten babies out of me before I know what's hit me. Is that right? Huh? When are we getting married?"

"We have a little time. Maybe we should elope before my mother tries to plan a coronation from her sickbed."

"I don't want to elope," he said. "I want to party! Please, Gracie, take off this dress! Let's do it, then we can argue about the wedding. I always get my way after I make you feel good." He kissed her. "I know *exactly* how to get my way." He pulled down the zipper on the back of her dress and helped her shimmy out of it. "God," he said. "I'm going to make you *very* happy."

George Lacoumette and his wife, Lori, insisted on taking Matt to the hospital…with a bucket in his lap. They didn't really think he'd cracked his head open, they explained. They thought the likelihood of concussion was lower than alcohol poisoning. But there would be nothing as awkward as the untimely death of a member of the wedding party. In an effort to protect Peyton's happy memories of her special day, they forced Matt into their car and then into the emergency room.

Matt was pissed as hell. He knew he'd been out of line and regretted it, but he wanted to be taken home. He still lived in the apartment he'd shared with his ex-wife, Natalie, a woman he still loved, except that he hated her. It was Natalie's fault that he'd gotten smashed at the wedding. They'd been married on the farm and he was still in a state of anger and depression over the divorce, which had come much too soon after the wedding.

The ER doctor started an IV, then left the room as a bag of fluid ran into Matt. He sobered up fast.

The doctor returned after a while.

"Wow," Matt said. "I only see one of you!"

"Welcome back." The doctor laughed.

"I didn't know you could do that! One IV, instant sobriety! Instant shame!"

"Yeah, it's magic. So, you have a headache?"

"Right here," Matt said, pointing to the back of his head. "Am I injured?"

"Possible liver damage, but we didn't see any blood or bumps. Let's check the eyes." The doctor waved a light across his pupils. "I'm going to go out on a limb here and suggest you bumped your head on the way to passing out. So—this a problem for you?"

"Hitting my head and passing out?" he asked.

"No, drinking like a pig and falling down," the doctor clarified. "Are you an alcoholic?"

"Ah, shit." He rubbed his head. "I'm divorced. I got married in that same orchard a couple of years ago. It didn't last long. The marriage, that is. It was kind of…what's the word?"

"Painful? Embarrassing? Grievous? Lonely? Regrettable?" the doctor tried.

"Yeah, those are the words. I might've overdone it a little tonight."

"So you're not adjusting well?" he asked.

"My brothers and sisters have taken to calling me Mad Matt. Does that tell you anything?"

"You might want to consider some counseling. Before you really hurt yourself."

"Doc, I appreciate your help, but if there's one thing I don't ever want to talk about it's my ex-wife and my divorce."

"Brother, there is life after divorce. I am living proof."

"You?"

"Me. According to my ex-wife I keep lousy hours, I'm inattentive off the job, I don't pitch in, I'm snarky and critical, a tightwad, insensitive, selfish, many negative things. The list is long."

"I didn't think anyone divorced a doctor," Matt said, sounding surprised.

"The divorce rate among doctors is high," he said. "I'm going to let you go home. If you have any problems or questions, call me. Don't sit and wonder if you're okay, just call me. And be done drinking for the day."

"Funny," Matt said, "the divorce rate among farmers is low. Yet…"

"Even if you were given a reason, that's just one opinion," the doctor said. "You going to be okay now?"

"Yeah," he said, sitting up. "I have to come up with a good apology for my sister, the bride. I don't think I'll see her tomorrow. There's the honeymoon and everything." And she wasn't the only one he should apologize to, but that other woman, whose name he never got, was long gone.

"Look, kid, you're young," the doctor said. "You'll get past this divorce thing. It happens to the best of us. The next time you'll be wiser and more patient about everything."

"Next time?" Matt asked. "You're kidding me, right?"

The doctor, who wasn't that much older than Matt, clapped a hand on his back and said, "You're like looking in an old mirror."

Matt had fallen in love with Natalie instantly. True, he'd been all of twenty-five, but if that hadn't been love he'd sure like to know what it was.

At the time he was giving a couple of lectures at Portland

State; his master's degree was in biology. His undergrad degree was in plant biology, he had minored in agricultural science and he was a farmer. He was also a visiting professor, which had made his father laugh. But Matt knew a lot about farming, pesticides, organic farming, water runoff, landscape contouring, animal husbandry, you name it. In pursuit of his degrees he'd studied agriculture, environmental science, and the care and breeding of animals, and that made him a valuable resource. It didn't hurt that his father was the owner of one of the most prosperous farms in the state, with two of his sons, Matt and George, being associates.

And Natalie had been a biology department secretary, also twenty-five, with the longest legs he had ever seen.

She was so pretty and fun-loving and dating her had been sheer bliss. He hadn't rushed into anything, despite that ER doctor's assumptions. They went out for months before they moved in together. She wasn't Basque, which suited him fine. She was of Swedish descent, with a few other European countries in the mix. She was very polite to his family but made it no secret, from their first date, she was never going to be a farm wife. He had no quarrel with that, either. He wasn't looking for a farm wife, just as his sisters hadn't been looking to marry farmers. She didn't want a slew of children. He was okay with that, but he wanted a couple of kids and so had she. *Later,* she'd said. No hurry.

Matt loved the farm. But in order to commit to a relationship, one makes compromises. He and Natalie didn't have to live on the farm. They'd build a house closer to the city, when they could afford it. He commuted from their small apartment near Portland and spent the occasional night on the farm when it was a real busy time—planting, harvesting or lambing. George had the sheep, but Matt was always there to help, too—with the breeding, shearing, lambing, inoculations, docking and castrating. Matt wouldn't marry Natalie until it was clear—he wasn't giving up the farm.

Knowing that, Natalie still wanted to get married. She chose the orchard as the venue—but the reception was held in a large hall in Portland. When a bee stung her forehead during the vows, causing a very large red bump, it should have been an omen. But even with that big red bump the size of a quarter right in the middle of her forehead, the wedding was a success. The wedding pictures had to be doctored, but they were beautiful. If you could predict the success of the marriage by the wedding, they should have made it fifty years. Not only were all the Basque relatives present but also every friend and family member Natalie had ever known.

Very soon after the wedding, before the last thank-you note had been written, Natalie was already growing unhappy. She didn't like his hours or the dirt under his nails or those big family dinners on the farm with all the noise and chaos. Being married to a farmer, even a commuting farmer, was trying and boring for her. He was up at 4:00 a.m. and home, exhausted and hungry, at five, and in bed by eight. She'd rather have brunch at the Hotel Monaco than dinner with the Lacoumette clan. She liked clubbing and dancing. And she'd appreciate it if he could stay awake through one movie!

Natalie had many suggestions for alternate careers. Matt could get his PhD and teach full-time, even head a department. He could consult for companies. He could go to medical school; his degree was a premed qualifier. Or he could go to work for one of the big food companies, like Harry & David. He'd be president in no time!

As for Natalie, she was only working at the college to supplement her income, most of which she spent on clothes, while she built her modeling career. It was important for a model to look good and she did. Well, she definitely had the body for it—tall and lean and beautiful. She'd had a few modeling jobs, but that career choice wasn't exactly taking off for her and she was already aging out of it. Matt tried to be supportive even though he thought her expectations were unreasonable if not delusional.

Thus, they argued quite a bit. Every day, in fact. A few times he'd stormed out and gone back to the farm for the night.

Though annoyed by the fighting, he tried not to take it too seriously. Sometimes he just laughed and kissed her ear. "I'll try to get all the dirt out from under my nails before I come home, babe." He encouraged her to do what she wanted and he would follow his dream and they could meet in the middle. He supported them and she spent her money on herself, which was perfectly fine with him. He just wished she could be more agreeable. He wasn't sure what more he could do.

Everyone in his family had an opinion about his disintegrating marriage. *There's a period of adjustment,* his mother had said. *Women have to think they're getting their way, at least most of the time*, George had said. *You're both young and need to mature*, Lori had said. *You have to talk to the priest*, Ginny had said. *You worked out these details before the wedding*, Paco had said. *Tell her a deal's a deal!*

But it all unraveled. The fighting escalated; cruel and terrible things were said and done. There were tears and the sounds of hearts breaking. They didn't make it a year. Both of them were in a great deal of pain with a complete inability to find any more compromises or solutions and, ultimately, an inability to forgive and repair the damage.

Matt spent many nights on the sofa while Natalie sobbed and raged. She wanted him to understand she felt trapped. She didn't want to be stuck in a small apartment with a bunch of kids, held captive in a life that she didn't sign on for, no nightlife, no romance, in-laws who treated her like an outsider—like a ridiculous child because she dressed nicely rather than in jeans and rubber boots. His work at Lacoumette Farms wasn't a job, it was a life sentence! She never saw him, they argued but never talked like they used to and he never saw the need to court her anymore.

Then one fateful morning when Matt could go no further, he got up at his usual 4:00 a.m. and left her a note.

I'll be at the farm if you have an emergency and need me. I'll stay there until you move out. Please let me know when that will happen. Or, if you want the apartment, you can have it and I will live at the farm. It's over.

CHAPTER TWO

The flower shop was a safe haven for Ginger. She couldn't possibly have handpicked a better place to rejoin the human race even though she found herself surrounded by pregnant women. She would have expected to be envious or frightened for them or thrown into worse depression over losing her own precious son. But strangely, it felt like exactly the right place for her, among this group of women. It allowed her to finally talk about her own pregnancy and childbirth, both of which were wonderful experiences. In fact, she had been so healthy and energetic, her son so perfect, he should be toddling around now, not gone.

Truthfully, she was a *little* envious. The caveat was she probably would never have the courage to try for another baby, even if she had the chance.

Talking with Peyton was particularly encouraging, however. Her medical training emphasized what Ginger had learned from the doctors and in her own reading—she had done nothing wrong. SIDS was extremely rare, one of those unpredictable flukes that was not likely to ever happen again in her family.

"As if I'd ever be brave enough to risk it by having another child," Ginger said.

"I can't imagine how fearful that concept must be," Peyton said. "But the next time you're blessed, your circumstances will be very different. You'll have a lot more support. Not to mention close medical supervision. Just getting over this one is a big enough job for right now."

And that's what she was finally doing, one day at a time. And in the best possible place—in a quiet shop that did brisk business but was not crowded with people all day. She was becoming skilled at building and even creating the arrangements that Grace sold and those hours she spent by herself in the back room with the flowers were important to her healing. She was productive and she could think, but she didn't think too much because Thunder Point was a town bristling with friendly people. Had she come here on her own, she might've remained a stranger for a long time, but she was living with Ray Anne. Everyone knew Ray Anne. And since Ray Anne had told her friends about Ginger's circumstances, she had frequent company. People would drop by the shop to chat, stop her on the street or in the diner to visit a little; they'd include her in plans, or sometimes Ray Anne would invite a small group of women over to the house. Rather than feeling self-conscious and marked as the one whose husband left and baby died, she had an almost instant sense of belonging. There was abundant nurturing.

And she was needed. Boy, was she needed! Grace spent every morning in the shop, usually starting early. But in the afternoons she had other tasks. She was trying to get the house out on the beach ready for her mother. She'd bought the house from Cooper—it was one of three spec houses he'd built and it was perfect for her needs. Grace's mother had ALS and was using a wheelchair most of the time now. Grace wanted her nearby—it was uncertain how much time the incurable condition would give her.

Grace made daily runs to the house to prod the workers and spent the rest of the time rounding up furnishings. Almost every day after school and on weekends, her fiancé, Troy, was pitching in at the house, trying to finish up. In what Ginger learned was typical of Thunder Point, Troy's friends were always lending a hand. Together the newly engaged couple put up drywall, textured, sanded, installed molding and painted, trying to get the entire house done before Winnie arrived, or at least to leave just a few decorating details on the upper and lower floors. Troy and Grace planned to move into the lower level because between the two of them and their tiny apartments, there was no space for a baby. The lower floor with two bedrooms, a large bathroom and a game room was perfect for them.

"Yes, it seems like half the town is pregnant, though it's only the three of them—Grace, Peyton and Iris," Ginger told her mother during one of their phone calls. "In fact, their due dates are so close together it makes one wonder if there was a blackout or bad storm during one particular week in early April."

"Maybe it was just spring," Sue said.

It was a beautiful spring. There was something about the feeling of rebirth that lent itself to Ginger's desire for a fresh start, a new beginning. And one thing she now knew for certain, she couldn't make it in that bedroom in her parents' house where she had lived when her baby died. Just that brief visit when she went with Grace to attend Peyton's wedding had made it glaringly obvious. It was time for her to move on.

She hoped Ray Anne wasn't feeling crowded in her small house. Given a little more time to get her finances in order she'd look around for an apartment or something. The woman never complained and seemed to genuinely enjoy Ginger's company, but Ray Anne had Al, her boyfriend, and Al had three foster sons at home. She was aware that time alone for the two of them was hard to find since Ginger had come to town.

Late afternoon was Ginger's favorite time, now that the days were longer and the weather milder. The middle of May was kind to the oceanside residents. Storms blew up at night sometimes but the afternoons were generally warm and sunny. Wild-flowers bloomed on the hillsides that framed the town and bay. When Ginger was pulling in the shop's sidewalk displays, people would stop to talk. Sometimes someone would insist on lending a hand. Waylan, a grizzly old coot who owned the bar across the street, had taken to her and she believed he watched for her to start her closing-time ritual so he could at least come pass the time. Al seemed to be mysteriously available as well, right when a strong arm would come in handy. Lou Metcalf often stopped by before heading out of town after her day teaching at the middle school. Lou was a close friend of Ray Anne's and had twice invited Ginger for a cup of coffee at the diner. And it was usually right about the time Ray Anne was quitting for the day and would drive that little BMW of hers to the flower shop to talk about dinner. Would they stay in, just the two of them? Go out? Get something from Carrie? Cook? Have Al to dinner? Should it be every man for himself tonight?

But as she pulled in the big wooden Mother's Day tulip, she saw a man walking down the street who looked vaguely familiar. Her brow wrinkled as she studied him. Where had she seen him? He was tall and handsome, she could see that much from a block away. Black hair, broad shoulders, jeans and boots, the common wardrobe around town, but a crisply pressed cotton shirt, sleeves rolled up to expose strong forearms and big hands. As he got closer she could see the jeans were in very well-preserved condition—this guy had not just stepped off a fishing boat. His hair, brows and eyes were black and he sported a slight, whiskery beard, a day or two's worth. The moment she found herself thinking he was heart-stoppingly sexy in a very exotic way she also realized who he was. *Oh, my God, it's Peyton's brother!* By then he was upon her and gave her a slightly shy but brilliant smile. Complete with dimples.

He nodded his head, almost a bow. "Miss Dysart… Ginger… I came to apologize."

She actually took a step back. "Um. Okay," she said a little nervously. "You came all the way from Portland?"

"I came to see my sister," he said. "And to apologize to you. To explain. I can explain."

"Water over the dam," she said. "You don't have to explain…"

"I was drunk," he said, as if he hadn't heard her. "Stinko. I don't get drunk and I don't like drunks. I got married in that same orchard a while ago and the marriage didn't take. I've been divorced over a year and it was bitter. I'm either going to stop going to those weddings or stop drinking. But I guess all the Lacoumettes are married now. If they have better luck than I did, we should be all right."

"I'm sure Peyton understood," she said.

He gave a bark of laughter. "She's my sister. She's going to make me pay for a long time. I didn't hurt you or anything, did I? Because I remember reaching for you. I think I was going to drag you onto the dance floor. I'm a clod."

"You groped me," she said. "You said your intentions were to drag me to the hayloft but you missed my arm and got my…" She stopped. But he understood.

"Oh, Jesus," he said, hanging his head slightly. "What an ass."

"No damage done," she said. "Apology accepted."

"Listen, can I take you to dinner? To make amends?" he asked.

"Not necessary, Matt. It is Matt, right?"

"Matt Lacoumette," he said, sticking out a hand. "I know it's not necessary, but it would make me feel better if I could do something for you. Peyton says you're one of the nicest women in town."

Ginger tilted her head and her eyes rounded in surprise. And right then she heard the beep of Ray Anne's horn as she pulled up in front of the shop.

Ginger still wore her green work apron. Ray Anne stood just outside her closed car door, the motor still running. "Quitting time?" she asked.

"Almost," Ginger said. "Ray Anne, this is Peyton's brother Matt. Matt, this is my dad's cousin Ray Anne. I've been staying with her in Thunder Point."

"It's a pleasure," he said. "I just invited Ginger to dinner and I'd be happy if you joined us."

"Oh, you sweet boy," Ray Anne said. "I just stopped by to tell Ginger I have plans for the evening, so you two go ahead. Ginger, I'll see you a little later, honey." She slipped back into her BMW and disappeared down the street.

Ginger looked back at Matt. "As it happens, it's been a really long day," she said. "I've been thinking about a quiet evening at home tonight."

"I promise not to keep you out late. We can walk down to Cliffhanger's or I can drive. I've only eaten there once before, but it was excellent. And probably the best way to get rid of me is to accept, let me make my amends, and then I'll go back to the farm and leave you alone."

"Matt…"

"I'll behave very well."

"Of course you will, but…"

"I'm kind of a pest until I've had a chance to apologize properly. Because, really—"

"That damn Ray Anne—she doesn't have plans," Ginger blurted. "At least she didn't until you invited her to dinner and then she got an idea that she could be sure I went and I'm really not keen on the idea. And I don't buy that you have to make amends over dinner or you won't sleep at night."

"Okay, you're right. It's not just amends. I really want to convince you I'm not a total asshole. I know how to treat women and I don't do…" He shook his head. "I don't do the things I did. Paco had his ways of training us in manners. In respect. Respect is very important in our family. I was disrespectful to you, to the bride and groom, to everyone. Paco has been reminding me daily."

That made her smile in spite of herself. She raised one brow. "Ice water?"

He grinned. And really, it was a convincing grin. As handsome as he was, it was boyish. "Whatever is at hand," Matt said. "Can I pick you up or would you like to walk down to Cliff's with me?"

"I think I'd like to go home and change. I'm just closing now. Give me an hour? I'll meet you there."

"Can I help you move this stuff inside?" he asked.

"Yes," she said. "Yes, you can."

Matt had pulled that off perfectly while giving the impression dinner had been part of his plan from the start. It hadn't been. The truth was he didn't remember Ginger very well. Big surprise, since he had been completely toasted. All he really remembered was a blonde in a purple dress. In fact, he remembered the dress better than the blonde in it. Then when he saw her in jeans, green florist's apron, simple knit shirt, so pretty, freckled, looking fresh as a schoolgirl, he was stung. He saw that she wasn't really blonde-blonde. There was a little red in that hair streaked with gold and it looked so soft. And those green eyes sparkled in the afternoon sun. She didn't wear much makeup—her cheeks were a peachy pink and her lips shiny. She had a fine arch to her light brows. And green stains on her fingers. At dinner, he would ask what it was like working with flowers.

When he got back to Peyton and Scott's house, Peyton was spreading butter on a French baguette for garlic bread. There was red sauce bubbling on the stove and two empty Ragu jars on the counter. Peyton was not the cook his mother was.

"I'm going out for dinner," he told his sister. "Sorry it's so last-minute—I hope that doesn't spoil everything you have planned."

"Out?" she asked.

"I went to see Ginger. I apologized and I asked her to dinner to make amends. Just here in town. That restaurant at the marina."

"Dinner?" she said.

"I thought it was the polite thing to do."

"Listen, Matt," she said, putting down the spreader. "Go easy on her, okay? She's a sweet girl but she's coming off some hard times. I'm sure she can take care of herself, but I don't think she's ready for a wolf."

"Wolf? Me?"

"Yeah, you," she said. "I know what you've been doing the last year and change. Chasing women, running through them fast, moving at warp speed…"

"That's ridiculous," he said. "I've been getting up at four and having dinner at the farm most nights. Dating hasn't been a priority at all. In fact, I mostly avoid women."

"Whatever," she said, picking up the spreader.

But she was right. That's why he kept the apartment he hated, to have a little privacy. He'd been whoring around since the day his divorce was final and he wasn't sure why. Oh, he had a healthy libido, he knew that. He came by it honestly—his people were like that. But it was possible he was trying to change the taste Natalie left in his mouth. He might also get a little satisfaction from thinking it would make her unhappy if she knew, but then he never prowled around in her territory. Or maybe he just wanted to prove to himself that he could get along fine without a steady relationship because taking a chance on another marriage was out of the question. And sometimes when he had a woman under him, he forgot. After what he'd been through with Natalie, he didn't even feel guilty. He did have the courtesy to warn them, however. He was temporary at best. It was amazing how many women were of a like mind.

"Come on, my hours are too long and dirty for women," he told his sister.

"Right," she said. "Be nice to Ginger or you'll be answering to me."

"You don't want to be answering to her," Scott said from somewhere. "She's relentless. She forgets nothing!"

Matt looked around. "Where is he?"

"Under the table," she said. "In the fort."

He heard giggling, and Matt went to the dining room table, which was covered with blankets. He pulled aside the flap and there were Scott and his kids, Will and Jenny. "You are a strange, strange man. Aren't you a little big for this?"

"We're all getting a little big for this," Scott said.

"Come on, you guys," Peyton said. "I told you to put the fort away so we can eat at the table."

"I'm not leaving for a little while. Want me to make you some bruschetta?" Matt asked.

She smiled. "That would be nice. You can have half of this baguette."

It was his peace offering to Peyton, his favorite sister, and he had four to choose from. Matt didn't need to be reminded that no one got away with anything with Peyton, nor that she was relentless and had the memory of an elephant. He grew up in that house, after all. Ginny was too bossy, Ellie was too critical and Adele was too much like him. But Peyton, several years older than Matt, had always seemed wise and he loved her independence, her strength. But she happened to be closest to George and Adele. And young Mike, who was getting his postgrad degree, worshipped Matt. Ginny, who got on Matt's last nerve, adored and pampered him and called him Mattie. And so it went in big families. Feuds, alliances, shared failures, victories, spats, celebrations and reconciliations. But they were family and Matt would go balls to the wall for any one of them.

After supplying the bruschetta, he chose to walk down to the marina. Though it was Friday night, crowded and the closest thing to fine dining Thunder Point had to offer, at least half the people present were dressed as casually as he was. He took a seat at the bar, ordered a beer and asked if he could get a table for two in about fifteen minutes. The man behind the bar said it was no problem.

It was only five minutes later that Ginger walked in, also early. And if possible, prettier than before. She looked a little fresher, like she'd fluffed her hair and wet her lips. She'd changed clothes. Still jeans, but this time with a jacket and boots with heels instead of clogs. He stood and smiled at her and checked her hands. They weren't green. He waved her over. "We're ready whenever you are," Matt said to the guy behind the bar.

"Hey, Ginger," the man said.

"Hey, Cliff. How's life?"

"Always good. Always. This a friend of yours?"

"This is Peyton Grant's brother Matt. Matt, this is Cliff. This is his restaurant."

After a little chat, mostly from Cliff about how grateful they all were that Peyton worked with Scott and that Scott had had the wisdom to marry her, though probably not for the sake of the town, he took them to a table in the dining room. He bragged a little about the lobster bisque, said anything on the menu with crab was outstanding and that there was mahimahi on the specials tonight. Ram—presumably the chef—didn't fry too much, he recommended the blackened salmon or Cajun ahi.

Then they were alone.

"I see you got the green stains off your hands," Matt said, smiling, making her laugh.

"Flowers are dirty work," she said.

"Tell me about dirty. I'm in fruit. And potatoes. And sometimes sheep."

"Sometimes?"

"I work with Paco on the farm and George, my oldest brother, he has the sheep end of the business. When it's time to shear or breed or anything real busy, I help. Everyone helps. And Uncle

Sal has the vineyard—we go to the wine harvest on and off between August and the end of September, the same time we're bringing in the pears. The whole extended family is running around the state—grapes here, sheep there, pears and potatoes."

"That orchard," she said. "One of the most beautiful places on earth."

Cliff brought a glass of wine for Ginger, and they both ordered the same thing—Cajun ahi. "There's a small butcher shop in Portland where you can get ahi steaks. They cost the moon but you can eat them with a spoon, they're that fresh and good."

"Portland? You live in Portland?" he asked.

"It's where I'm from. I live here now. I really hope it works out and that I can stay. At least for a long time. I love the town, the shop."

"Tell me about flowers," he said.

"What can I tell you? I work for Grace, who owns the shop. I've only been there a short time but I'm learning to make very nice displays—bouquets, centerpieces, wreaths, wall hangings. I love it when she gets an order from a big hotel or resort and we do something huge, like an underwater obsidian stem in a tall cylinder glass vase. It's more of a sculpture than an arrangement."

"How'd you know you wanted to do that?" he asked.

"I didn't," Ginger said. "I was visiting with Ray Anne, just sitting around completely unmotivated while she went to work, and she told me I had to do something, no matter how small it was. That very day Grace asked me if I'd consider her shop. She was in desperate need of help and I had absolutely no experience. Honestly, I took it because it was there. I had no idea I'd like it. I shouldn't be surprised—I like all those sorts of things."

"What sorts of things?" he asked.

She laughed a little uncomfortably and looked down at her hands. "For lack of a better description, girl things. I've worked in retail, in clothing, in housewares, in domestics. I'm the youngest of three with two older brothers and am the only member of the family who doesn't work in the family business, my dad's trucking company. Small but pretty successful. My dad runs it, my oldest brother is the comptroller, my other brother is operations VP and my mother has been the dispatcher and scheduler since he had one truck. And I, the baby of the family and a girl, never found my niche. I've taken some college courses, never found a degree program. But boy, can I organize the house! And I know how to change the oil in the car, landscape the yard, bake a soufflé, hang wallpaper. The joke around the family is that since my mother has always been at the company, working with Dad, I am the only housewife in the family."

"Landscape? Ever have a garden?"

"I rented a small house and planted flowers around the border."

"You'd like my mother's garden," he said.

"I saw your mother's garden. A small farm! Looking at it made me hungry!"

"We grow things for a living," he said with a smile. "What was your last job before coming here?" he asked.

"I worked in a department store in the bridal registries. But I needed a change."

Then it came to him suddenly. "Jesus, what a dunce! Dysart Trucking!"

"That's right," she said. "You've heard of them?"

He grinned. "We use them, Ginger. They take our crops to market. They're a good-size company."

"Locally," she said. "My dad started with one truck."

"My grandfather started with a small grove and a few sheep and a lot of debt, but every time he had two nickels to rub together he bought more land."

"He invested in himself," she said.

"He invested in his sons. My dad has the grove and sheep and potatoes, Uncle Sal has grapes, Andreas has a couple of fishing boats. As you no doubt noticed, there's quite a lot of family."

Then his phone vibrated in his pocket. He pulled it out and looked at it, sent the caller to voice mail, put it back in his pocket. Lucy. They'd gone out a few times. She'd like to go out a few more. Time to move on.

"I don't mind if you take that call."

"That's okay, I'll call back. So, everyone works in the trucking company…"

"Except me. I'm willing to help out but I don't have any talent for it, except maybe washing rigs." She laughed. "I'm very good at all the things people don't get paid much for—cooking and cleaning, that sort of thing. I suppose when my parents are very old and infirm and I'm an old maid, I'll be the one to take care of them. And all your family is involved in the farm?"

"No, only a couple of us. Peyton is here, Ginny and Ellie are homemakers and their husbands are not farmers, Mike will be a professor married to a professor, Sal is a CPA for a large winemaker in Napa. He'd like to buy a vineyard someday. I guess, named for Uncle Sal, it makes perfect sense. He's good with numbers and has a very good nose. They're all pretty successful. My parents pushed us hard."

Through dinner they talked about their families, some of their childhood experiences, what movies and books they liked. He told her he was a part-time teacher and she told him about her three best friends from high school and how they'd all left Portland for big careers. He made her laugh and he was mesmerized by her sweetness and charm. They had a cup of coffee but neither wanted dessert. Two hours had flown by. She told him that as apology dinners go, this was the best she'd ever had.

"So," he said, "what is it you like so much about this little town? Why do you want to stay?"

"The people have been so lovely. And that flower shop—it's perfect for me. I'm around people sometimes but I spend a lot of time alone, making up arrangements, cleaning up the cooler and back room. I need that time—time to think. But I shouldn't have too much time or I get caught brooding."

"And what does a pretty girl like you have to brood about?" he asked, flashing his dimples.

"Peyton didn't tell you anything about me?"

"Come to think of it, she told me you'd had a bad year and made me promise I wouldn't be a wolf."

"Well, we have maybe a couple of things in common. I'm also divorced. Just over a year."

"Is that so? I'll tell you mine if you tell me yours?"

"You first," she said.

"It's not that interesting," he said. "Everything Natalie and I talked about for the year leading up to our wedding, we agreed on. Immediately following the wedding, she was unhappy. She didn't want to be married to a farmer, I got up too early, went to bed too early, had dirt under my nails, shit on my boots. She wanted me to go to med school or get a PhD and teach. She wanted fancy cocktail parties rather than big hoedowns at the farm. She was intimidated by the sheer size of my family. So we fought, and fought and fought. We'd married the wrong people. It was a damn shame, but there it is." He shrugged. "See? Not interesting. Make yours at least interesting."

She took a breath. She twirled the coffee cup around on the saucer. "Maybe I shouldn't…"

"You don't have to," he said.

"I married the wrong person, too. I married a musician. A singer/songwriter with the voice of an angel. The first time I heard him sing was in Portland at a fair and he sang 'I Guess The Lord Must Be In New York City.' My bones melted and I fell right in love with him. I was young—twenty-one. He was older and had been trying to make a breakthrough in the music business for a long time. He traveled a lot but when he was in the Pacific Northwest, which he called home, we'd see each other. After a couple of years of that he suggested we live together,

though he would continue to travel for every gig or business opportunity. He moved all his things into my little rented house.
That went pretty well for a while. In fact, there were times it
was a lot of fun—lots of musicians around, lots of music, a real
party. We got married and he sang to me at our wedding. He
also notified the newspapers and had a couple of photographers
there. He was going to be the next Eric Clapton. I worked in
a department store and he made a pittance on his gigs, barely
enough to keep him in equipment and plane tickets. He did sell
five songs to a big country star, they just never made the charts.
That's when I started to realize what a mistake I'd made—he
made a hundred thousand dollars and bought all-new equipment.
It was all about him. The big break that would set him up for
life was always right around the corner. But of course marriage
didn't work. He didn't want to be a husband. His music came
first. He said, 'I told you, Ginger—I have to concentrate on my
music and I thought you were on board with that.'"

Matt gulped. Had he put the farm ahead of his wife? Would
everything have been different if he'd given her ideas a try? "I'm
sorry, Ginger."

"Well, time to move on, right?" she said.

She was obviously trying to brighten up. He thought the pain
of divorce must be much fresher for her. His phone vibrated and
he looked. Lucy again. He'd call her later and explain he wasn't
in Portland and she'd have to find someone else for the night.
He put the phone back in his pocket.

"Really, it's okay…"

"Just my kid brother," he lied. "I'll call him back."

"What if it's an emergency?" she asked.

"If it was an emergency, I'd hear from Paco and Peyton and
I'd answer for them because it would obviously be important.
He probably has a work-related question. He's working on a
biochem degree. He's researching."

"Wow. You really do have an impressive family."

He laughed. "So do you, Ginger."

He walked her to her car. She told him again that it was the best apology dinner she'd ever had. "With my sister living here, we'll see each other again. I can always apologize again."

"You really don't have to," she said with a laugh. "Would you like a ride home?"

"No thanks. I like to walk, especially at night."

"All right. Have a good visit then." She put out her hand.

He pulled on that hand gently and kissed her cheek. "Thanks. Take care." And he walked off into the night.

When he got back to Peyton's house, it was kind of dark. They'd left the outside porch light on for him and when he went inside he found Dr. and Mrs. Grant were curled up together watching a movie. Peyton instantly put the movie on pause, flicked on the table lamp and sat up straight. "You're back," she said.

"I'm back."

"Did you have a nice dinner?"

"I had a very nice dinner," Matt said. "Have you ever tried the Cajun ahi at Cliff's? Because it's really good."

"I meant with Ginger!"

"Did you realize that she's Ginger Dysart of Dysart Trucking?"

"Who's that?"

"The trucking company we use to take our crops to market. The company we rent our flatbeds from to take Christmas trees to market."

"Huh. I didn't realize."

"You could've told me she was recovering from a divorce, just like me. I might've understood why you were acting so protective of her."

"Well, it was a bit more than that. She told you about the baby?"

"What baby?"

Peyton sighed as if trapped. "Well, everyone knows. It's been easier for her, really, since everyone knows and no one asks. She got pregnant and her husband left her, I don't know the details. She said he didn't want children. He wanted to devote his time to his career. So he left her."

"Where's the baby?" Matt asked with a sinking feeling.

"She moved back with her parents, had her baby as a single mother, and he died of SIDS at four months. That was almost a year ago. She's just coming back to life."

Matt thought he might throw up. "God."

"She's doing well now, considering. But you can see why I didn't want you to be your tomcat self around her."

"For the last time, I'm not a tomcat," he said.

But he was. And he was damn lucky he hadn't offended Ginger for the second time because he found her very attractive. Very desirable.

But now, knowing what he knew, he was going to get out of town and get back to Portland tomorrow. He'd make some excuse. He wasn't staying the weekend, after all.

CHAPTER THREE

Grace walked around the great room of the new house. It was freshly painted. She hoped her mother would approve of the colors she'd chosen—ivory with dark brown accents in the great room. Taupe with just a touch of mauve in it, dark accents, ivory ceiling in the master bedroom. It was restful, she thought. On Monday they would install the kitchen cupboards and light fixtures and continue work on the shower in the master bath. The thing she thought was the smartest and most practical—a curved glass cinder block wall rather than a shower door for accessibility and also for the elegant design—that was taking the longest. Workers had spent days on that one small project.

Troy was taking advantage of a warm sunny Saturday with only a light breeze rather than strong winds off the Pacific to seal the deck and steps to the beach. The sealer dried so quickly he was already on the second coat and it was early in the afternoon. Sealer had been sprayed on the underside of the deck before Troy brushed on the topside. Spencer, their next-door neighbor and Troy's colleague at the high school, was at work on the steps—fourteen from the deck to the lower level, four-

teen from the lower level to the beach. The main level of the
houses was thirty feet above the beach.

She found herself standing just inside the great room doors
watching Troy. His jeans were ripped at the knees and he wore
a T-shirt with the sleeves torn off, exposing those biceps and
forearms she loved so much. The jeans fit perfectly on his booty.
He wore a cap to cut down on the glare, but he yanked it off
regularly to wipe the sweat from his brow. He was just as sexy
sweaty as he was all primped up.

He caught her staring and shot her that dazzling smile of his.
"What are you looking at, little mama?"

"Dinner, I think." And then she bit her lip.

There would be enough to do to keep them busy for quite a
while, but she thought she could get her mother in the house
in two weeks. And she suspected that her former skating coach,
Mikhail, would be staying with them for some time. He had
said, "I will come to this place if you could secure a little room
in a cheap hotel. Just a bed is all I need—I despise to sleep on
the floor. Someone should help get her settled. Winnie can be
difficult. Then I will leave."

Difficult? She could be a nightmare! But Winnie was ill now, losing her physical stamina, failing as ALS took over and the fatigue she suffered from made her more docile. It was true she
had always listened to Mikhail. And Mikhail had said he was
coming for two or three days and he'd been there over a month
already. She'd better get that second upstairs bedroom and bath
finished for him. She had a feeling Mikhail planned to stay much
longer than he let on. There was an affection between Mikhail
and Winnie that Grace couldn't really identify. Not romance,
certainly. Friendship, but more than the usual friendship. Part-
nership. Mikhail had been Grace's coach for years, from the
time she was fourteen until she was in her early twenties and
quit competing, and through all that time he had stayed close
to both Grace and Winnie.

Virginia, Winnie's assistant, would stay in her position until that big albatross of a house in San Francisco was closed and all the possessions were dealt with. There were a few pictures Grace wanted for this house, but the rest of her mother's art was going to a fine-art museum on long-term loan—it would be displayed as *The Banks Collection*. With the help of the now part-time housekeeper, some things were being packed and shipped to Thunder Point—just a few treasured pieces of furniture, some dishes, kitchenware, her mother's precious bedroom rug, a valuable Aubusson. Then there would be an estate sale—the furs and most of the jewelry would be included. Grace would have to make a couple of quick trips to look through things—there were undoubtedly photo albums, books, mementos and keepsakes that should be preserved.

Virginia was looking for a roomy flat in the city where she could live and work until the estate was settled. Then Grace just might ask her if she wanted to continue to manage the estate after Winnie was gone.

Meanwhile, that handsome history teacher on the deck was trying to get a binding pre-nup. He wasn't looking for half, he was looking for nothing. He never wanted it even suggested that he was interested in Grace's legacy. That would be the money she would inherit because as of now she had a flower shop and about a year's income in the bank, cautiously invested. Troy had been intimidated by Winnie's house and furnishings. If he ever saw the actual bottom line, the net worth, he might stroke out.

Oh, they were going to make interesting neighbors. A teacher and flower shop owner, now expecting. A diva with ALS who would probably sit on the deck in a wheelchair wearing furs and diamonds. Full-time nursing help. And a little Russian coach who liked raisins in his *wodka*.

"Troy!" she called. "I think I'm going to do a little painting in the loft."

He straightened and pulled off his cap. "You paint nothing!

There are fumes. You can sweep. Or go arrange flowers. Or call your mother and tell her how helpful I am."

"She already likes you more than she likes me," she muttered.

"As it should be," he said.

"Wow. Good ears!"

"I'm a high school teacher! I have to hear everything!" he shouted.

"And so do I," Spencer yelled from the bottom step.

Matt Lacoumette had one of those grueling weeks where he had to be everywhere at once. There was fertilizing to do in the orchard—the flowers were giving way to buds of fruit and it was a delicate time. Some of George's ewes had lambed but there were some late breeders ready now. He liked to shear the ewes to make their lambing easier, and Matt helped with that. Then they liked to get the ewes delivered so they'd be ready to breed by fall. Everything happened in spring and fall, over months—the planting, the harvesting, the pears, the grapes, the lambing, the breeding. And things were not going to calm down anytime soon—there was more shearing to be done after lambing so the sheep could grow nice coats over summer. On top of that, he had to teach a couple of classes before the end of term.

If all that wasn't enough, he had to deal with Lucy, who kept calling him. Despite the fact that he'd been clear he was not in the market for a girlfriend, Lucy, like so many women, thought he'd change his mind. So she cried and he had to do his best to assure her there was nothing at all wrong with her—she was lovely and smart and sexy. It was him—he was not going to be anyone's boyfriend. It was brutal.

And then, after leaving his last class of the week, he left the building to find Natalie leaning against his truck. She was sporting yet another hair color and style—this time it was jet black. The last time he'd seen her it was brown with red highlights. When they were together he'd gotten the biggest kick out of her change in looks, every variation beautiful. There it was again—he was feeling both lust and rage.

"What is it, Nat?" he asked.

"I thought maybe we could have a cup of coffee," she said.

"Because...?"

"Because having you hate me is killing me! Please, Matt!"

He took a breath. "I don't hate you," he said patiently. It was a lie, he really did hate her. The problem was that he was also still drawn to her. He could love her if he'd just relax and let himself, but he'd be damned if he'd even entertain that notion. "We're not having coffee. We're not trying again or patching things up or being good friends. We thought we felt the same way about things and it turned out we felt the opposite way about important things. We made a mistake, Natalie. I have to go now. It's been a long week."

She didn't budge. "And you have to get to bed!"

He ground his teeth. "I'll call campus security," he threatened. "And I'll tell Dr. Weymouth I can't give any more classes because his department secretary is harassing me."

"You wouldn't do that."

"I would. I should. Now get out of here and please, no more of this."

"But when are you going to forgive me?" she said, crocodile tears running down her cheeks.

"There's something I just can't forgive. Everything else is a distant memory, but that one thing—"

"God, who knew you were so *Catholic!*"

He clenched his hands into fists. They'd been over this, too. It wasn't religious or political. It was his personal ethic about marriage, their marriage in particular, about how marriage had to work. There had to be give and take, they had to talk about deeply personal issues, they had to find a way to compromise. There had to be trust. They couldn't lie to each other. They failed at marriage and it had nothing to do with his religion. As far as he knew every religion shared similar if not identical ethics.

He took out his cell phone.

"What are you doing?" she asked.

"Calling campus security. Then Dr. Weymouth…"

"Ugh!" she grunted, moving out of his way. Then she stomped back toward the building in her high heels with ankle straps, her short skirt and long legs more than distracting.

He grimaced. He should probably quit this gig anyway. He sure didn't do it for the money. Most months of the year he could slip it into his schedule easily but spring and fall especially, it was a real inconvenience. It was just that he liked the students. There were only a few who took these particular classes to check off a box or try to get by with an easy class. Most of them were either premed or heading into agriculture or environmental science. They asked stimulating questions, created interesting dialogue and arguments, gave him something to think about. They were sharp.

He thought about going out for the evening or back to his apartment. Instead, he went to the farm even though he'd been there all morning. The nice thing about the family home, he didn't need a reservation. The door was never locked; there was no possibility his parents wouldn't be home. If they had plans, somewhere to go, he'd hear about it weeks in advance.

He walked in, found his mother in the kitchen and gave her a kiss. She acted like she barely had time for the kiss. "Coffee? Wine?"

He looked at his watch. "Wine, thank you. Rioja. The red. Do you have a full table tonight?"

"George, Ginny, their families. I have no trouble squeezing in one more."

"Thanks. I'm starving."

"And, as you can plainly see, I am cooking. I'll have you some tapas in a minute." She put a glass of wine in front of him. "You usually move in and out of this house without a word, unless it's business. Tonight is different. You're friendly."

He laughed. His parents could really read their kids. Even as adults! "I wanted to speak to Papa but you'll do. I want to give up that apartment—it's too much trouble. But I don't want to live in the house. What I'd like to do is build on Lacoumette land. If there's a space that can be allotted to me for a house."

Her eyes lit up and she was clearly excited. "For a family?"

He shook his head. "For me. Maybe someday there will be a family. But Mama, I still have wounds to heal, so not now please."

"These wounds, Matt," she said. "If you feed them too much they can heal on the outside and keep getting worse on the inside. Then you're in trouble."

His mother, who was not well educated in the traditional sense, knew all. "Yes, Mama. I'll watch for that."

"Paco will be so happy to give you your choice of land. Not too close to the house, eh? So we don't see the hundreds of girls come and go?"

He laughed. He was going to change that, as well.

Then his brother and sister and their families started trooping in. George shook his hand and thanked him for the hundredth time for his help with the ewes. Ginny kissed and hugged him. Lori, George's wife, did the same. The kids pretty much ignored him, as he was not an uncommon sight around here. Then Paco came in and gave him the traditional greeting, a hand on the shoulder and a swat on the cheek.

"Matt wants to build a house on the farm," his mother said from the kitchen.

And Paco, surprised and clearly thrilled, grabbed his son and kissed him on each cheek. Then did so again. "There is a woman?" he asked.

"Just me, your bachelor son."

"Good then. We'll get you ready for a woman."

★ ★ ★

It was about nine forty-five when Ginger's cell phone rang. She didn't recognize the number—it wasn't a family member or Grace. She was in her room, reading. Ray Anne and Al were having a "date" up on Ray Anne's private deck atop the garage. Ginger was committed to not getting anywhere near them. She was locked away so they could be alone. She wouldn't even go to the kitchen; she did not want to hear moaning, panting or giggling.

Thinking it must be a wrong number, she answered uncertainly.

"Hi, Ginger. It's Matt."

"Matt?" she asked, sitting up on the bed. "Did I give you my number?"

He laughed. "You did not. I got it out of my sister and I had to swear I would be a perfect gentleman or she was going to do to me what we do to goats we're not going to breed."

"Ew."

"Exactly. You tell her I was less than perfect and I'm a eunuch."

She couldn't help it, she laughed. "Gee, and Peyton seems so sweet."

"Ha. Don't let her fool you. She was the oldest of eight and could be mean as a rabid dog. She'd do unspeakable things to her younger brothers and sisters as long as there was no possibility she'd get caught."

"You must have a reason for calling…"

"I do. Don't think I'm a loser, okay? I had a really crazy week that ended pretty good and here I am, home, and have no one to talk to but my mother!"

"Your mother is there?" And she couldn't help it, she thought *red flag.*

"No." He laughed. "I had dinner at the farm, which I do a lot. There's always plenty of good food and an unpredictable number of family members. And I talked to my mom for a while. But seriously, Ginger. A little chatting it up with Mom is not what I'm looking for and I remembered we had a pretty cordial conversation."

"But what about Peyton?" she asked. "I bet you could talk to her anytime."

"Peyton? The pregnant newlywed who threatened to castrate me?"

She settled back against her pillows. "Right. So what did you want to talk about?"

"My week was nuts. I was all over that farm and had to help George with shearing some ewes who came into season late and were just now ready for lambing and the fruit trees are budding early and had to be aerated around the roots and fertilized. Dirty work. And I had to teach a two-hour class at the college—I should give that up—it's inconvenient. But it's also dangerous. My ex was leaning against my truck when I came out of the building. She's done this a few times—she wants to talk. I had to threaten her with campus security to get her to go away..."

"Oh, you didn't!" she said. "Oh, Matt, she must be so desperate!"

"Well, that's not what I wanted to talk about, but yes, she's desperate. But why? I mean, we had that talk—we shouldn't have gotten married and were not happy. We were worse than unhappy, we were miserable. But that's not what I called about. I wanted to tell you something important."

"Okay..."

"Shit," he said. "I'm an idiot. This probably won't be important to anyone but me. To me, it's big. You'll probably think it's just dumb. Or a big nothing."

"You're so dramatic," she said. "Just tell me."

"I hate this little apartment I live in. It was my concession to Natalie. I'd be a farmer, but wouldn't live on the farm. When we split up, I stayed here because she couldn't afford it, but I hate it. I wasn't cut out to live on top of other people. I can't be happy without land. So I had this sudden epiphany and made a decision—I'm going to build a house on the farm. My father was so excited, he almost kissed me on the mouth! He wants to get together tomorrow to look at the land. George is the only other Lacoumette living on the farm and Paco is ecstatic. And guess what? I'm pretty excited, too. Of course I'm a year away from making the transition, but I just had to tell someone. I'm going to live in my favorite place."

"You could live with your parents until your house is built," she said.

"No, none of that," he said, laughing. "I'm almost thirty. I'm not living with my parents. I do stay over when things are crazy at the farm, when we're tracking possible bad weather at pear harvest or bringing in lambs or something that requires twenty-four-hour vigilance. But I need a little privacy, you know? But a house on the land…"

"The most beautiful place in the world," she said.

"You think so?"

"I can't imagine how much work it must be, but it's incredibly beautiful…"

"Those pear trees don't blossom year-round, you know."

"It's not just the blossoms, although just the scent is hypnotic. I love Portland in the spring when the fruit trees all over the city are in bloom! Everything about your farm is lovely—the house, the barn, the chickens…"

"The *chickens*?" he asked.

"I bet you take them for granted," she said. "Fresh eggs in the morning…"

"Fresh chicken at night," he added with a laugh.

"I hadn't thought of that, but yes, I suppose…"

"Peyton hates killing chickens. My mother doesn't like it, but she does it. If George is around the house she'll send him to round up a few and she'll cut them up and freeze them. She protects her best laying hens. It's about time for her to hatch a bunch of eggs, replenish the henhouse—there's an incubator in the barn."

"I would love to see that, baby chicks," Ginger said, a little breathless. "I don't think I'd like killing them, either."

"Maybe you're just not a farm girl. Not everyone is. Peyton can do anything there is to do on the farm but she doesn't like it. She's funny, she loves the farm—she wants the fresh food, wants to snuggle the new lambs—but our Peyton, her majesty, does not shovel shit. She's what we call a gentleman farmer— wants the land and animals, wants to pet the animals and eat the food, and other people have to do the work."

"Can't you be a farm girl and not like killing chickens?" she asked.

"The cycle of life is important on a farm," he said. "You grow it, eat it, grow some more. We're a commercial farm. It's not just about fresh eggs for breakfast, it's a business and has to support a lot of people. It has to support the land, too. We can't deplete and not replenish or it will be a one-generation farm." He paused and silence hung between them. "I'm sorry, I'm boring you."

"No! No, you're not. I'm really interested, believe it or not. I probably don't have any intelligent questions to ask but I like hearing about it."

"But you'd like to see the chicks or new lambs?" he asked.

She sighed. "I would love that. Maybe I'll visit my parents on a weekend when that's happening and I could come by the farm on my way back to Thunder Point. If that's all right?"

"It would be great. You have to eat, however. No one comes to the farm without eating something."

"I wouldn't want to impose…"

"Didn't you notice how much my family loves feeding people? Not everyone enjoys it, by the way, but it's possible Scott married my sister for the food."

"Tell me about the classes you teach."

"I just guest lecture in the biology department. I usually talk about either plant biology or animal husbandry. I can lecture on the biology of the farm, the microbiology of soil. The students love talking about cloning and two-headed sheep. We're making great progress as a biological as opposed to organic farm because we still use small amounts of chemicals and we immunize the sheep, but we're cautious. We fertilize mostly with chicken manure, kill pests on the trees organically, stick to nature where we can."

"Sure," she said. "You have to take care of the fruit…"

"We have to protect the bees. If we kill the insects and the bees disappear, we're doomed. The balance is delicate and the health of the plants and animals and consumers is… Am I putting you to sleep?"

"No!" she nearly shouted. "I never thought of farming as a science…"

"It is indeed a science. Paco is not a scientist but his experience and instincts are flawless. Everything he taught me holds up scientifically. Almost everything, at any rate. It is not true that if you put a statue of Saint Isidore the Farmer in the yard you will have a good crop year."

"Is there a statue of the saint in the garden?"

"My mother has one in the garden, yes. Also Saint Maria and the Virgin. Not overwhelming in size, but obvious. And her garden is plentiful."

They were quiet on the phone for a moment. "Matt? Why did you really call me?"

"Peyton asked the same question."

"What did you tell her?"

"I told her there was a special bonding moment when I groped you and you knocked me out…"

She laughed almost uncontrollably for a moment.

"Really," he said. "It's because you felt like a friend. Strange as it might feel to you, I think we somehow became friends. I hope you're okay with that."

She smiled. "Everyone can use a friend."

Ray Anne had a sweet little hideaway on top of the garage, a deck. From there she had a great view of storms rolling in over the bay. Or, when it wasn't storming, just starlight so deep and wide it was otherworldly. She and Al dragged out the bean bag chairs, he had a beer and she had a glass of wine. They reclined together, talked about their week, he told her about the boys and she reported on Ginger, who seemed to be doing better all the time. They kissed and fondled and made sneaky love under a blanket, then talked some more. It was almost eleven when Al carried down the bean bags and blanket and Ray Anne carried her glass and his bottle. They stood in the kitchen for a moment, safe in each other's arms, reluctant to say good-night.

There was a sound in the house, a soft lilting coming from the bedroom. They both froze to listen.

"Oh, God, that's Ginger!" Ray Anne said. "She's crying!" She turned to go to her.

Al grabbed her hand, stopping her. "Ray," he whispered. "Listen!"

She froze and listened. With their arms around each other's waists, they moved closer to the bedroom door.

"She's laughing," Ray Anne whispered. "She's talking on the phone and laughing!"

Al smiled down at her. "I don't think she needs rescuing."

"Who in the world is she talking to? Laughing with?"

"Maybe if you're very sneaky, you can worm it out of her."

CHAPTER FOUR

Matt had talked with Ginger for over an hour and he'd congratulated himself that he'd been right—she was a genuine person who could be a friend with no agenda to redesign him. She wasn't a woman who wanted to sleep with him and then change him into at least a boyfriend, at best a husband. They didn't talk about it, but it was implicitly understood they were both too vulnerable to take on new partners. Ginger, like Matt, was in recovery from her own short, extremely disappointing marriage. And yet they had so many things in common. More than Ginger realized. No doubt she thought it was just their divorces. That was enough.

But Matt, who had dated half of Portland, knew it was more. It was as though it balanced with his loss somehow. She'd wanted a family and fate had cruelly snatched it away from her. He wanted a family and hadn't had a chance at that.

They might never talk about these things, he realized. He really didn't want to tell her or anyone how selfish and cruel his ex-wife had been.

But here was Matt with a new friend and he felt very tender toward her. He wasn't about to get involved, but she had already changed everything. He was going to stop fucking everything that moved, for one thing. That hadn't worked for him and he'd probably hurt people in the process. He was going to clean up his act, show gratitude for friends and family and carry on in a much more chivalrous manner. He'd done a few insensitive, careless things himself—he wasn't proud of that. Somehow Ginger reminded him that at his core he was a good man. He would at least behave in a way that wouldn't shame his mother and infuriate his father.

Matt already had an idea of where he'd like to build a house, if Paco agreed. On the far side of the orchard, just within sight of his parents' home, there was a perfect spot. From the front he would see the grove, from the back, the mountains, to the west the big house. He'd have to grade a road. He tried sketching out a floor plan. He had inherited many of his father's ways, but living lean to the bone wasn't one of them. He was frugal but he intended to have plenty of bathrooms in the house and an indulgently big master bedroom and bath. He'd be more than happy to extend the use of those extra bedrooms to the family who showed up at shearing and harvest to help them. Even though he didn't watch a lot of TV, there would be at least two in his house. And they would be large.

Later in the week, he called Ginger again. "I've taken to sketching out a floor plan that I think I like and I've learned something important."

"Oh? What's that?"

"Architects are geniuses. Do you have any idea how hard it is to string a bunch of rooms and hallways together? The rooms I want to be the largest look the smallest on the drawing and vice versa. I think I took mechanical drawing in high school. How come I can't do this?"

"Just be sure to put those sliding shelves in the kitchen," she said.

"Huh?"

"Well, you open a lower cupboard door and pull the shelf out instead of getting down on your hands and knees and practically crawling in to find what you need. They're so awesome!"

He was quiet for a moment. "Ginger, I'm going to live next door to my mother, who will probably cook almost every meal I eat. I won't even be able to fill the kitchen cupboards."

"That may not be the case forever," she said. "I know you don't think so now, but you might actually get over this marriage phobia and meet someone nice who wants to live on the farm. And cook. In that kitchen."

"Highly unlikely. Will you? Get over it? Try again?"

"Sure," she said. "When I'm fifty."

"I might just look you up when we're fifty," he said. "Then if it works out, *you* can put in the sliding shelves."

"That seems pretty reasonable," she said. And they both laughed.

"What's happening in Thunder Point?"

"A lot, as a matter of fact. Grace has been spending a lot of time at the new house so she can get her mother moved here. You know, I told you, her mother has ALS and is weakening by the day. Grace's fiancé is helping her whenever he can because he really wants Grace to meet his family and they're having trouble finding a time to do that. She can't move her mother into the house and leave her to go south to meet Troy's family. And he hasn't told his family that Grace is pregnant because he said they will all immediately pile into cars and head this way, invited or not. So…everyone around town is putting every effort toward getting that house ready for them. Even me. That stretch of beach has taken on a life of its own—it's like a barn raising."

"Sounds like the Lacoumette family," he said.

"Peyton confirmed that. Except for the cultural dress, wine and dancing, it looks like it, too."

"Peyton is out there, too?"

"Sometimes. She's busy with the clinic and Scott's pretty

busy with the clinic and being on call. But they can't seem to stay away. If they're not out there working, they're checking on the progress."

They talked for over an hour and covered every subject. They laughed a lot; they were both good at puns. There was even a little cautious flirting going on, starting with hooking up at the age of fifty and touching on her reassurance that she was now convinced he could be a gentleman.

"Didn't you tell me you're usually asleep by eight o'clock?" she asked.

"I think I've been a little excited about the prospect of getting out of this apartment. It's almost ten. Late for me," he said.

"For me, too. I've been getting up very early to get into the shop and get things rolling so that when Grace comes in, she feels comfortable leaving it in my hands so she can do what she has to do."

"You're vying for employee of the year," he said.

"I'd far rather be awarded friend of the year."

When they hung up Matt lay on his back on his bed with his phone in his hand. The phone was hot. Matt was hot. *I have to stay away from Thunder Point*, he thought. Very scary place to go.

Ginger was so sweet. So kind and generous. Here she was, still hurting after being treated like crap by her husband and losing a baby she was devoted to, and what concerned her most right now was helping Grace and Troy, helping her new friends. Ginger didn't have a single sharp edge anywhere. She was pleasant, soft, unselfish…nice. She was nice.

Mad Matt never thought about that when he thought about women, at least not lately. He thought about long legs and perky boobs. He thought about pretty, buoyant, confident and lively. When he fell for Natalie he was willing to make almost any compromise to keep her satisfied, to keep her home, but he hadn't ever once thought about if she was unselfish or how caring. He thought about not forcing her to deal with his overbearing family too much, about trying to balance her need for fun and a social life with his need for sleep, about trying to be sure none of the farm stayed on his hands or boots when he went home to her.

Ginger was so nice, but she was not bland. When laughter took her by surprise, she sounded wicked and playful, which triggered his memory of her smile. Her smile could melt a man's heart. And he loved those freckles. Maybe it was the freckles that made her seem almost childlike to him, innocent, in need of a strong arm.

Stay away from Thunder Point, he told himself.

The thing about Matt—he'd been with a lot of women, before and after Natalie. He wasn't bad-looking, he was pretty smart, usually stable. Before Nat he was probably searching for someone permanent without really acknowledging it. After Nat he was looking for a way to get over her. But there was one thing, probably a cultural thing, a family trait—marriage was sacred. He didn't need a High Mass wedding to feel that way, it was just a thing with him. Once you pledged yourself to a woman, she became everything. Naturally it followed that he would be her everything, that she would do anything to see him happy and content. Between them there would always be complete honesty, trust. Everything would be shared, discussed, dealt with as a team. It was true that he had some firm, unshakable beliefs. That kind of went with the Lacoumette territory, especially the men. Stubbornness and passion might prevail, they might act like the king of their castle, but it was all a show. The women ran the castle. The men worked tirelessly to support their families and they *served* their women.

He spent Saturday around the farm though his father and George hadn't been expecting him. If it wasn't crazy season, he usually took a couple of days off a week. On Sunday morning, he woke at four like a bad habit. He showered and got in his truck. He grabbed a fast-food breakfast he could eat on the road and he drove south. Fast, along a deserted highway. He was in Thunder Point before nine in the morning. He drove right out to the parking lot behind Cooper's place. It was no mystery where the action was—there was already a lot of activity around the third house down from the bar.

The garage door stood open, and three men he happened to know were armed with paint rollers and painting the inside walls of the garage. A truck holding four large ceramic planters filled with small trees was parked on the road.

"Hey, what are you doing here?" Cooper asked Matt.

"I heard there was a barn raising and I was curious, thought I'd check this out. And since I'm here, maybe you can use a hand."

"I didn't know you were coming down," Scott Grant said. Scott was covered in paint and it was still early. "Are you staying over?"

"Can't. Monday morning Paco is snapping his whip early. We're temporarily caught up at the farm and I had a day, so…"

"Does Peyton know you're here? Did you stop by the house?"

"I didn't. Didn't call her, either. Spur of the moment. What can I do?"

"I don't know," Cooper said. "Project manager is Troy. Really, it's Grace, but she's letting him think he's running things. Last time I saw him he was struggling with the light fixture in the kitchen. Apparently it's complicated…"

"I got that," Matt said with a laugh.

When he got inside, Troy was apparently supervising while a big guy in a blue T-shirt was on a ladder installing track lighting. He was introduced to Al, whose name he'd heard in conjunction with Ray Anne. The great room was cluttered with furniture covered in plastic, several boxes and picture crates. And a lot of women with rags, mops, brooms and shelf paper were opening boxes, looking things over, organizing.

"Matt!" Troy said in surprise.

"Matt?" a tall curly-haired woman he couldn't remember asked.

"Iris, this is Matt Lacoumette, Peyton's brother," Ray Anne Dysart said. "I can't believe you're here."

"Last minute, I know, but I thought since I had a day, maybe I could help."

They all eagerly accepted the offer. Ginger, a kerchief tying back her strawberry-blond hair, flushing slightly under her freckles, just smiled at him. He smiled right back at her.

"We're down to finishing touches," Grace said. "*Lots* of finishing touches. Furniture was just delivered, my mother's assistant shipped some personal and household items that have to be put away after the cupboards and closets are cleaned, the basement and garage are getting painted today, light fixtures and bathroom fixtures have to be installed as well as washer and dryer hookup. And obviously serious cleanup. What's your pleasure?"

"I can clean like I was trained by Corinne Lacoumette and I'm pretty fast with a screwdriver."

"Great. You've got bathroom fixtures. Four bathrooms, the fixtures all in boxes in the bathrooms. One loft bathroom, master and main floor bathrooms, one bathroom downstairs."

"I'll go get my toolbox," he said, leaving them. As he was walking out to his truck, he heard the unmistakable sound of women giggling and whispering. And it made him smile. He remembered something Paco had told him long ago: *try fooling women all you want, you'll never get away with anything.* How true. He wanted to stay away from Ginger; he wanted to be with her if he could.

Everyone worked ferociously and work crews came and went. Cooper went home to take care of his little daughter and tend his bar while his helper, an old guy named Rawley, replaced him. Al left to go to work, Devon left to go home and Spencer replaced her—someone had to watch the kids and this "work in progress" was no place for little ones. Peyton showed up and apparently got the word Matt was on the premises right away because she found him in the downstairs bathroom, head in the cabinet under the sink with a wrench, fixing a leaky pipe.

"I suppose you think you're fooling someone," she said.

He sat up abruptly and hit his head. He scooted out cautiously. Women, it seemed, were a serious threat to his cranium. "I don't know what you're talking about."

"Why are you here?" she said.

"Ginger told me about this project, about the urgency because Grace's mother is not well, and I am a very neighborly guy."

She completely ignored his virtues. "You're pursuing Ginger and I told you not to. It makes no sense. It's not like you two got off to a good start."

"Peyton," he said very patiently. "Boxers are sometimes friendly outside the ring. On weekends defense attorneys play golf with prosecutors. But you're wrong, I'm not pursuing her. We've talked a couple of times and neither of us is interested in a new relationship. For obvious reasons. We've sworn off, all right? But we're friends now."

"This is a bad idea."

"Bugger off," he said. "And don't piss me off."

"Or what? Huh?"

"I will do something terrible to you, without causing you any distress to your pregnancy. But you'll never forget it, it will be so bad and dangerous."

"How can you talk like that to your pregnant sister?"

"Gee, I don't know," he said. "Didn't you threaten to castrate me? Now, leave me alone. I can pick my own friends. And for your information, Ginger is very nice."

"I *know*!"

"And she likes me!" Matt said, standing up and facing her. "Why is it you're so upset at the idea of me being friends with her? I admit, I made an awful mistake at your wedding, but she's accepted my apology and I've been perfectly perfect."

"That's now," she said. "You've been… Well, Matt, you have a reputation. A love-'em-and-leave-'em reputation. That's the last thing a nice girl like Ginger needs right now."

He got it. Everyone thought he left Natalie because of a lot of annoying arguing. Because no one knew the whole story. And no one could know. "Okay, okay. I give you my word, we're friends and I will not do anything to hurt Ginger. I like her. She's a good person. I'm here today because she told me how everyone is helping Grace and Troy so they can get their families together and get married and I thought it was sweet and kind. She told me you and Scott were helping, even though you have little kids and a clinic to run. She told me she was going to be here all day working, even though she worked all week at the flower shop. I came to help. *That's* why I came."

"You swear?" she asked.

"I swear. Now, can I get back to my plumbing?"

She gave him one last withering glare, then left him. She was no longer his favorite sister. He rubbed his head. He bet no one ever accused Peyton of being a kind girl. No one who was related to her and really knew her at any rate.

After the plumbing fixtures, he helped finish installing a couple of light fixtures, something Troy seemed to find a challenge. Cooper's wife, Sarah, brought over a huge tray of sandwiches from Cooper's bar. Right behind her was Cooper with a cooler full of cold drinks for everyone. The work party moved out to the deck to picnic in the warm afternoon sun, and Matt had to focus his attention on the men because his nosy sister wouldn't leave.

After lunch, they were down to cleaning so that the area rugs could be rolled out, furniture uncovered and placed, kitchenware and linens put into drawers, closets and cupboards, beds made up. The cleaning went from top to bottom, cupboards, countertops first, floors last. He bravely took his life in his hands and joined Ginger in the kitchen.

"I was so surprised to see you," she said. "What a good guy you must be, driving all the way down here to help out."

"Tell my sister, will you? That I'm a good guy."

"I have two brothers," she said, laughing. "I know about that brother-sister thing. Not easy. You'll just have to be satisfied that I think you're good."

"Thank you. I have to drive back tonight. We start early on Monday mornings. But I brought a change of clothes. I could clean up at Peyton's house and we could go out for something to eat. Something casual. Mexican? You like Mexican?"

"I love Mexican!"

"That'll save us a phone call."

"You know a place around here? Because I'm new in town," she reminded him.

"I'll find one. Someone around here will know a good place."

"I don't want you to stay too late and drive home tired..."

"But I'm here, Ginger. Let's do something. Fun. Let's have some fun."

"Aren't you having fun?" she asked him with a wicked grin.

He leaned toward her. "I'm glad to help, but I came for you. Just, don't tell my sister."

"Why not?"

"Because Peyton thinks I'm a bad bet. And I'm getting real sick of hearing about it."

Peyton watched Matt and Ginger from the deck as she swept up crumbs and collected empty cans and plastic bottles from lunch. Scott and Spencer carried a large potted plant through the house and out to the deck, placing it where they'd been told to. Then Scott was by Peyton's side.

"If you frown and scowl and brood like that any longer, you're going to wrinkle," he told his wife.

"As soon as Matt leaves Ginger alone, he's going to get an earful of my opinion of his behavior," she muttered.

Scott grabbed her by the shoulders and turned her to face the bay. He put an arm around her, holding her there. "No. He's not," Scott said. "You're going to keep your mouth shut."

"Huh? Listen, I can handle him."

"I said, no," Scott said firmly. "I command you."

She glanced up at him and laughed.

"Figures you would think that's funny. I want you to listen to me, Peyton, because when it comes to your family, you're a little on the blind and deaf side. He might be a little brother to you, but you're not in charge of him anymore. You have to leave him alone. He's thirty and he's obviously experienced some difficult times."

"He's been divorced over a year. And that marriage, it was very short and very miserable. And—"

"I've only known the Lacoumette family for a year and the whole time Matt has been silent. A little cranky. Very absent. Your mother and some of your sibs have apologized for him, said he was one of the best-natured men in the family. That short marriage obviously took its toll and he's been nursing some big wounds."

"And he's been coping by having a different woman every week!"

"Peyton, he's smiling. He's laughing. For that matter, I haven't seen Ginger look so good since I've met her—she's smiling and laughing."

"Hanging out with my brother, she could get hurt!"

"If you get in his business any further, *you're* going to get hurt. You're going to get spanked!"

"And just what big man is going to do that?" she asked, laughter in her voice.

"This big man, your lord and master," he said.

"Oh, you're really pushing it…"

"We're going to finish up here, grab the kids from next door where they're watching a movie and we're going to go home, without saying one word, because if it were you in there, flirting with me, and someone got in your way, you'd be furious. They're adults. They appear to like each other. They're two people who have been through a lot and they're having a good time for once. I suspect they know more about what they need right now than you do." He shook his head. "You've got a really scary big-sister thing going on. Don't be a bully."

She gasped. "I just don't want either one of them to go down the wrong path with the wrong person. It seems dangerous to me. And I don't approve of the way Matt has handled himself the past year or so, but he's my brother. I love him. It won't make me feel good to see him hurt, either. After all, the past couple of years has been hard on everyone."

"I know. Letting go isn't easy. But I'm right about this. He has to find his own way. And Ginger does, too. You told Matt about Ginger. Matt isn't going to use and abuse her. Can you really imagine he would? He might be your naughty little brother, but I've gotten to know him."

"He probably wouldn't," she relented.

"I saw a sweetheart side of Matt today I didn't even know existed and I've known him for a year," Scott said. "He's not fooling anybody—he's here because he heard about this barn raising from Ginger."

"He says they aren't involved," she said. "That they've sworn off relationships."

"And maybe they have. But something there is helping them heal. When I let you turn around, look at them. They're enjoying each other, enjoying the day. They're up to their armpits in hard, dirty work and they're smiling like kids. Honey, I want you to do something you have a hard time doing. I want you to have no opinion."

"Oh, now—"

"None. Zero. Nada."

"Now you're making me sound like a real buttinski! Like I'm in everyone's business!"

"You're related to half of northern Oregon, Peyton. And you are certainly not the only one in the family who butts in."

"Well…it's a hot-blooded family."

"Will you stay out of his business? Out of hers?"

"All right, all right. Hey, you don't have some kind of spanking fantasy, do you?"

He grinned at her. "Only if it's you spanking me." He turned her around. "Look," he said, indicating the couple in the kitchen. Ginger had a knee on Matt's shoulder while she reached for the highest cupboard above the refrigerator with a rag; he braced her with hands stretched up and holding her at the waist. He snuck one hand upward to tickle her ribs, but he held her safely. She laughed as she wiped out the cupboard, and he lowered her to the floor gently. "You going to leave that alone?" Scott asked Peyton.

"Yes," she said tiredly. "And I'm not spanking you."

"Oh, nuts," he said, laughing at her.

The house on the hill above the beach was empty of helpers now. Smoke was rising from Cooper's grill on his deck two doors down. There were people walking along the beach and as the sun set, lights from the town were starting to pop up like fireflies. Grace sat on one of the newly acquired chairs next to the newly acquired outdoor table, facing the ocean. Troy trudged up the outside deck stairs, wiping his hands on a rag.

"That's that. Downstairs bathroom is scrubbed and outside deck swept. I haven't put the sheets on the bed down there, but it wouldn't take five minutes if you want to stay here tonight. Makes more sense to go to your loft, though, where all your stuff is. We can get moved in this week, unless you changed your mind…"

She looked at him with moist eyes. "They did this for us," she said softly. "They cleaned, installed, unpacked, hung pictures. The window guy is putting in the shutters tomorrow. It's ready, Troy. Our friends got it ready."

He sat down in the chair next to her. "Because they don't want us to say 'I do' minutes before I have to rush you to the hospital. You really want to move here right away? You don't want to let your mother settle in first?"

"Once we have furniture in the game room it'll be just like our own apartment. You can store your toys in the garage. After we let your parents use your apartment for their visit, we can bring your couch over for downstairs. Then you can give up the apartment and we can live here."

"Listen, we've talked about this a little bit, but this is serious business. Even though that downstairs is like a private residence, we'll be living with your mother, your old Russian coach—because we both know he's never leaving—and there will hopefully be nursing help. I can't have my pregnant wife making them all comfortable, directing traffic or waiting on an invalid day and night. We're going to have to agree on how we're going to handle this situation. Gracie, it's not going to be easy. It usually takes a staff of five to manage her."

"I know. I think we'll be okay. School's out soon. Maybe we can tell your family on the phone, move into this house, let your family use the apartment and the loft for a visit and just get married while they're here. On the beach?"

He pulled her close. "I married you in my head weeks ago. We should give my son a proper name."

"It's a girl, Troy."

"It's a boy, Gracie. I know it."

"It's a girl. Bet?"

"When can we find out?"

"I don't know. Twenty weeks? We have things to do, Troy. Next we have to make a baby room."

"We've just done so much. Can we have a day off?"

"I'm going to call my mother tomorrow and tell her the house is ready. I think she can be up here by the end of the week."

"I'll call my mom and dad tomorrow, too," he said. "Are you going to insist your name be Gracie Dillon Banks Headly?"

"I'm going with Headly," she said. "The most adorable history teacher at Thunder Point High."

"Not adorable, Grace. *Hot*. The girls think I'm hot."

CHAPTER FIVE

"When I was a little girl I made very little houses," Ginger told Matt. They sat at a small table in a dimly lit Mexican restaurant. She nursed a glass of wine and he had a beer and there were chips and salsa on the table. She had a plate of enchiladas and he had a mammoth burrito. "I made miniature houses and people out of everything—Q-tips, cotton balls, pipe cleaners, shoe boxes, paper cups and paper clips. I used twigs and flowers and leaves and gum wrappers. Eventually, when I had the supplies, I used cardboard, paper and glue. In winter when I was outside I used snow and made castles. When I was about seven my parents gave me a great big dollhouse for Christmas—the obvious gift, right? And I wanted nothing to do with it. It just sat in a corner of my bedroom because I liked the sloppy little houses I built."

"All little girls play house," he said. "My sisters played house. Peyton was *always* the mother. And she was a very strict mother."

"What's your earliest memory?" she asked him.

"Hmm. I'm not sure if it's an early memory or some family story that's been repeated so often I think I remember it. It might be when Mikie showed up. My parents had two cribs and a bassinet in their bedroom. We were all lined up to meet him. Ellie was two, Sal was one and Mikie was in the bassinet by the bed. My mother said, 'This is your new brother, Michael, and from now on your father is sleeping in the barn.' I didn't know what that meant for a long time. Eight kids in a little over ten years."

She laughed happily at that.

"You have little leprechauns in your eyes."

"My mother's side of the family, I guess. We're the only green-eyed members of the family. And I've met most of the Lacou-mettes—no leprechauns there, I think."

"That's for sure," he said. He put down his fork. "What happened to your marriage?"

"The marriage?" she asked, like that was an odd question. "Matt, I told you, I fell for a musician. A singer with a guitar. He played other instruments, too, but mostly guitar and piano. What I didn't tell you, I was a groupie. He was in and out of Portland and for three years I followed his gigs. He called when he was in town or even near town, like Seattle or Vancouver or Astoria, and would ask me to come. It was nothing for me to drive three hours just to be with him. On and off, off and on. He's ten years older and even though he's had a few breaks here and there, he doesn't really have a pot to piss in. He wasn't interested in marriage or family or settling down, though he did move in with me because I had a freestanding garage he could use as a studio. So one night when he said, 'Hey, babe, maybe we should just get married,' I jumped on it. Brilliant, yes? I was all over it because hey, I was over twenty-five by that time and all I'd ever really wanted was to be a wife and mother. So I married a self-centered, absent, maybe even adulterous musician who rarely remembered to even call me. My mother thought I'd lost my mind. My brothers hated him. My father still wants to kill him. I married him as fast as I could before he changed his mind. We were married for seven days when he got a job in San Francisco of uncertain duration and he not only took it, he said I wouldn't enjoy myself, given his terrible hours, and besides, I had to work. He said he'd probably be back in a few weeks. Turned out it was sooner, but he left again a week later, that time for a month. When I tried to talk to him about it he said, 'Hey, I told you I'd be a lousy husband. I'm just not into it. My music is really important to me and I'm so close. Baby, I'm so close. And you love my music.' Also, he usually needed money. And I stupidly gave him what I could."

Matt's mouth hung open. He was speechless. If there was one thing about the Lacoumette men, they would die before they'd live off a woman. "You're making this up."

She gave him a rather patient smile. "I could not make it up. I fell for a singer because he had what I thought was a beautiful voice and I believed that once he saw how happy I could make him, he would never want to leave me again. Oh—he would write music and play music, but our love for each other would come first. That was the lie I told myself. There was one part of the equation I hadn't taken into consideration. He didn't love me."

"You married him when he hadn't even said he loved you?" Matt asked.

"Of course he said it," she said. "He said it all the time, along with a lot of beautiful things. Sometimes I even heard them again and again in songs he wrote. He was extremely romantic. But he didn't mean them. He's a poet, Matt. A dreamer. A liar."

"And you left him?"

"Sort of. I left after he told me he just couldn't do it—that whole traditional marriage and family thing. He sat me down, told me how wonderful I was, how he didn't deserve me—boy, wasn't that the truth. And he said it just wasn't for him. No wait, he said it wasn't his *scene*." She took a sip of her wine. "I thought he'd change his mind, come around. He didn't. I know you know, Matt. That I lost a baby to SIDS."

"How do you know I know?"

"Because everyone knows. It's kind of strange—I thought that might be terrible, having everyone know. But it's not. It's easier, in a way. Because I don't have to explain to anyone that yes, I have baggage. Heavy baggage. My newly pregnant friends are so careful—they try not to talk about their happy new pregnancies too much. I wish they didn't have to guard my emotions like that. But it's so thoughtful, don't you think?"

"I'm sorry, Ginger. Sorry for your loss. Yes, Peyton told me. If she hadn't, I don't know how I would have guessed. You seem…" The sentence trailed off.

"Normal?" she asked. "Catch me some early, early morning when I wake up from a dream and can't breathe. Or maybe on a sunny afternoon when I wonder if he'd be walking yet. Or in a store when I see something that would look so cute on him." She took another sip of her wine. "Or maybe, take a look at me having dinner with a beautiful man I can never be more than friends with because my track record is…just…too much. I don't even make sense to myself. What was I thinking?"

"You have to remember, my track record sucks, too," he reminded her. "How long did it last? Your marriage?"

"About three years."

He smiled. "I made it seven months. I didn't fall for a singer but I did fall for the prettiest girl in the biology department. She was a part-time model. Completely self-absorbed. She thinks farming is inconvenient, dirty and boring. We have completely different values."

"Maybe we should introduce her to Mick. He's anything but boring."

"Wait a second. Mick?"

"My ex. Mick Cantrell. His real name is Edward—he changed it to Mick because he thought it was sexier."

"You're kidding, right?" he asked. He dunked another chip. "I should've known better. Hell, she told me she didn't want to be a farm wife."

"And Mick told me being a husband and father wasn't his *scene*."

"I hope you're not still in love with him," Matt said.

"I don't think I am. Not only wouldn't I give him another chance, he doesn't want one. But don't give me any credit for being smart there—just look at what I put up with first. But you? Are you still...?"

He shrugged. It would be terrible to lie to her. "Some days," he said. "When I have those days that I don't understand why everything went to hell. My hours were terrible before we got married and I thought we were happy. She was the one who wanted to be married so bad it made her teeth ache. Why the hell would she marry me? I was the worst person for her to marry. And now she wants to have coffee. Or drinks. She wants us to be friends, to get over it, even try again..." He shook his head. "Aw, God, don't tell Peyton that, please. I don't want to talk about that with my family."

"I'm not going to say anything to anyone about this conversation. But can I say one thing? It's good to have someone like you to talk to."

He reached for her hand. "We have some things in common. But Ginger, once we've gone over the details of all this crap in our rearview mirrors, we're going to talk about other things."

She squeezed his hand across the table. "Like what?"

"Like, can you still make little houses? Do you read anything I might like? Is there time in your life for adventure? Would you have a dog? Or a cat? Or a bird? Are you sensitive to insect bites?"

She laughed at his questions and the twinkle in her eyes was back that fast. "Do you have a dog?"

"We have working dogs, a bunch of 'em. I don't even know how many. They're mostly with George—they mind the sheep. There's a golden and a black Lab around the orchard—they hunt and keep predators away from the chickens. There are no animals in the house."

"Well, I want a dog in the house," she said. "On the bed, in fact. And on the sofa! I want a good old happy dog who looks at me with sad loving eyes no matter how late I get home…"

"And dog hair in the soup."

"And dog hair in the soup," she agreed, laughing.

He lifted his beer. "You're all right, Ginger," he said before taking a drink.

The conversation blessedly turned from bad marriages and other catastrophes to family humor—what her brothers did to her miniature people and houses, what his sisters did to him. Peyton and Ginny were older and tried to dress up the little boys like dolls and make them play roles as their babies. He had her laughing hysterically at the tales of ten people and one bathroom. She told of the fun game her older brothers had of tossing her back and forth, until someone missed and she broke an arm. Matt told of numerous fractures on the farm, all from doing things they were forbidden to do, like swing on the rope in the barn from the loft to the ground.

They had each driven their own vehicles to the restaurant so that when Ginger went home Matt could just head north to his apartment. He walked her to her car and stood with her right outside the driver's door. He put his forehead against her forehead. "For the first time in a long time, I'm a little bit happy. Because you're my friend," he said.

"Me, too. Will you do something for me?"

"Sure, Ginger. What do you need?"

"When you get home tonight will you give me a call? Just so I know you made it without problems. I promise not to keep you on the phone."

"Sure," he said. He looked at his watch. "I'll be waking you up in about four hours."

When he called her, it was already after eleven. And then they talked for two hours.

★ ★ ★

Thank God for Ginger, Grace thought for the millionth time. She was in charge of the flower shop while Grace was at the new house preparing a nice dinner for her mother and Mikhail. And sadly, she was hoping that Winnie would prove to be too fatigued to be argumentative, demanding or feisty, because there were things she had to be told right away.

Oh, how she hoped her mother liked the house. They'd all worked so hard.

Troy had gone to the airport to fetch them. Winnie and Mikhail had come by private jet. She was standing in the kitchen when she heard the garage door slide up, the hum of the Jeep as Troy pulled in and she went to the kitchen door. She saw Troy get out and go around to the passenger side. He lifted Winnie into his strong arms and carried her into the house.

"We're here," he announced to Grace. "Let the party begin!"

And Winnie, God bless her, blushed and slapped at him. "Stop it, Troy! My partying days are long over."

Grace kissed her cheek while Troy still held her very capably. "I'm so glad you're here. How do you feel?"

"Oh, you know. Just always so tired." And then she looked around the great room and kitchen. "Very nice, Grace," she said.

And Grace felt every tight muscle in her body relax. She was surprised she didn't sink to the floor in sheer relief.

Troy put Winnie on her feet then helped her to the chair near the open French doors, facing the ocean, and Grace pushed the ottoman over, lifting her feet up. Winnie shrugged out of her wrap while Grace sat on the ottoman and pulled off her mother's shoes. She held Winnie's feet in her lap and gently massaged them.

"You used to do this for me when I had a long day of skating," Grace said.

"Seems so long ago now," Winnie said.

"You'll want to see the rest of the house but we'll take it a little bit at a time. It's actually a large house, but everything you need is on this floor. I've cooked us a little dinner…"

"I'm not very hungry, darling," she said.

"I have a little soup if you're tired and don't want much to eat. But I hope you have enough energy to hear some news. It's going to be a little exciting around here soon—and we'll try to keep it manageable with regard to your health. We're going to get married, Mama. We want to get married anyway but we're going to put a little rush on it because I'm pregnant." She covered her belly with one hand. "Due around Christmas."

Winnie looked up and over her shoulder at Troy. "You do realize she's never been in a relationship before, don't you?"

Troy's eyes shone. He gave a nod. "She's very good at it," he said.

"And she obviously knows nothing about birth control," Winnie added.

"Or I don't," Troy suggested.

"I'm just going to let all that go," Grace said. "It won't be flashy, Mama. I think we'll get married on the beach, right in front of the house, as soon as possible. School is out soon. While you're still up and about and can enjoy it if you squeeze in a good nap. Troy's family will come but I think they'll stay in town, maybe at his apartment and my loft above the store. I promise to keep your stress low."

"My dress," Winnie said. "You'll want my dress!"

Grace shook her head. "It's not necessary. I'll find something much simpler."

"My dress is simple. We can take off the train and pitch the head gear. I hated that head gear anyway. My mother insisted on that. You need something more your style. But the dress is one of a kind."

"I wouldn't want to get sand and sea all over it…"

Winnie laughed, and her face looked bright. "Why not? Did you think I was going to use it again? Now, if it's the matter

that you don't really like it…of course we'll alter it. I don't care
what you do to it, but if it can work for you in any incarna-
tion, it's yours. Before you decide, look at it. I'll have it sent."
She looked around. "This is a nice little house, Grace," she said.

"We have the downstairs," Grace said. "It's large enough for
me, Troy and a baby. And the top floor—two bedrooms and a
small bath—perfect for Mikhail."

"Excellent," he said. "I might stay day or two."

"Maybe we should get the luggage inside and then toast the
new house," Troy suggested.

"Excellent," Mikhail said.

"Troy, darling," Winnie said. "Before you do all that, is there
a chair on that deck out there that could accommodate me? If
it's warm enough, of course. Could you take me out there first?"

"Of course," he said. "Gracie, can you pull the cover off that
chaise?"

"Absolutely," she said. Then she added, "Troy, darling."

Troy scooped Winnie up in his arms and carried her to the
deck, gently placing her on the chaise.

"My daughter was definitely thinking of me when she let
herself love you," Winnie said. "I think I'll be very happy while
you're around."

Troy winked at Grace.

Flirt! Grace mouthed back.

"And my phone," Winnie demanded. "Who has my phone?"

Mikhail took it out of his pocket and handed it to her.

"Virginia still works for me, doesn't she? Because I have things
for her to do."

"You know she still works for you, Mama."

The luggage was brought in, unpacking was accomplished,
drinks and tapas were served. The sun was beginning to set,
making the beach and the deck bright. Troy put out the awning to provide a little shade. Winnie tried the soup Grace had
on hand but though she claimed it was delicious, her trem-

bling made it a messy dish. Grace made her a new plate—very small portions of roasted chicken, scalloped potatoes, steamed asparagus—just a few bites of each. The others loaded up their plates and enjoyed chocolate cheesecake from Carrie's deli. Troy, Grace and Mikhail carried their plates to the table outside while Winnie balanced a tray on her lap and enjoyed the sound of the waves and the sinking of the sun. Troy showed her the corner where an outdoor hearth would be built and described the activity on the beach in the summer and fall. He explained all the neighbors and his job three doors down at Cooper's beach bar.

"I've asked Virginia to send my dress," Winnie said. "You can do anything you want to it—it's yours. Rip it up or store it away and forget about it, I don't care. And I asked Virginia to make arrangements to reserve that condo in Bandon for your family. It's the least I can do—I've contributed nothing to my only daughter's wedding. Shall I send a jet for them?"

"Oh, Jesus, no!" Troy said in a panic. Then more calmly he took Winnie's hand in both of his and said, "Winnie, best not to flash too much around here. People won't know how to act. My family in particular—they aren't used to a lot of material wealth. It might make them nervous. It might make them not themselves."

"Is the condo all right?" she asked, suddenly concerned.

"It's not necessary," he said. "Thank you. But we have room for them in town. My parents and brother will be fine in Grace's loft and my sister and her family will be very comfortable in my apartment. They'll be close to the beach and this house. But I promise I won't let them overrun you or tire you out."

"I'm such a burden," Winnie said. "I hate being a burden!"

"You're no trouble at all, Winnie. I don't want you to worry. It's a real pleasure having you here. We're living in your house, after all."

Winnie turned her eyes to Grace. She smiled. "I think you did all right for yourself here, Grace. This boy is just what we need."

It was still early when Winnie was settled in bed. Since there was no staff or nursing help, she had her cell phone handy and could call Grace's cell phone if she needed water, or to get up to use the facilities, anything that required assistance. Winnie thanked Troy a hundred times. And Mikhail retired to a room that boasted a very fine flat-screen with a satellite connection and access to all sorts of entertainment.

The house fell quiet before nine and Grace crawled into bed, content that she'd done a good job. She placed her cell phone beside the bed so she could hear if her mother called. Then her fiancé crawled in beside her. Naked.

"Winnie thinks you're a nice boy," Grace said, laughter in her voice.

He pulled her close. "That's good. Let her think that. That will make life easier on you than if she knows the truth."

"That you're just a dirty bad boy?"

"Excellent," he said, affecting a Russian accent. "We toast that!"

Matt's curiosity was piqued. He'd never heard the name Mick Cantrell, but that didn't mean anything. He wasn't into music to that degree. Now, if you asked him the name of the head of the Arizona State University Research Farm, he had that. Or even the name of the PhD in Australia studying and publishing on biological farming. And of course he probably knew every Oregon botany PhD publishing in the state. And he was up to speed on environmental policy, growing sustainable food in the US and many other subjects.

He was not up-to-date on rock stars.

He researched Mick Cantrell and found a website and many hits on Google. It appeared he was a minor star. He had a lot of pictures posted on his website and Facebook page, a few showing him on stage with a huge audience, but on his events schedule there weren't too many listings. His bio made him sound like Bruce Springsteen—he played to thousands, had several CDs, wrote songs for major stars… Matt had heard of the stars but not the songs. But what had Ginger said? He did sell some songs but they never made the charts.

It appeared his gigs were mostly around the Pacific Northwest and he happened to be playing in a Portland nightclub in a week. On a Saturday night.

"What are you up to this weekend?" Matt asked Ginger during one of their phone conversations.

"I'm going to be busy with the shop," she said. "Grace's mother has arrived, there's a fever in the air as they try to pull together a wedding in just over a week. Troy's family will descend on the town and everyone will be busy. I'm going to do as much as I can to free Grace."

"I bet she's so grateful you stumbled into her life," Matt said.

"That makes two of us. I love her flower shop. What will you do this weekend?"

"Me?" he asked. "Oh. There's stuff to do. I'm needed on the farm."

CHAPTER SIX

Ginger had to string together a series of lies in order to have the weekend she planned, a weekend that could bring disastrous results. But she had to do it, had to. There were things she had to know.

She was driving to Portland where she would stay one night with her parents. She planned to have an early dinner with them on Saturday night then, she told them, she was going to meet a couple of girlfriends she hadn't seen in a very long time. She said she probably wouldn't be late. She cringed to see how happy her parents were to hear this! She looked better, said she felt better and now she was putting her life back together with old friends. Her mother's eyes got teary and her chin quivered.

Ginger wasn't meeting girlfriends. The idea actually appealed and she made a mental note to pursue that in the not-too-distant future. She'd get in touch with those few friends who had nothing to do with Mick or with the baby. She might have to reach all the way back to high school or maybe even junior high, but it was a worthy notion.

But on Saturday night she dressed to go to Roy's Theater. It was part club, part dance hall, part theater. For big acts they could open the whole place up and seat more than a thousand. For popular dance bands, they could accommodate a couple hundred and a large dance floor. And for entertainers somewhere in between, especially those with a strong local grassroots following like tonight's act, it could be as many as three hundred in their nightclub.

Mick was performing. Roy's had always been one of his favorite venues. He was bringing a backup band and singers. Ginger knew that was not a traveling band. It was made up of friends he jammed with and he'd give them a couple hundred bucks each. That meant his set list would be deep, including songs he was known for twenty years ago. And of course his own songs, which were only appreciated by his die-hard fans. His most popular performances were the classic artists—James Taylor, Eric Clapton, Gordon Lightfoot, Bruce Springsteen, Harry Nilsson. He even had a Josh Groban piece with a guitar accompaniment that she had heard on the radio from time to time. It was actually cleverly done.

She had seen him twice since the divorce. Once when the baby was born, once after the baby died, but not for the funeral. Mick had had a gig on the day of the funeral. When he showed up a few weeks after the funeral there was nearly a brawl when her brothers, outraged by the fact that he'd played the dead baby card at his last several concerts, threatened to beat him to death. A long time, then. She couldn't remember the last time she'd seen him that things were good between them. Sometime before she was pregnant.

She probably should've worn baggy jeans and a paint-splattered shirt. She didn't. She wore the purple dress with gold piping.

"You look so beautiful," her mother said. "I should get Ray Anne to take me shopping, she's that good."

"I really love this dress," Ginger said. *Do I hope to make him notice me?* she asked herself. Because it was unlikely he would even know she was there. She'd find a secluded place away from the house lights. She was in no way reaching out to him. She just had to know one thing—after all they'd endured, did she still feel anything at all for him?

There was a line to get into the theater. It wasn't long, but there were some people who wanted to get there early for Mick so they could have seats close to the stage. She even recognized some of them; she'd seen them over the years. They weren't exactly friends, though some had shown up at her house when there was partying or jamming going on. She'd see them at various concerts. It had been a long time and thankfully no one spoke to her. It was possible she wasn't recognizable. Also possible she'd only blended into the background of his celebrity, no more important than part of his crew, a mostly volunteer crew. She caught a whiff of marijuana. Several people held beers and since the club wasn't open yet, they were obviously brought from home.

Once inside there were lots of options and she knew each one. There was theater seating in front of the stage for those dedicated enthusiasts. Then there were booths and tables for general music aficionados. And at the back of the room, a couple of long bars, for those live music fans who had nothing better to do on this Saturday night.

She found a small table for two at the far left end of one of the bars. It was a dark little table and when someone asked if she needed that extra chair, she gave it up happily. She ordered a glass of white wine and one ice water. Then she blew out the candle on her table. The waitress relit it and when she was gone, Ginger blew it out again.

It seemed to be a very long time before that rush ran through the crowd, the anticipation of his appearance when the house lights went down. Her wine was half-gone. She couldn't even summon a memory of the way it had felt years ago when she'd drive for hours to be one of many, heart fluttering in excitement because he was going to sing! Then afterward they'd party with some of the superfans. He'd like to smoke a little pot, and after a long, long night he'd take her to bed and make love to her. She never failed to feel like she'd gone to heaven in his arms.

Where was it? The rush? The thrill? She expected to at least feel some nostalgia. Instead she felt only embarrassment, but she wasn't sure for what. For being caught up in his charisma? Hell, she was hardly the only one—he had quite a following of young women. Sadly for Mick, he didn't have quite enough charisma to make him famous.

He finally strode onto the darkened stage to the roaring applause of his audience, especially those down front. One lone spotlight shone on him. He carried his guitar and sat on an ordinary wooden stool, his microphone wired to him. He looked good in his signature jeans, ordinary T-shirt, suede vest. He wore cowboy boots but no hat—he wasn't a country singer, though he had some great country numbers and his biggest sale of original songs had actually been to a country artist. But he was too vain to cover up that silky, thick, honey-colored hair. He wore it just a little long, but he always said he wasn't the hippy-dippy type—no ponytail. He'd chosen blue eyes from the optometrist. Startling blue eyes that were, without the contacts, ordinary hazel. He was damn fine-looking, she could admit with complete objectivity.

He began to sing one of his old selections, a Harry Nilsson award-winner with a lot of fancy guitar work. It was a whole two seconds before the crowd recognized it and burst into applause. In his casual way, he didn't even look up; he concentrated on the music. Or at least appeared to.

There was a time when her love for him was so overwhelming it felt like a great balloon had been expanded in her chest and left her aching when it was ripped out. Then there was the profound sadness of not having enough of him; it hurt so much. That was followed by the crushing pain of being rejected, retreating to the safety of her mother's house to give birth alone. Then briefly, the euphoria of holding a part of him in her arms. She had accepted that she couldn't have him in her life, but she'd found a certain peace. He had been the love of her life, she'd never get over him or find another but she didn't have any more sacrifice in her. She had to find a way to move on. With her son.

Then, not long after little Josh died, the hurt and anger rose up in her. Not so much at Mick but at herself because look at what her romantic delusion had cost her! Years of her life gone trying to find ways to finally deserve his love and devotion. And then a baby ripped from her life and no father to grieve him.

She shook her head. What a profound waste. She sat in the darkened club, hands folded in her lap, and listened to his sweet, melancholy voice, heard the women cry out in adulation and, no doubt, powerful desire. And she just shook her head. *Poor fools*, she thought. *He's not real, can't you see that? He'll never give anyone anything. He'll suck the life out of anyone who dares love him.*

And she felt nothing.

Matt purposely stayed in the back of the crowd entering Roy's. Of course he'd been there before—he'd grown up in the area, and this was a popular hangout; Natalie had loved it. He only wanted a glimpse of this Mick, this mediocre guy who could screw up so many lives and then just trot into the sunset strumming his guitar. Who was this dude? The Rhinestone Cowboy? So it was his plan to stand in the back, maybe just inside the door. He might have a drink, listen to two or three songs, take a look at how much people appreciated his modest talent, then get the hell out of there.

If only life could cooperate with him for once. He stood at the end of the bar, ordered a Cutty on ice and before the house lights dimmed, he saw Natalie with two of her girlfriends at one of the tables near the front. So it might be only one drink. At least she was far away. And then, because he supposed he deserved to be punished for something, there was Lucy in the theater seating down front. There were so many females down there he wasn't sure if she was with anyone.

Well, they were both so far away and the house lights went down, so he was safe. But he wasn't going to stay long. It was too risky.

But then he saw Ginger. She sat at a table alone, her hands primly folded in her lap, watching Mick walk onto the stage. She was wearing that dress, that sexy dress. He frowned considering this—how a dress with a high, mandarin collar could be so damn sexy. Her sleek and soft blond hair moved gracefully as she shook her head while watching Mick. Just a little thigh and knee were visible, her calf shapely in her ordinary heels. There she sat with a half glass of wine, pretty much covered up, not dolled up in spike heels with ankle straps, no boobage on display, and he just wanted to grab her into his arms on the spot. Really, she wasn't as beautiful as Natalie on the surface. Why she seemed ten times more so completely confused him.

"Matt?"

He turned to find Lucy standing in front of him. "Well," he said uncomfortably. "Hey."

"You a fan?" she asked.

"Me? Hell, no. I mean, I just wanted a drink and I thought I'd see if there was any talent here. You? You're a fan of this guy?"

"I like him, yeah." She shook her auburn curls. "Not huge, but my girlfriend is really into him."

"Well, I'm not staying so you should get back to your girlfriend…" Then he winced. He could be such a rude bastard.

"You could stay long enough to buy me a drink," she said.

See, this was the problem, he found himself thinking. Lucy should tell him to just go fuck himself instead of calling him, asking him to buy her a drink. He wasn't worth her time. She shouldn't waste her time on a guy who wasn't treating her right. "What would you like, Lucy?"

"Just a chardonnay," she said, and smiled.

He waved to the bartender. He ordered and fished out his wallet. He put a hand on her upper arm and gave her a soft stroke. "Listen, Lucy, I want you to be careful tonight, okay? Don't drink too much, don't take chances around here. Lot of hungry wolves here tonight and I can't hang around to look out for you."

"That's so sweet," she said.

"No, it's not—"

"Well, at least you're not sitting on the farm, drowning your sorrows," a familiar voice said.

Right beside him stood Natalie. She must have grown attached to the ebony hair, short and spiky. Now, here was boobage—Natalie's top was cut down almost to her navel, outlining her small breasts perfectly. Since he'd been married to her, he now knew the tricks—a little fashion glue would keep the silky fabric from sliding or gaping and exposing her. The outline of her nipples was intentional, as was the slit up the thigh. Her eyes were huge and lashes thick—thanks to the augmenting of a few extra lashes and the artwork of liner and shadow. The shoes were attention-getting—four inches, ankle straps, pointy toes. Hell on her feet, though.

"Isn't this an interesting reunion. Lucy, this is my ex-wife, Natalie. Nat, meet Lucy, a friend of mine. In fact, I met Lucy in a place a lot like this, didn't I, Luce?"

"Rosewood Ballroom," she supplied with a smile.

He could see by the expression on Natalie's face, the narrowing of her eyes, that information speared her in the heart. He was always too tired to party when married to her, but after the divorce he'd been to clubs and dance halls? And here he'd been trying to stay away from Natalie. Even though little Lucy couldn't hold a candle to his ex in the looks department, it felt good to have her know he wasn't lonely. Or bored. "Can I get you something, Nat?" he asked, playing off her momentary jealousy.

"Cosmo," she said, her voice crisp.

He hailed the bartender again, fished out money again. He wasn't going to hang around waiting for a bill.

"It was a friendly parting, I take it?" Lucy asked.

"Actually, it was acrimonious," Natalie said frostily.

"But, as you can see, we're working through that," Matt said, passing the drink.

"And what do you do, Lucy?" Natalie asked.

"Dental assistant. I work for a local periodontist. And you?"

"I'm a model," Natalie said, stretching to her full five-eleven in four-inch heels. Then she stared daggers at Matt, daring him to point out that she'd had only about a dozen jobs for catalogs and ad brochures. There had been nothing with national exposure.

The uncomfortable chitchat and buying of drinks lasted through two songs and then the lights went up and Mick Cantrell started working the crowd, coming down from the stage while the lights revealed his backup musicians. He shook some hands, kissed a few cheeks, asked people where they were from. He wore his guitar on his back and microphone hooked around one ear and hovering over his lips. He was so happy to see them all. Who came the farthest? he asked. Ah, there was a pretty young woman who'd come all the way from Chicago!

"Well, there was a big surprise for me tonight. The most beautiful woman I've ever known is here and I have a gift for her," he said. "A little something from Dr. Hook…"

The band began to play behind him, a spotlight suddenly shone on Ginger, and she actually jumped in surprise. It looked like she was going to make a run for it but seemed to think it through and settle into her chair, polite as always. And he began to sing "Sharing the Night Together."

Matt thought he saw her wince. But, with hands still folded in her lap, she looked up at Mick and let him sing. She blessed Mick with a small smile. Matt could hear the sighs of women

in the audience while Mick crooned that he'd like to be holding her, he'd like to take somewhere, he'd like to share the
night together.

It was the longest three minutes of Matt's life, watching that.

"That was so beautiful," Lucy said. "They must know each
other."

Mick ended his song by whispering to her and giving her a
sweet little kiss on the cheek to the applause of many. Then he
turned away from her, heading back to the stage and launching
into "When You Really Love a Woman."

The minute the audience was again focused on the stage, and
the light and the attention was off Ginger, she stood and left her
table. She was getting out of there. She was going to walk right
past him. Though her head was down and she was concentrat-
ing on an open exit path, she lifted her gaze briefly and saw
him. She stopped short, her eyes wide with not just surprise but
chagrin at being caught in a lie. Her cheeks colored under those
adorable freckles and she continued at a brisk pace.

"Well, ladies, you'll have to excuse me. I wasn't planning to
stay and I'm outta here. Enjoy the concert," he said.

"Wait!" Natalie said. "We have to talk, you and me. Alone!"

He turned to her. "No," he said. And without further expla-
nation, he turned his back and strode out.

It took a moment to spot Ginger. She was moving quickly
and was already down the street. "Hey! Ginger!"

Oh, she knew it was him because she never even turned. She
strode on, head down.

"Ginger!" he tried again.

Nothing.

"Crap," he muttered and broke into a quick jog, catching
up with her in another block. "Hey!" he said, reaching for her
elbow. She turned around, her eyes cloudy, her mouth fixed in
a line. "Come on," he said. "I'm not going to let you run away
from me like that! What's the matter?"

"Nothing. Nothing. I—" She took a breath. "I'm sorry I didn't tell you I'd be in Portland."

"That's okay, Ginger. You don't have to tell me all your personal business."

"But that was humiliating," she said. "Catching me looking at my useless ex-husband like that. Secretly."

He chuckled. "First of all, he's not completely useless. He does a pretty good job of stirring up the girls. They don't know it won't get them anywhere. And second—those girls I was standing between? One was my ex and the other was a young woman I briefly dated and don't want to date anymore."

She was speechless for a moment. "Seriously?" she finally asked.

"Seriously. For about thirty seconds I was wondering why I couldn't just die. I had absolutely no idea they would be there. I'm pretty good at identification and avoidance of trouble. I don't want to be around either one of them."

"Then what were you doing there?"

"Same as you, I bet. I wanted to catch a glimpse of that character. Mick. I wanted to see what he had. Is that what you were doing there?"

"I don't know. I can't explain it very well."

He smiled at her. She was the best sight he'd seen in more than a week. Just her presence took all the stale, dark air of the club out of his nostrils. "There's an all-night diner a few blocks from here—on Washington. It's called Spoonin' or something."

"Noonan's," she corrected with a laugh.

"That's it. Good coffee, mediocre pie. Want a cup? With a friend?"

"Yes," she said. "Yes, I do. Can I ask a favor?"

"Sure."

"Can you try to not ask me to explain why in the world I'd want a look at my ex-husband? Because I'm not sure I can do an adequate job of it."

"Ginger, our talking has been easy. I don't make you talk about things you're not ready to talk about and you don't push me to uncomfortable limits, either. That's why it's working between us. Come on, I'll walk you to your car."

Seeing him was a rush, that's all there was to it, Ginger thought. Even though when she first spied him she felt caught in a snare. Oh, God, caught sneaking around to see her ex! She had no intention of being busy at the flower shop; she had planned that trip to see Mick perform at one of their old haunts.

But Matt was there. Why did he care to see Mick?

He left her at her car. She didn't know where he'd left his truck but when she parked beside the diner, he pulled in beside her.

"This is such a great rescue," she told him.

"Not something I'm known for," he admitted. "I'm glad to be of service. It was a provocative night—he sang to you." He held open the door for her. "He sang you a love song."

They settled into a booth—old red vinyl benches, scarred laminate tabletop, jukebox. The waitress was there in an instant and they ordered coffee and pie.

"He sang a love song to you," Matt said again. "Women were fainting all over the place, each one wanting to be you."

"It's what he does for a living," she said. "It probably did more for his image to sing a love song to me than to anyone else. Everyone reacted just as you did. Wow, he sang that woman a love song. And by the way, it's not much of a living."

"I haven't figured out that part," Matt admitted. "I looked him up on the internet and he sounds like a major star… There are pictures of him singing on a big stage to what looks like millions…"

"He's opened for a few big bands," she said. "Fifteen minutes to a sellout crowd before the big guys take over for a two-hour concert. He's got good PR and it costs a fortune."

"Well, he didn't turn me on, but he was breaking hearts all over the room. I don't know if he's good—I don't know that much about music. Sounded okay to me. I mean, I hate him, but I think it sounded good."

"Why do you hate him?" she asked.

"He didn't treat you right," Matt said. He shook his head. "He must be a little crazy. Or very stupid."

"Or I am." She put cream and sugar in her coffee. "The women surprised you, huh? The exes?"

"Oh, yeah. They shouldn't have. First of all, I met Lucy in a place just like that. I had gone there looking for women. Or, to be more specific, a woman. And Natalie wanted to go to places like Roy's. All. The. Time. Every night of the week, if possible. Them being there was far more predictable than me being there."

"And yet, you wanted a look at Mick?"

"I did. I wanted to see what kind of fool would give you up. What kind of lamebrain would walk away from his wife, his child? It makes no sense to someone like me. In our family if a guy did that, he might be shunned."

"But you did," she said.

At first he looked at her in shock. "Natalie didn't want kids. At least not for quite a while," he said quietly. He stared into his coffee cup for a long moment. "Ginger, you won't understand this. I can't explain this without telling you some things I swore I would never talk about. All I can say—I had to. There were lies and betrayals I just couldn't get over. I admit, that's on me. Being married means being able to forgive and I couldn't. She wants another chance. I wouldn't dare."

She sat back. "Then it wasn't just a simple matter of marrying the wrong person."

"Is it ever simple?"

"Does seeing her hurt?" she asked.

The pie arrived. The check was slapped down on the table as

if the waitress could tell they were engrossed in a serious conversation.

"It didn't. No. How about you? Did seeing him hurt?"

She smiled at him. "That's what I came for. To gauge the
pain. I invested a lot in that man. Years and years. Promises
and patience and vows and sacrifice and I wanted to know if I
still longed for him with every piece of my heart. I looked at
him and felt nothing. Well, that's not really true. I felt a little
shame—I was a complete fool. I should have known better—he
never lied about who he was."

"He said something to you," Matt said. "He kissed your cheek
at the end of the song and said something."

"Uh-huh. He said, 'Wonderful to see you. You look beautiful. Thank you for coming.' And then he turned and began to
sing to a woman two tables away." She laughed and shook her
head. "He thought I came for him. Of course."

"And you went for you."

She nodded and cut off a forkful of pie. On its way to her lips
she paused. "Have you ever had your heart broken so badly you
thought you might die? That you wanted to die?" He nodded
solemnly. "Every time Mick couldn't really be mine, when he
finally said it just wasn't his *scene*, my heart hurt so bad I wondered how it hadn't killed me. How does it beat through that?
The whole time I mothered my little son I was so grateful to
have him, but my heart still ached for the man I had believed
in. I decided it would take willpower to let go, but I was getting over him—so slowly, but I was getting over him. Then
the baby died."

She paused for just a second because she couldn't miss the fact
that Matt's black eyes glittered, like they might be getting wet.

"He just didn't wake up in the morning," she went on. "Softly,
simply, sweetly, like he had just moved on. No cries, no struggles, no gasping. Just a gentle sleep. Then I knew pain. And
grief. All I could think of while I was going through that—not

winning Mick was *nothing*! I couldn't even remember what it was I thought I loved. Well, that's been a while now. It's going to be a year this summer since Josh passed away. I thought it was time to see Mick, but I didn't want to talk to him. I didn't want him to see me. I didn't want to hear how he's got a great deal he expects to sign in a month or less. I wanted to see him so I could know once and for all if I'm finally past that insanity that is Mick Cantrell. That's why I went. I just want to be free."

"And are you free?"

"Pretty much," she said, smiling. She sipped her coffee. "He can still manage to annoy me, the arrogant bastard. But for the most part, I rarely even think about him."

Matt smiled. He took a bite of his pie, and they sat in silence for a moment, enjoying coffee, pie and the company.

"There are new lambs and chicks at the farm," he finally said.

She gasped, and her face lit up. She smiled brightly.

"Maybe on your way back to Thunder Point you could drop by."

"Yes," she said. "If it wouldn't be too much trouble for you and your family."

CHAPTER SEVEN

Matt sat with Ginger for two hours, two pieces of pie and far too much coffee. They passed through the emotional and sentimental stuff and got back to their comfort zone—laughing and teasing.

Thanks to caffeine, he couldn't sleep. He didn't nod off until the time he usually woke up. He slept until eight in the morning and in a panic, called her cell. He couldn't have her beat him to the farm.

"Don't worry," she said. "I slept a little late myself. I'm having breakfast with my mom and dad, then I'll be headed your way. I won't be there before ten."

"Are you sure you remember where the farm is?"

"I'm sure," she said, laughing. "Don't rush me now. I'll be coming when I'm done visiting with my parents."

She was the bravest woman he'd ever met. Strong to the bone, that's what Ginger was. She was the epitome of womanhood in his mind—after all she'd been through, after all she'd had to overcome, she could still be so sweet, so funny, so positive. Her scars were not thistles, they were velvet artwork on her heart.

In the whole of his extended family he could only remember

the loss of one child, one of his distant cousins, an infant who had been born with serious birth defects and had lived only a year. Every woman in the family rushed to the young parents. They came from as far away as San Francisco and Reno with food and prayer beads. The Jews and sitting Shiva had nothing on these Basque women. But as far as he could recall, it was only that one time. And it was fated. The poor child had not been expected to live; a year had been a miracle.

Ginger faced her demons head-on. She even talked about it. Honestly. Matt hadn't been able to do that yet. He was a master of evasion. *I can't explain, but I had to,* he'd said. How flimsy. Ginger would wonder what kind of problem would cause a man who professed to put marriage and family first to turn and walk away. But she hadn't even questioned him.

He sat on the front porch steps, waiting for her. Just like a kid waiting for the Easter Bunny.

She finally pulled up in her well-used gray Audi. She stepped out and gave him a little wave. He took a deep breath and smiled; she was just about the prettiest thing he'd ever seen. She wore a lacy sundress that fell below the knee. On her feet were knee-high boots and she wore a blue denim jacket. Her blond hair lifted in the breeze. It curled a little today, like maybe she hadn't straightened it out with the blow dryer or something. He wanted to grab her up in his arms and smother her with kisses.

"Hi," she said. "You're a little impatient, aren't you?"

"I didn't want you waiting for me. That would be bad manners. Want to see the chicks first?"

"Shouldn't I say hello to your mother?"

"They're not back from morning mass yet, but the house is already full of good smells." He looked her up and down. "Why don't I go get the Rhino?"

"The what?"

"It's like a mini-Jeep—gets us around the farm. You're too pretty to tromp through a farm."

"These are my most comfortable, toughest boots. I'm prepared to tromp."

Not like Natalie, is she? he thought. She'd show up in her fancy heels and he could tell his mother was biting her tongue against asking what she used for a brain. It was a farm, not a runway.

"And the dress?"

"Not new. Very durable. Come on, let's go."

He kept his hands in his pockets because he really wanted to hold her for a minute. Oh, hell, he wanted to make out for an hour or three. He'd wanted to kiss her last night, even though her ex-husband sang her a love song, even though she talked about her misfortunes and how she struggled to get beyond it all. But he had put her in her car to leave without taking any chances.

They walked to the coop where a few broody hens were keeping a lot of chicks warm, but the chicks were a couple of weeks old and were peeping and climbing all over the hens and each other.

"There must be two dozen!" she said.

"Adoption," he said. "Sometimes my mother will just let them hatch, sometimes she'll take delivery of some new chicks and if she has a broody hen, slide them under the hen at night when she's docile and most of the time the hen will take over. A good broody hen can sit on ten eggs or chicks. Sometimes she incubates a couple dozen and either tries an adoption or keeps them in the brooder—it's a pen—until they're bigger and can fend for themselves. I'd take one out for you to hold but broody hens are a little temperamental and you don't want me pecked."

"Thus, the term 'henpecked,'" she said.

"It's no laughing matter. Once they're big, it's pretty communal. You have to remember, these hens are here to work and these chicks are being raised to lay eggs, then they're dinner."

"You're just trying to shock me," she accused. "I do understand where the chicken breasts I buy come from."

After she sighed and fussed over their cuteness, he told her they should go see the lambs. "George has the lambs. It's almost a mile. Should I get the Rhino?"

"Not for me," she said. "Lead the way. Unless you're in a hurry?"

"I have all day, Ginger. But some women don't enjoy plodding through a pasture or orchard."

"I don't have all day," she said with a laugh. "I have a four-hour drive ahead. But there's no rush." Then she drew in a deep breath. "Does it seem like the air is fresher here, on the farm?"

"There are still some blossoms and other flowers," he said. "There's also fertilizer and droppings, so watch your step in your comfortable boots."

He walked beside her, shortening his stride so she wouldn't have to jog to keep up. She brought up the prior evening and how awkward it was that they were all there alone and yet ended up being a group of exes. You couldn't plan something like that.

"Are you anxious to get back to Thunder Point?" he asked.

"To my friends and the shop and Ray Anne, yes, always. It turned out to be such a good move for me. And believe me, I was against it from the start. I just wanted to be left alone."

"But you did it," he said. Impulsively, he reached for her hand, holding it. "You picked yourself up and made yourself do it. I think maybe you're the strongest person I know."

"No," she said with a laugh, shaking her head. "Not me."

"Yes, you. Look at yourself. You somehow pulled yourself together and tried. I'm so impressed by you."

"You should have seen me the day I arrived in Thunder Point. Ray Anne was appalled. For one thing, it took me far longer to get there than it should have and Ray Anne was ready to call the state troopers to ask if there had been any accidents. I told her I stopped to look at the ocean, which was true. What I didn't tell her was that I had contemplated just throwing myself off a cliff."

He scowled. "You're intentionally scaring me."

She ignored him. "I had lost a lot of weight since the baby died and was swimming in my clothes. I was pale because I hadn't been eating, hadn't left the house in months. My hair was… I can't even describe it. *Neglected* is probably the kindest word. I could have made a public service commercial for severe depression."

"Yet, look at you a few weeks later." He gave her hand a squeeze.

"Ray Anne couldn't stand looking at me! She took me, kicking and screaming, for a makeover. She warned me that it might not help the mess on the inside but we had to spare the public what I was showing on the outside. She had a point. Even I find it easier to look in the mirror."

"And how about that cliff thing?" he asked.

"I'm not suicidal," she said. "The only thing I really want, suicide wouldn't get me. I want for it never to have happened. I'm afraid that's not possible."

He stopped walking and faced her. He took her other hand. "I want to tell you something. I can't even explain the dark place I was in a few months ago. I didn't go through nearly what you did but I was in a black, foul temper I couldn't shake. I did a lot of stupid self-destructive things and didn't just hurt myself—I hurt other people, too. And then I met you and things began to change. Just knowing you, talking to you, looking forward to the next time we'd talk or get together—it pulled me out of the hell I was living in. Ginger, I don't want to heap any more trouble on you, but if I didn't have you right now, my family would still be calling me Mad Matt. I rely on you. You lift me up. And the best part is, I don't think you really even mean to. It's just your nature. You're the kindest person I know."

"Matt," she said. "Oh, that's so nice of you to say."

"I'm not being nice, Ginger. We connected. Maybe it was out of shared troubles but maybe that's not all it is. Maybe when we're done surviving this, maybe we go on to find new reasons to connect."

She laughed softly and blushed a little; looking at her feet. Then she lifted her eyes to his. "There's something I should tell you. There was another reason I went to Roy's last night. It was true, I wanted to see him and know that I didn't want him anymore, didn't grieve him. It was also something else. I started to have warm feelings for another man. A dear man who is not dark or angry or mad. I had to be sure that one look at Mick wouldn't throw me back into that spiral I was once caught up in. I wanted to be sure what I was feeling was real."

A half smile played on his lips. "Was it?"

"I believe so, yes," she said.

They stood on the dirt road between the orchard and the pasture that led to George's barn. Maybe halfway there.

"Has it changed things for you like it changed things for me?" he asked.

"Yes. Remember we joked about trying again when we're maybe fifty?"

"Uh-huh."

"I'm down to forty-nine and a half."

He just smiled. Then he leaned toward her and pressed his cheek against her cheek. He let go of one of her hands and slid his around her waist to the small of her back, just enough to hold her while he felt the softness of her cheek and the tickle of her hair. He hummed softly, content. They stood like that for a long moment. Then he slowly pulled back and while looking into her beautiful eyes, touched her lips with his. He felt her lean into him a little and watched as her eyes slowly closed.

He didn't push his luck. He pulled back. "Was that okay?" he asked.

She nodded. "Lovely."

"How do you feel about us now?"

"Maybe forty-nine."

He laughed loudly. "Not even forty-eight and a half? We didn't even get a whole year? I obviously have work to do with you."

"Be careful you don't drive it in the other direction."

He laughed and led her down the road toward the lambs. Matt had never had to be careful before. He'd had almost legendary success with the girls, then the women. This one wasn't going to fall into his lap. He didn't want her to, he realized. He wanted to work for her. Earn her. Deserve her. Be good for her. "You're going to love the lambs," he said.

It was such a perfect June day to gambol about the farm, Ginger thought. And that was really what they were doing, she and Matt, hand in hand, walking at a leisurely pace, visiting the new lambs and the not-so-new lambs. The babies were in the lambing pens inside, though they were big enough to be outside in such perfect weather. There were just a few late lambs; most had been born at least a month earlier.

The weather wasn't the only thing that was perfect. Ginger had begun thinking that while there were people in her life she trusted and could talk to, for some reason this new friendship with Matt was deeper and more trusting than anything she had known. She assumed it was because they were recovering from similar heartaches. But they only visited those subjects a little bit, then moved on to other things—his family, his education, her family and how everyone but her seemed consumed in the family business.

"How long have you known this was what you wanted to do—farm?"

"I think I was born knowing," he said. "I never wanted anything else. I only write, research and teach occasionally to stay well-rounded. It's important to stay involved in the community. We go to a lot of town meetings—things like zoning, environmental issues, property tax, lots of things to stay on top of. I grew up knowing these things."

"I envy that," she said. "I'm the only person in the family who hasn't found any study or industry that would be fulfilling for a lifetime. I've had jobs, and while none of them were going to make me rich or successful, I was satisfied."

"Did your parents ever push you?"

"There was the occasional comment asking if I didn't think about college. I took a few classes. I was interested in literature but not English or composition. I liked some history but most of it put me to sleep. I've never been any good at geography. And math? Forget it."

"Science?" he asked.

"Yes, anatomy. Basic biology was okay but I spent four weeks in chemistry before I just panicked and dropped it."

He laughed. "Because it was hard?"

"Hard and intimidating!"

"I wonder how you'd feel about botany..."

"Now that I've visited a real working farm and work with flowers, I might find it interesting..."

They looked at George and Lori's house, but just from the outside. Ginger remarked on the small garden on one side.

"That's George. His wife isn't too interested in that sort of thing. George says she won't plant or cultivate but she's good at picking for dinner. She, like Peyton, is more inclined toward medical pursuits. Lori is a physical therapist and has worked since they got married. Peyton, I have no doubt, will continue to work with Scott even after they have more children. She loves her work."

"Where is everyone?" she asked. "I expected a lot of action around here."

"By now I think they're all at the big house. It's not the biggest house—George's is actually bigger, but it will always be the big house because my parents are there and it's built for an army. Only seven rooms, but they're huge rooms. On Sundays when the farm is quiet, no planting, breeding, lambing or harvest, the family just maintains. There are daily chores but it's the only day of the week there's actual rest. They take care of the animals, then go to mass, then have an early dinner. It's the only day of the week the family eats before six. I left a note for my mother that you might join us, but it's up to you. There could be a lot of them."

"Really?"

"George's family, I have two sisters nearby, Ginny and Ellie, but they divide their time between my parents and their husbands' families. You know the food will be great but I don't want to overwhelm you."

"If you're sure I wouldn't be imposing..."

"I'm sure it would be a challenge to get you away from them. My mother especially. She lives to feed people, especially people who are at her table for the first time."

"That would be so lovely."

"Does your family have traditions like that? Sunday dinner together?"

"My married brothers have split all the holidays with their wives' families, but we have some. Then there's the occasional gathering—a backyard barbecue, a Sunday brunch and numerous company parties, often at one of my brothers' homes. Richard has a boat and RV—there are family trips to the lake now and then. It's nothing like your family. I was at the reception, remember."

"That's not a typical family dinner. But when we're harvesting, that's when everyone turns out—we need the help. They work like mules, men, women and kids. Then they eat like vultures. Then they drink and dance."

"I did see some of that at the reception," she said with a laugh.

He took her hand and they began to walk down the road to his parents' house. "Sunday is different. It's the only day Paco sits in his favorite chair and spends hours on the newspaper. Or he might read his magazines—all about agriculture. The television stays off and doesn't come on until *60 Minutes* when he argues with the TV and accuses them of having everything wrong, but he never misses it."

"We have that in common," she said. "My father does the same."

She enjoyed the walk, the hand-holding, the fact that they had everything and nothing in common. There'd been those divorces, but that seemed to be where it ended. Their families were completely different but both had built family businesses. Her family was so vanilla and ordinary while he had that rich Basque culture. Between them there seemed to be a unique understanding that allowed them to explore each other's lives and emotions.

When they got to the house they found it bursting at the seams. She had trouble counting them all—it was the mother lode. Matt reintroduced her to people she'd met at the wedding reception—the women were in the kitchen, the kids were all over the place, everyone was smiling a little wildly as they said hello and she knew, then and there, they were hopeful that Mad Matt had found a woman. What the devil was she to do about that? They had gone over that—they weren't about that, they weren't able to couple up, even though just for a moment she thought about how comforting that could be.

"They set a place for you," he whispered to her.

That's when she was able to count. There were nineteen plates on the long oak table. *Nineteen!* Soon she was settled into her place next to Matt, beside his mother, his father not far away. There was a momentary silence for a brief blessing. Then everyone was again talking at once. Paco was pontificating to one of his sons-in-law while simultaneously loading up his plate, mothers reprimanded children, women laughed, kids argued. She looked at them, seeing a few pale brunettes and blondes among the in-laws and children. Serving platters and tureens crowded the table and people moved them around quickly. Much to her disbelief, Corinne picked up Ginger's plate and served her, heaping a little of every dish, filling her bowl with soup, tearing off crusty bread with her hands and placing it on the bread plate. Her glass was filled with white wine.

"Oh, no," she protested. "I have a long drive ahead!"

Without a word, Corinne switched wineglasses, taking Ginger's full one and pouring a small amount into her empty one, then placing it in front of Ginger.

"Don't worry, you don't have to eat it all," Matt whispered to her. "And you don't have to drink the wine. I want you to have a safe drive."

The plate Corinne had filled was placed in front of her and she stared at it in disbelief. There was enough food for at least three meals before her. She looked at it uncertainly. She picked up her fork, not knowing where to start.

The table fell silent, even the children. They were all staring at her—she could feel their eyes. Ginger sampled what she believed to be a chicken dish, though what kind she had no idea. She slid the fork into her mouth and the flavors seduced her instantly. "Mmm," she said, letting her eyes close briefly.

Everyone immediately began talking again, laughing, gossiping, lecturing. She looked at Matt in confusion, her brow furrowed.

He laughed and whispered, "Everyone wants to know if you like our stuff. Our Basque stuff. She overfilled your plate, don't hurt yourself. Be glad she's not spooning it into your mouth."

"Is this like an initiation?"

"Yeah, something like that. Don't worry now. You gave the approved response."

She wanted to ask if Natalie almost fainted from the beauty of the food, but of course she couldn't. Maybe during one of those late-night phone chats she'd brave it. Mick would have loved it; he'd have written a song about it because everything was all about him. He would have played his guitar and sung for them.

She ate a respectable amount, joined the conversation to talk about the flower shop and Grace, spoke admiringly of the new chicks and lambs, even commented on the amazing June weather. She poked at a rich desert, feeling stuffed. When dinner was done she insisted on helping in the kitchen where there was no dishwasher and many difficult roasters and pots to scrape. They shooed her away but she wouldn't go. First of all, she liked them and second, it was bad manners to ignore the cleanup.

Eventually, before the meat and sauces were blasted out of the huge pans, Matt rescued her. He held her denim jacket and said, "Come on, everyone, Ginger has a long drive ahead and needs to be on the road."

They all chimed in. *Of course! Please go before you miss the light! Thank you for everything! You are too wonderful to help!*

She hugged each one, thanking them for making her so welcome, for sharing their amazing Sunday dinner. Matt walked her outside where she paused beside her car and took a deep breath of the clean air. Then she turned her startled eyes to Matt. "Oh, Matt! I wanted to see where you were going to build your house! How did I forget that?"

"Next time," he said with a smile. "We were too busy for that today."

"Next time? Your family will think I'm a freeloader!"

"*My* family?" he asked, laughing. "You're lucky they didn't hold you down and stuff you! You complimented them very nicely without even knowing it. My mother will be ecstatic."

"Thank her again for me, will you please?"

"Of course. I'm glad you had a good time. Will you do something for me?"

"What's that?" she asked, wondering if she should send Corinne a thank-you note.

"Will you call me when you're home? You don't have to call

the second you arrive, but tonight? Maybe we can do a post-mortem on your visit to the crazy Lacoumette farm."

"It was far from crazy," she said. "I'm so glad I saw you last night. So glad I came today."

He had a hand on her waist and leaned his forehead against hers. "It was a nice day."

"Perfect," she agreed.

"Will you kiss me goodbye?" he asked. "It won't obligate you to anything."

She put a hand against his cheek. "I don't have anything."

"Not yet, maybe. But we're pretty lucky, you and me. Our time together has been good. For both of us, I think."

She pressed her lips against his. Briefly. Softly. "Okay," she said. "Forty-eight."

"I'm flattered. Drive carefully. Slowly. Call later."

"I will."

Inside the house, several people were crowded at one small window, carefully peering through the sheers, not moving the curtains. Corinne and Paco, Ginny and Ellie, Lori and George. A couple of kids. They watched the goodbye at the car.

"They look like dawn and dusk," Corinne said.

"The princess and the dark knight," Ginny said.

"Matt and a second chance," Ellie said. "She's so lovely in her heart, isn't she?"

"Do you think he knows he's in love with her?" Lori asked.

"He's a blockhead. He won't know for months," Paco said.

"Paco!" three people admonished at once.

"He's stubborn! You think I don't know my son?"

They saw the kiss, saw him smooth her hair, watched him turn from the car and walk toward the house. They all scrambled away from the window. Even Paco moved at warp speed to his chair, looking all innocent.

When Matt walked in the house, everyone was occupied. No one looked at him.

"Uncle Matt, do you know you're in love with her?" Ellie's nine-year-old daughter asked him.

"What?" Matt said.

"Paco said you won't know for months because you're a—"

There was a sudden plague in the room, a burst of heavy coughing. Ellie whisked her daughter away.

By the time Ginger made the freeway, there were tears on her cheeks. The Lacoumettes were so wonderful, all of them. Matt was such a lovely, strong man and what she felt for him was growing in her heart. She wondered what it might have been like to begin her romantic life with someone like him. If her baby was destined to die, how would her life have been different if she'd had a loving husband to hold her through the pain and tears?

She might be falling in love with him a little. She was very afraid to love again. She was afraid she wasn't very good at it. And when she screwed it up and made mistakes, the next pain would be even worse.

CHAPTER EIGHT

On Monday morning, Ginger made it to the shop early. Of course Grace was already there. Who knew how early she had arrived? She was standing in the back room wearing a wedding dress. A sheet was spread out on the floor beneath her to keep the hem of the dress and its train clean. Iris and her mother-in-law, Gwen, were looking at the dress.

"Good morning," Ginger said uncertainly.

"It's going to be madness this week," Grace said. "Utter madness."

"Um, beautiful dress," Ginger said.

"Not quite yet, it's not. It's my mother's dress. It's not really to my taste and it's certainly not right for a wedding on the beach, but it would make her happy if I wear it. She has no problem with me altering it, but..."

"I don't know that I can," Gwen said. "It's a little complicated."

"What do you want to do to it?" Ginger asked.

"I like the basic lines, but these puffy sleeves are atrocious. These gathers in the back over the butt, ack. And we can't have a train—this thing is long and heavy and I'm not dragging it through the sand. The deep cowl neckline and bodice—nice. I think I want about four yards of satin removed from this thing."

"Little cap sleeves, gathers smoothed and no train but maybe three inches longer in the back than in the front and maybe some lace appliqué right under the bust," Ginger suggested. "But not an empire waist—that's too sixteenth century. Fitted, sliding right down your hips. Some seed pearls around this stunning décolletage would be nice. You're not showing yet so it should be sleek. Simple, clean, brilliant white satin, smooth lines. A couple of small flowers in your hair."

Everyone just stared at her.

"What?" she said. "Just an idea…"

"Perfect." Grace looked at Gwen. "Can you do that?"

"I don't know," the older woman said. "It terrifies me. This is a designer gown!"

"I can do it," Ginger said. "I sew. But I don't have a machine with me or any supplies. I didn't even bring a pair of scissors—and this fabric would need especially sharp scissors. I'm just not set up for it…"

"I'll fix you up," Gwen said. "I'm a quilter, I have everything and what I don't have we can buy. We can do it at my house and I'll help with the handwork. Oh, my God, it will be beautiful! But I'm not cutting it, not me! I think that dress must have cost a million dollars!"

"For all I know…" Grace muttered. "Ginger, please be sure the front door to the store is locked."

"It's locked," she said.

Iris and Gwen helped Grace out of the dress. "Are you sure? Are you willing to alter it?"

"I'm sure I can do it," Ginger said. "Are you sure you trust me with it?"

"You may have saved my life—again."

"But your mother may not recognize it with all those

changes," Ginger pointed out. "She'll recognize that beautiful cowl neckline but nothing else."

"That's not the most important thing," Grace said. "If I can swear to her it's her dress, that's all that matters."

"Good then," Ginger said. "We'll save and preserve the removed pieces so your daughter can use them someday. And we'll need an industrial-strength steamer—no iron is getting near that fabric."

"Anything you need." Grace got into her jeans and shirt. "I have to get out to the house. A nurse is meeting me there at nine—she's going to take care of mother during the day. Peyton and Scott recommended her. Another woman is coming at three—she could be an evening and weekend nurse if we need her. We don't need round-the-clock coverage yet but Peyton says there's an excellent agency with lots of good part-timers when we do have a need.

"Troy's parents will be here on Wednesday and his brother, sister and her family arrive on Thursday." She stopped dressing and stood stone still. "I'm sorry, Ginger. It's going to be madness."

Ginger smiled despite her nerves. "It's going to be beautiful. Try not to worry."

School was out. Troy was around to make sure his family had everything they needed and Iris was off for the summer and offered to help in the flower shop. Ginger and Iris wanted the wedding flowers to be perfect. And, as if having an important wedding wasn't a big enough issue with Ginger, the dress was top priority.

"It will be such an intimate event," Ginger said.

"There is no such thing on the beach," Iris said. "Trust me, I've lived here all my life. If they marry on the beach, everyone will know about it and they'll either be invited, come even if they're not invited or be hurt that they weren't invited. I warned

Grace—she's going to have to tell Carrie and Rawley to be prepared to cater to a crowd. God, I hope the weather holds…"

"What happens if it doesn't?" Ginger asked.

"They get married in the living room and depending on the weather, food is served on the deck or in the foyer."

"Oh, my," Ginger said.

"It'll hold," Iris said, tenderly placing the dress in the large hang-up bag.

The week started out crazy and definitely didn't ease up, but Ginger was so happy to have something new to talk to Matt about that she didn't care. She explained all the excitement and complications of the week, how every hand was needed to make this happen quickly so Troy's family could meet Grace's family before health issues got in the way or, God forbid, Grace was as ripe as a melon!

"You're on speaker," she told Matt. "No one's here at the moment, but you're on speaker because I'm sewing seed pearls around the neckline of this dress. The dress lives with Gwen during the day and then after dinner I bring it home so I can look it over, fit it to Grace and do a little handwork at night."

"You must be exhausted," he said.

"Not yet, but I'm working on it. I just want this wedding to be wonderful for Grace. And if you could have seen my hand tremble as I was about to take the scissors to this one-of-a-kind gown… I tried not to let it show I was scared to death. But it's going to be beautiful."

"You're full of surprises."

"Tell me everything you did this week," she said. "While I go blind on these itty-bitty pearls, tell me everything."

"I don't want you to fall asleep while you're supposed to be sewing."

"Tell me," she said.

"It's June, the farm is stable. We aerate, irrigate, spray for bugs here and there. George has turned out the lambs, Paco is watching for potato worms and other pests. We make our own compost and it's a double-edged sword—we don't run the risk of transplanting pests from commercial products but sometimes we create a haven for our own pests because we stay away from the chemicals that will kill them. Our potatoes are well-known for being big, healthy and tasty. During summer, we mind the pears and potatoes, we have a small cherry orchard, some apple trees. We're watching the crops. George has needed a hand with the lambs—a little docking and castrating."

"Um, docking?"

"Cropping their tails. If they're left long, they get messy back there, if you get my drift."

"Poopy is the drift, I take it."

He laughed heartily at that. "You don't want poop on your sweater."

"Why do you castrate them? Where do you plan to get more babies?"

"George has a couple of very happy rams."

"They take care of the whole flock?" she asked, stopping her sewing for a second. She had seen the flock. It seemed there were hundreds of them.

"They're *very* happy," he clarified. "The lambs of these rams grow bigger and faster. George has a very successful business, his sheep are high quality and healthy. I'll spend a couple of days this week helping him vaccinate, too."

"Wow. I wish I could watch all these things. Maybe not the castrating part. I think farming sounds fun."

"I think it's fun. No offense, I have no interest in watching you sew seed pearls onto a wedding dress."

"No offense taken. Watching sewing is like watching paint dry."

"When is this wedding, exactly?" he asked.

"Saturday at four. I just want her to be beautiful and happy, then my work is done."

"It's a nice time at the farm. We just watch the weather, which has been predictable, and do our chores, which are manageable. When can you come back up here? I can think of things to show you. It's only peak of summer and dead of winter I'm not running around like a maniac getting things done. I can show you the plans for the house."

"You already have plans?" she asked.

"Not official. I have a rendering. I'm trying to keep it from being just another farmhouse."

"How do you do that?"

"Glass. Views. Modern kitchen and bathrooms. Sliding cupboard shelves…"

She laughed.

"There's no reason it can't be a beautiful house just because it's on a farm, right?"

"Tell me about it," she said.

Almost an hour later, after having made suggestions to the construction of Matt's beautiful house, she was ready to put the wedding dress away, get in her pajamas, get an ice water for her bedside table.

This had become a nightly event, talking each other almost to sleep, filling each other in on everything from their deep emotional issues to the mundane events of seed pearls and sheep docking.

"Are you okay?" he asked her. "Surrounded by wedding plans and pregnant women?"

"I am," she said. "As Ray Anne says, we're stuck with life so we have to live it. I've been okay since I came to Thunder Point."

"I'm glad," he said. "I better go then. Pears, potatoes and sheep get up early."

She snuggled down into bed and wondered if this habit, the phone calls that reached into the night, was a rite of passage. She needed to get back to having girlfriends to share some of this information with. Since she married Mick, they had drifted away or she had drifted away from them. She'd ask Grace. Maybe Iris.

In eighth grade she had a boyfriend named Bruce and she remembered talking to him for what seemed like hours. Sometimes they just found recorded songs to play to each other because they had nothing more to say. Sometimes they just listened to each other breathe. They weren't nearly as exciting face-to-face.

Matt was so protective. *Are you okay? Surrounded by wedding plans and pregnant women?* What a darling.

Her cell chimed and she smiled. She clicked on. "Forget something?" she asked.

"Yeah. I forgot to tell you how awesome it was that you came to my gig."

Mick! Holy crap!

"You looked so awesome. More beautiful than ever. It made me remember how much you inspire me. I'm never better than when you're in the house. Oh, babe."

"What do you want?" she asked.

"I'm going to be in the area for a few weeks and I thought we should get together. You can come to a couple of shows. We have a lot of history, good history. Might be time to have another look at that. It's good for me so it's gotta be good for you. Right?"

She started to laugh. She couldn't help it—it was so Mick. If it was good for him it must be good for everyone else. *Right?*

"I was there to meet a guy. We didn't know you were the show or we would've picked another bar."

"What? A guy? Since when?"

"Since a very long time ago. I don't live in Portland anymore. And the last thing I'm ever going to do is get together with you to talk about our *history*. Lose my number!"

"What? Where do you live?" he asked.

"Houston!" she yelled, hitting the end icon. She turned the phone to vibrate and turned off the light.

It vibrated at once. A text was coming in. Why hadn't she changed her number? Because she hadn't needed to! Mick never called.

Baby, what's wrong? Wasn't that the right song for you? For us? I thought it was just right! I thought about At This Moment. What's wrong?

She couldn't resist. She knew it was futile, that he'd never get it, that he was a self-absorbed cretin, but she just couldn't resist.

What's wrong? Gosh, let's see. You divorced me when I was pregnant with your child, you brought me flowers at the hospital and I didn't hear from you again until you sent a card a month after his funeral! And it wasn't even in your own handwriting! What could possibly be wrong, you stupid, arrogant asshole!

Hey, I paid tribute to him in the next four concerts! I played Tears In Heaven!

I must have had a mental break, she thought. *Brain damage, that's what it was. How in the world did I ever think this idiot was a real man?*

Go away. Never contact me again. My boyfriend will kill you. Then my brothers will chop you into little pieces.

Whoa, baby, you got some hostility.

It was hard to sleep after a phone call like that. Then when Ginger did finally nod off, she was restless with anxiety dreams, the one that finally shook her awake being the worst. It was so vivid, so colorful. And shamefully real. Their house and the free-standing garage where Mick liked to jam with his friends were both full of people, spilling out into the yard. A lot of people gathered around to listen to him play, sing, talk about the business, gossip about artists he knew. *Yeah, that's when I met The Boss…he really liked a few of my songs…wouldn't be surprised if he wanted to buy a few.*

It was getting a little loud. Mick was playing some rock, the speakers making the walls shake. She was getting nervous. They were supposed to keep the weed outside and the noise down. They were going to wake the baby! And the windows were open! These fumes—could hurt the baby! The noise wasn't good for him! She went to Mick and appealed to him to clear the place out if he couldn't manage them, the people who gathered around. But he didn't acknowledge her. Her ears were ringing and she decided it would be best if she gathered up the baby and went to her mother's house, but she couldn't find the baby. She should call the police or run to the house next door—but the neighbors were also in her yard, enjoying the music.

She was trying to get to her car but her legs wouldn't carry her and her car wasn't where it was supposed to be and she had no baby. She wanted to call for help but she just cried like a little fool. Mick was telling her to settle down, she wanted this. This is what you signed on for, he reminded her, frowning at her, going back to his guitar and singing. Then he was kissing someone, some woman she'd never seen before.

Her stomach was in a knot and she was gasping for breath. Her head hurt. In the way dreams can be wild, she was pregnant, then she was searching for the baby and couldn't find him.

Her eyes flew open. She was trying to catch her breath, as if she'd been running. Her heart was pounding relentlessly and it took her a second to realize it was all a dream.

Instinctively, she rolled over, looked at her phone, saw Matt's number and hit the redial. His groggy voice answered instantly. "What?" he said. "What's the matter!"

"Oh, God," she said, suddenly aware she was calling him in the middle of the night. "I wasn't thinking. I'm sorry. I'm so sorry. It's nothing."

"It's something," he said. "What is it?"

"It's nothing," she said, willing herself to be calmer. She tried to slow her breathing. "I had a bad dream. I just reached for the phone. And woke you. Jeez—they're going to lock me up. I'm crackers." She ran a hand through her hair. "My God, I'm just plain nuts."

"It's okay," he said more calmly. "It's okay. Just tell me what's wrong and we'll talk it through."

She looked at the clock. "Never mind. You have to wake up in two hours and I'm fine."

"I can sleep in. Till, like, four thirty."

She laughed in spite of herself, wiping her cheeks. "I bet you wish anyone but me had knocked you out at your sister's wedding."

"That is a privilege I would grant *only* you," he said. "What did you dream? Was it about the baby?"

"Yes and no. It was about my early years with Mick, back when we moved in together. Our house was a party house. It was my house. I rented it. When he was around, every night was spent rehearsing. There were always people around—sometimes a few, sometimes a crowd—groupies, musicians, you know. Music, noise, smoke, drugs. I wasn't into drugs, by the way. I tried some pot once, drank a little too much a few times, years before starting a family, but…"

"I was in a fraternity," he said. "You don't have to explain."

"Sounds like a never-ending college party, right? I thought it would change when we got married, but it didn't. Why did I think it would change? He never said it would. In my dream, I was concerned about the baby, about the noise and the smoke and the baby and he was telling me to chill. And then I couldn't find the baby," she finished in a weak whisper.

"Matt, I never had the baby in that house with the parties. I left when I was barely pregnant. I told Mick I was going to stay with my parents until he could wrap his head around the fact that we were having a family and the lifestyle wasn't healthy. I couldn't be around all that second-hand smoke and I needed to sleep! That's when he told me it wouldn't work for him. He was sorry I didn't get it, but that whole family and baby thing just wasn't for him."

He was quiet for a second. "The stress," he said. "I think all the stress is getting to you, Ginger. The wedding, the dress, the pregnant girlfriends…"

"No, no, that's not it. He called me. Right after we hung up, Mick called."

"What did he want?" Matt asked, sounding more alert now.

She laughed a little. "He thought it was so great that I came to hear him sing. He thought we should get together. To talk about our good history."

"And you said…?"

"I called him an arrogant asshole and hung up on him, then he texted me and said I had some hostility."

"Jesus," he muttered. "You know, I've made some incredible blunders, but that defies imagination."

"It does, doesn't it? He used to bring his guitar to holiday dinners with my parents and brothers and serenade them. He didn't notice that they rolled their eyes and wandered away."

"Always a show, eh?" Matt asked.

"How did I not know how ridiculous he was?"

Matt laughed. "My ex used to tiptoe through the goat shit in her spike heels when she'd come to a family dinner with me. High heels, tight, short skirt, nails like red talons. Everyone in the family looked at her like she was a clown, dressed for the circus, but I didn't even notice how inappropriate she was. Well, not for a year or so…"

"What do you suppose happens to us?"

"I don't know what happened to you but I was pumping about a thousand pounds of fresh testosterone," he said. "I figured it out, just not quick enough."

"Is that why you divorced? Because you finally figured it out?"

He thought for a second. "No, Ginger. Because she wasn't just fancy and self-absorbed on the outside. I'd have been happy to carry her through the muck and offal of the farm. But then I found out she was like that on the inside."

"I never would have guessed how much we have in common."

"You have no idea. Now put your little head down. See if you can get some sleep…"

"I'll say good-night," she said.

"You don't have to say good-night. Leave the line open. I'll be right here if you need me."

"We can't do that," she said. "Our phones will run out of juice and then we won't be able to call anyone."

"You think you'll be okay?"

"I'm fine. Kind of embarrassed. That was impulsive. I'm not usually that impetuous, calling a man I hardly know in the middle of the night."

"Hardly know? I can't think of a woman I know better," he said. "We know each other very well. If we sign off will you promise if you need to talk, you'll just call back? No matter what time it is?"

"Sure," she said. "But I'll try not to."

"Sometimes talking helps," he said. "God, never tell anyone in my family I said that, okay?"

"Okay," she said with a laugh.

Matt held the phone against his chest. *Look out*, he told himself. *Danger, danger*. He wanted to be there with her. If he was there, she could roll over, and he'd comfort her. He wanted to get his arms around her, hold her, whisper to her that what she was feeling seemed reasonable. And that she was no longer alone. He'd take that job in a heartbeat.

CHAPTER NINE

The fatigue of ALS might've slowed Winnie down but it didn't keep her from staging her own wedding festivities. She rested in the morning after breakfast and a bath, generously tended to by her new full-time nurse, Lin Su. Then she was good for a little company and lunch and with an afternoon rest, she had at least a few hours of socializing and dinner. Winnie's schedule of meals and rests had to be carefully monitored and protected to ensure she wasn't weak or fatigued because she had planned activities!

"As if I'm surprised," Grace said.

Grace had every reason to expect the Headly family to be wonderful. After all, Troy was. What she wasn't prepared for was to find them more wonderful than she could have imagined. Troy's mother, Donna, was thoughtful, funny and clearly a strong head of the family. Burt Headly was a big, good-natured cuddle-bear, always smiling, always hugging, perpetually laughing, grandchildren climbing on him all the time. When Troy and twenty-one-year-old Sam stood beside their father, the resemblance in looks and temperament was so obvious people would put them in the same family without knowing them. Troy's sister, Jess, was very like her mother in both looks and that quiet authority. Her husband, Rick, the firefighter from Morro Bay, fit into the family perfectly—strong, good-natured, patient. And the three children, ages two, four and six, had piles of energy but Troy, Rick and Burt ran them up and down the beach until they were sandy, gamey and worn-out. When they came to what was Winnie's house, the Headly adults kept a hand on each child, careful that they wouldn't mess up the place or tire Winnie.

Donna and Jess were the most interested in Grace's skating career. "I would give anything to see you skate," Jess said.

"And I'd be happy to do that for you, but Troy might have a fit," she said, smoothing a hand over her tummy. "It's not as though I'd take a hard fall and hurt the baby, but he's gotten very protective."

"I have the matter taken care of," Winnie said. "I had my assistant from San Francisco send us the DVDs."

"Mother, you didn't," Grace said. "We can't ask the whole family to watch home movies!"

"But we'd love to," Donna said. "And after the baby comes, once you're on your feet and have had a chance to practice a little, we want the real thing."

"The girls are going to be so excited!" Jess said.

After a family dinner that Donna and Grace joined forces to cook, the women and kids sat around the great room with the DVDs playing on the big flat-screen, exclaiming over each jump, spiral, arabesque, axel and double axel. After just a few minutes, the men were on the deck with drinks, except for Mikhail, who was giving commentary on the skating. Pretty soon the little girls and Jess's four-year-old son were twirling around the living room, making them all laugh.

Troy, Donna and Burt hustled everyone out of Winnie's house before it was very late and Grace was able to help her mother get ready for bed.

"When we're not in wedding mode, Lin Su will be able to settle me for the night," Winnie said apologetically.

"I'm happy to do it, Mama."

"I've had many reasons to resent this blasted condition, but I think tonight brought home to me the best reason to resent it." She sighed. "I think you and Troy will have lots of children. I think you'll be wonderful with them, even if you don't have the stamina to turn them into great athletes." She sniffed. "I hope heaven has a good window, Grace. I really want to watch them grow."

"Oh, Mama…"

"We're not going to snivel and drown in self-pity," Winnie said. "Instead we're going to get you married. You picked a good one. How you did that without my advice, I'll never know."

Grace laughed through sentimental tears. "It's a wonder, isn't it?"

"His family," Winnie said. "Nice people. I think they like you."

"I hope so."

"They're going to tell all their friends that you're a champion," Winnie said. "You'll be a better mother than I was."

"I'm not so sure about that…"

"Work on it, then. I was better than my mother, you'll be better than I was, your daughters will be better than you. But Grace… Izzy," she said, adding the name Grace had gone by as a girl. "Tell me one thing. I was a hard mother, I know, but did you ever doubt I loved you?"

Grace shook her head. "No. Your love was fierce."

"Ah," Winnie said, satisfied, settling back and letting her eyes close softly.

"A little controlling," Grace added.

"A *little*?" came a voice from the bedroom doorway. Mikhail stood there watching them. He held up a DVD in a plastic sleeve. "If the Empress is ready for bed, we will watch another show together. Now the house is quiet and the little dancers have gone home to bed. I can tuck her in for you."

"Do you feel up to it, Mama?" Grace asked.

"I'm fine, Grace. But you must be tired. I remember—that was the first thing about being a little pregnant—so tired. Go and rest. Leave any more cleanup to the baby's father."

Grace kissed her mother's forehead while Mikhail settled into the comfy chair beside the bed.

Grace didn't bother with anything in the kitchen or great room. She wasn't too tired to think about the way things had turned out. She felt reasonably sure this ALS, with the limits it put on Winnie's life, had softened her. Winnie had always been a difficult, stubborn woman; their relationship had been challenging. If Winnie wasn't sick right now the chances were good that they'd be fighting over all these details—the wedding, the groom's family, everything. That was the history they'd had— one power struggle after another with very brief periods of affection.

Now, when it was almost too late, Winnie was becoming the kind of mother Grace had always longed for. Tolerant. Warm.

Rather than cry about it, she'd be grateful for this. It was a gift.

Winnie sat up in the bed. The television was a gray blur; the DVD had stopped playing. She looked at her phone—it was the middle of the night. It was the snoring combined with her full bladder that had roused her. She turned on the light and stretched a leg toward Mikhail's knee, giving him a kick.

He jolted awake, startled. "Shits of the gods," he grumbled.

"You should go to bed. You're snoring."

"You are sure it wasn't you, snoring?" he said.

"The snoring had a Russian accent. Go to bed," she said, looking at her phone.

"What are you doing?" he asked.

"I call Grace when I have to get up, when I need something," she said.

"Ach, let the girl rest. I will get what you need."

She smirked. "The toilet?"

"I will take you."

"Don't be ridiculous! I'm not peeing in front of you!"

"Of course not!" he barked. "I take you, you hold the bars, I leave, I close door, you sit, you make it rain, you do what you do—I suppose you don't shake it off like a man. Then you can pull yourself up on the bars. Then what? Whistle?"

She was shocked silent for a moment. But then she smiled. "I'll call Grace."

"No, let the child sleep. You want I should get you some water?"

"First the bathroom," she said, scooting to the very edge of the bed.

He stooped, put her slippers on her slender feet and pulled her up. "Lean on me," he said. "I'm not a young man to carry you, but you can still walk ten steps. You'll be fine, then back in the bed, yes?"

"Mikhail," she said with a laugh. "Make it rain? Really?"

"You have trouble to understand meaning of this? I trust you know what to do."

"I'm going to do it right here if you keep making me laugh," she said.

"Please, no," he said. "I am wearing the stocking feet."

Winnie did all she could to comply, though a middle-of-the-night trip to the bathroom had never been so entertaining. She did as he suggested, holding the handicap rail beside the commode until he left. Then, adjusting her nightgown, lowered herself, made it rain—with a little laughter at the thought—and then stood. And flushed. Oh, how she wished she could whistle.

There was a little light tapping.

"Yes, come in. I'm waiting for you," she said. "I'm going to get a whistle!"

"Shits of the gods," he muttered. "Come, your highness," he said, tucking her arm in his. "Is not good for your rest to have so much talking in the night. In bed you go. Come, come."

He held the sheets back, lifted her feet to help her, took the slippers off and covered her up. Then he returned to the chair, pulled the throw over him and stretched his legs out. He crossed his arms over his chest.

"What are you doing?"

"Going again to sleep."

"Go to bed! That's uncomfortable!"

"Ach, is perfect. Is excellent. I never had better sleep. Stop with the talking."

"You'll never sleep!"

"You are correct! I will never sleep! Someone cannot shut her royal mouth! Enough!"

She looked at him for a long moment, then reluctantly turned off the light and lay down.

In the dark he said, "If I am right here, I'll know if you're dead," he said.

"How will you know?" she asked.

"It will finally be quiet."

Troy, his brother and dad, Cooper and Spencer, set up on the beach for the wedding. There were tables for the food, provided by Carrie. An arch that Iris and Ginger had covered with flowers had to be anchored. There was a stack of beach blankets that Cooper stored in the basement of the bar and a pile of canvas and aluminum beach chairs for people to use. There were a few picnic tables around, too heavy to move closer to the party but useful just the same.

The flower van was parked in the drive of Winnie's house; the catering van would be parked on the beach as the time

drew near. In addition to food and flowers, Cooper arranged
for a couple of kegs and several large bottles of wine. Twenty or
so people had been formally invited, another twenty-five had
been informally invited, still another twenty-five would probably show up.

Troy was told to get ready downstairs in their little apartment
while Grace would be on the main level with her mother. Because it was her mother's event, too, a beautician had been called
to do hair and makeup. Winnie could not have done it herself
and God knew Grace couldn't do it for her. Iris and Ginger came
over early to bring flowers and help; Ginger brought the dress.

Several times during the week Grace had looked at her wedding gown, a work in progress. She'd tried it on a couple of
times and been happy with it. It was so different now, less than
an hour before the vows, Grace's hair pulled back and caught
up in curls that cascaded down in back, makeup finished. She
stepped into the dress, Iris closed up the many small buttons in
the back, and she turned toward the mirror on the inside of the
closet door.

"Oh, my God," Winnie said in a breath. "Stunning. Beyond
stunning."

"It's beautiful, Ginger," Iris said. "You're amazing."

"Thank you," she said a bit shyly. "It was a joy."

"It almost looks like Pippa Middleton's dress," Grace said.
"Oh, Ginger, I'm never going to be able to thank you properly
for all you've done for me."

"Well, that goes both ways," she said. "I came to this little
town to get a break, a changed perspective, and look what I
found. A job I love, good friends, a new lease on life. A lot of
that is made possible by you, Grace."

"You do love that little flower shop," she said. "You treat it
like your own."

"I love it," she said. "If you think I could stay on awhile, I'm
willing."

"There's a place for you as long as you want it."

"Thank you, I've been very happy there. When the wedding is done and things calm down a little I might look for a small apartment or something. I should give Ray Anne her life back." She laughed conspiratorially. "Ray Anne and Al must really have to plot to have any time alone together."

Grace's eyes lit up. "I know what I can do," she said. "When the wedding is over and Troy's family leaves, he's giving up his apartment. There's no point in paying rent there while we're living here. The first thing we're going to do is bring his big leather sectional and TV over here for our downstairs."

"I'm going to need to find something furnished."

Grace raised one brow. "Does it have to be large? Could a studio do the trick?"

"Sure. Of course. I hope I'll continue to spend lots of time with Ray Anne and some of my new friends. It's just where I hang my hat…"

"How about my loft above the store?" Grace asked. "Troy's parents are using it while they're in town, but soon it will be empty. I don't have any plans for it."

It was first shock and then her features were taken over by disbelief. "You'd let me rent it from you?"

"No, I'm afraid not, Ginger. I will only let you have it if you continue to work in the shop and it will be rent-free."

"I couldn't!" she protested. "That's just too much."

"Nonsense," Winnie said. "What use does Grace have for it now? Well, we could store my furs there…"

"Mother!" Grace said with a laugh. She looked at Ginger. "There won't be furs to store," she said. "My mother was very fond of them, overly fond, but we agree there is no use for furs here. We'll keep her warm."

"But you'll keep at least one to remember me by, won't you?" Winnie asked.

"Absolutely," Grace said. "If it will make a good rug."

"You're incorrigible. I spoiled you as a child and what has it gotten me?"

There was a light tapping at the door. Mikhail poked his head in. "There is time before the vows and a groom is pacing out here. Put his mind at ease, my dove. Tell him you still agree to this marriage."

"Is he showered and dressed?" Grace asked. "Because no one touches me unless he is showered and dressed."

"I'm showered and dressed!" Troy yelled from the other room.

"He has the nerves. Come and soothe him, *pupsik*. He's making me want a drink."

Grace walked out to the great room where she noticed that Sam and Rick were sitting patiently on the sofa while Troy appeared to be pacing. When they saw her, they jumped to their feet.

"What in the world is the matter?" she asked him. "Are you having second thoughts?"

"Me? God, no! I just want to get this done before you come to your senses!"

"Well, I was all settled until I met your family and now…" She grinned at him. "I'm thinking I could be better off with young Sam."

Sam grinned hugely. "Awesome."

"Don't even joke about that," Troy said. "He has no morals." Then he reached for her hand. "Come with me." They walked outside onto the deck. Below them on the beach they could see the wedding activities—Carrie's buffet tables, the bridal arch, people beginning to gather.

She smoothed his collar; he wore the shirt she had ordered for him, a black linen Tommy Bahama beachcomber style, a stark contrast to her white. He ran a finger around the low-cut cowl neck of the wedding gown. "You're so beautiful," he said. He pulled a box out of his pants pocket. "Let's see if this works."

He opened the box to her gaze, and she sighed. It was a beautiful string of pearls. "It couldn't be more perfect."

"I had a little help. I asked the girls. Do you like them?"

"They're beautiful. I feel bad, Troy—we've been so rushed, I haven't gotten you a gift."

His hand slid down over her tummy. "Oh, I think you have."

"It's going to be the gift that keeps on giving, too," she said with a little laugh. She turned so he could fasten the pearls around her neck. Then he put his lips there. She leaned back against him for a moment.

"Tired, honey?" he asked, his arms circling her waist, holding her.

"When this is done, I'm going to sleep for a month."

He turned her to face him. "Did you eat anything?"

She nodded. "I know how something like this will go. I might not get a chance to sample our own wedding food."

"We're going to have a nice big plate made up and I'll sneak it into the house for later. We can have a picnic in bed."

She laughed and touched his cheek. "Your favorite kind of picnic."

"Luckily, the bride and groom get to sneak away. We don't have to be the last to leave."

"Iris and Seth are going to take the arch and van back to the flower shop and Carrie assures me there is nothing for us to help with—she's got it covered. She has a little help. Once we go down there, we're off duty."

"Except for Winnie. Rick has Cooper's little Rhino all cleaned up and parked in the garage. He's going to be in charge of getting her up and down the hill. Lin Su is going to come to the beach for a while, then she'll help Winnie settle in for the night. You can start your month of sleep right after you promise to love me forever."

"I think I did that already."

"Gracie, I didn't think I could be this happy. Thank you. I love you."

"Took you a while to get right with that idea, didn't it?"

"A couple of days, maybe. You haven't doubted me since, have you?"

She shook her head. "Not for a second. You ever doubt me?"

"No, Gracie. Not for a second." He glanced at the beach. "In fifteen minutes the judge will be here, everyone will be ready and we can do it. Should I pull the trigger on this event?"

"Do it," she said.

He left her on the deck and went inside. He told Rick to deliver Winnie to the beach where a comfortable chair waited for her—she insisted there would be no wheelchair at her daughter's wedding. It wouldn't do much good in the sand anyway. Iris got her flowers and handed a beautiful bouquet to Grace. Ginger and Mikhail got ready to make their way down all those stairs.

"Showtime," Troy said.

Ginger wept a little when the vows were exchanged, but not because she was seized by sadness from her own past. Just the opposite. She'd never been to a wedding quite like this. It was more than a union of lovers, almost as if best friends were joining together to make a perfect family life. She was so moved by the loving exchange between Grace and Troy, by the joy shared among the guests, a tear or two escaped. And she was hardly the only one. As she glanced around she saw that many shared her sentiment. They were indeed a beautiful bride and groom.

The only person who didn't seem to be completely charmed by the casual beach wedding was Ray Anne. "I don't go to weddings in flip-flops," she groused. "I can't even move in these shoes." Quite a few of her friends and Al found humor in the fact that if Ray couldn't dress up and wear her spike heels, it put her out of sorts. Everyone else seemed to be delighted by the circumstances. Even the bride was soon carrying her sandals in one hand, lifting her gown with the other. But Ginger noticed that before long Al was carrying Ray Anne across the beach to the stairs to Cooper's bar where his truck was parked.

Ginger enjoyed the goings-on. Children ran and played and there were lots of children—Troy's nieces and nephew and tons of local kids whose parents were at the wedding. People gathered around the few picnic tables, on beach chairs, enjoying an endless supply of drinks and delicious finger foods. She had on a strappy sundress she'd found in her closet from years ago, something she hadn't fit into in a long time but had always loved. It was flattering with a jagged hem that fell in an asymmetrical pattern below her knees, like many overlying scarves. The straps crisscrossed in the back. It was an emerald color that really brought out her green eyes. And the late-afternoon sun and breeze gave her a rosy glow. She started out in sandals but in no time she was barefoot like so many others.

She enjoyed the party, brief though it was. Sam flirted with her. Well, Sam flirted with everyone and a couple of hours into the reception he seemed to have found himself an interested young woman. Ginger didn't know if she was a guest or one of the many who happened down the beach and took advantage of the party. She was wearing a summer dress so Ginger guessed—guest. This was by far the largest gathering she had attended so she was able to visit with new friends and meet a few people for the first time. The couple who had once worked for Winnie and had later trained Grace in the flower business were there. Cooper had taken it upon himself to tend bar, assisting Rawley and Carrie. All her new women friends had their men present—Lou brought her husband, Gina was with Mac, the former town deputy. The Grants were there and Spencer, Devon and the kids. All the usual suspects.

It was around seven, the sun barely lowering in the sky, when the crowd began to thin. Winnie was whisked away in the Rhino, Mikhail was climbing the stairs to her house, the bride and groom were saying goodbye, the bridal arch was carefully loaded into the flower van. Cooper and some of the men were taking charge of trash while Carrie was packing up the little remaining food and Rawley dismantled the serving tables. They were drifting away in all directions—some going up the stairs to Cooper's because there was a parking lot behind the bar, some heading down the beach to the marina lot, some taking off in their beach-mobiles or vans.

Since Ginger had come from the flower shop in the van with Iris, she was on her own. Iris offered to drop her at home or the shop, but Ginger was quite content to walk slowly across the beach and just enjoy the early evening. The beach was a beautiful place, in all its moods—gray and chilly, stormy, sunny or wet. She strolled, kicking along the cold water's edge.

When she got near the marina, she saw a familiar face. He was leaning against the front bumper of his truck, one leg crossed over the other, holding a bottled water, watching her, smiling. Matt.

"Let me guess. You're stalking me," she said.

"Nah. Just happened to be in the neighborhood."

"What are you doing here?"

"I wondered how you'd feel after the wedding. You wouldn't go to Peyton's ceremony. Memories, you said."

"You should have told me you wanted to drive down. I could've invited you. I was allowed a guest."

"I knew you'd be busy," he said. "Working."

She tilted her head to one side. "What if I'd been with a guy?"

"If you'd planned that, you would have mentioned it. I don't know everything about you, Ginger, but I know you're honest. And up front. You've told me a lot more about your issues than I've told you about mine."

"I noticed that. So, you're here because…?"

"You might want someone to talk to," he said with a shrug. "How was it?"

"It was perfect," she said, smiling. "Very informal and perfect. It was almost like a bunch of people were having a party on the beach and two broke away from the gathering to get married. People were standing around, visiting, having a drink. Then the judge—the same judge who married Iris and Seth, I take it—stood by the arch, cleared his throat and it began. Troy and Grace stepped up in front of him, the traditional vows were repeated, they said a few sweet things to each other and that was it. A kiss—extralong, I think. Then it was back to mingling and enjoying the day." She looked up and around. "Perfect day for it."

"It does seem perfect. Want to go for a ride?"

"Where?"

"Up the coast a little bit. Or maybe down the coast. Just to a lookout to watch the sunset."

"Sure. You came a long way on a bet. I might've been busy."

"I know. In fact I thought you might be. I thought maybe it would go on for hours. Or maybe you'd be out with friends from the wedding or something. It was just a spur-of-the-moment thing."

"And if I was busy? You'd turn right around and go back?"

"I could. Or I could call Peyton and see if she'd put up with me for the night. She has mysteriously stopped lecturing me. I suspect Scott."

With a hand at the small of her back, he directed her to the passenger side of the truck and helped her up and in. Then he got in the driver's side and buckled up. "Do you care where we go?"

"You decide. We could just go to Cooper's."

"I thought after a day full of people you wouldn't mind a little quiet."

"Good idea," she said. "I'm tired, that's for sure. It was a packed week of work, sewing, trying to keep track of wedding-day details to help Grace, lots of flowers. Iris and I decorated the arch they used—it was so beautiful. And it's such a funny place—Thunder Point. They invited a few people and everyone else heard about it or saw it and just came. Grace was ready for that," she said with a laugh. "She and Troy ordered up enough food and drink to accommodate a huge crowd."

"In my family, if one person has an event, there is no possible way to keep it small. If you're invited and don't go, you better be prepared to bring your X-rays to prove you had a broken bone. And if you're not invited, you're obligated to start a riot within the family. Nothing like a good feud."

"Does that really happen?" she asked.

"You must have a very small family, if you have to ask."

"It's just us, mostly. The extended family is shrinking. All of Ray Anne's immediate family have been gone a long time and she never had children. My grandparents are gone. My folks are in their sixties, my brothers almost forty..."

"All it takes is one renegade who decides to have a bunch of kids and suddenly you're a country," he said.

She laughed. "In the Basque culture, that's not really a renegade, now is it?"

"My generation hasn't been as prolific as some. Most of my brothers and sisters want a reasonable couple of kids. Except Ellie—she already has five and wants more. She started real young. Peyton wasn't going to have any—then she met Scott and got knocked up before the wedding. But she doesn't have time for too many. Plus, she loves that little clinic. She's not going to trade off her medical profession for the mommy track."

"What about you?" she asked. "Do you want children?"

"I certainly did," he said. "But I'm a little old-fashioned. First I'm going to have to find a happy marriage. And just like you, that's not going to happen soon. We're stung, Ginger. We're both still in recovery. Bad time to try to partner up with happily ever after in mind."

"I suppose it is," she said.

"This looks like a good spot," he said, pulling into a wide lookout. He maneuvered the truck around and backed in.

"It's going to be kind of hard to see like this," she said.

"Wait, you're going to love this." He jumped out of the truck and ran around to her side, helping her out. He directed her to the back, lowering the tailgate to the truck bed.

Inside the bed of the truck were a couple of lounge pillows, blankets and a cooler. "Wow," was all she could say.

"This was how my parents went to the drive-in movie. For myself, I've never been to a drive-in movie, but my dad explained courting in his day—couples couldn't be alone in the backseat of a car, which is why drive-ins were invented, I think. So they got cozy in the back of a truck."

"I'm kind of dressed up," she said.

He smiled. "And beautifully, too. I've got you covered," he said, and jumped into the truck bed. He unrolled and spread out a sleeping bag on the bottom of the bed, shook out a blanket and covered the lounge pillows, then jumped out. He laced his fingers together to assist her in getting in. "Hand on my head and up you go."

"Is this legal?" she asked.

"What? Parking at the lookout? Why not?"

"I don't know. Seems kind of..."

"Naughty?" he asked with a grin. "Come on, up you go."

She climbed in, laughing as she kneeled and then, adjusting her skirt, crawled to the front of the bed where the pillows were. She couldn't stop laughing as she sat down against the pillows, smoothed her skirt and relaxed. He sat beside her, and when she rubbed her arms because she was a little chilly, he grabbed another blanket and spread it over her, tucking it around her shoulders.

"This is genius," she said.

He lifted the lid of the cooler. "Drink?"

"What have you got in there?" she asked, peering into the cooler.

"Water, soda, tea, a couple of juice drinks."

"I'll pass. After all, being a guy, you can pee out of the back of a truck. Life isn't that simple for a girl."

"We're completely alone," he said, mischief in his smile. "You could safely manage nearby."

Just as he said that, a car pulled in the lookout not far from them and an older couple got out and walked to the edge of the lookout. The gentleman had a very large camera hanging around his neck. They waved hello, then went about the business of photographing the sinking sun over the Pacific.

"Well, we'll be alone again in a few minutes."

"I'll pass," she said.

But it was sunset. And sunset over the Pacific was a good show. There wasn't exactly a crowd, but there were quite a few cars that pulled in to watch. Some folks got out and walked around, some stayed in their cars, and every time a car pulled into the lookout, Ginger laughed. At one point she wanted her cell phone to take her own picture and realized that, of course, she hadn't taken a bag to the wedding and had no phone. Matt got his out of his pocket and handed it to her. "Click away and send them to yourself."

Cars came and went, and Ginger took a few pictures of the sunset. It was better out here than at Cooper's, probably because it felt closer, there being no beach or bay between her and the setting sun. She snuggled under the warm blanket and before long darkness overtook them.

And they were alone.

Matt put an arm around her and pulled her closer, up against his big, warm body.

"If you do that, I might fall asleep on you," she said.

He gently kissed her forehead. "You fall asleep if you want to. You're safe."

She felt safe. In fact, she felt cherished. Protected. It was a feeling she hadn't had very often.

They were alone, quiet in the dark, and she felt a contentment wash over her. She'd like to stay here, just like this, forever. He turned toward her and gently kissed her forehead, her temple, her cheek, her ear. She lifted her lips, and he touched them with his. Then he adjusted slightly to take her into his arms and cover her mouth with a sweet and thorough kiss, holding her close.

Oh, God, he was a very good kisser. She let her lips part slightly. Very. Good.

She escaped the warmth of the blanket to wrap her arms around his neck and hold him closer. She gave herself to his mouth, his arms, and it was pure heaven. She tried to think when she last enjoyed physical affection like this and it was blurry. Long before she got pregnant. Oh, there'd been sex. But that feeling of being adored, of being swept away, of falling into some kind of bliss, that was long ago.

Headlights strafed them, causing them to reluctantly break apart. A highway patrol cruiser pulled up beside them. The spotlight at the top of the car shone on them. The trooper got out and stood up, looking at them over the top of the vehicle. "You folks okay there?"

"Well, we were," Matt said with a laugh.

"What's going on there?" he asked.

"We were making out, if you need to know."

"Drinking?" he asked.

"No, sir," Matt said. "You're welcome to check. Got a cooler of drinks here—water, soda, et cetera. We're enjoying the sunset. And then some."

"Well, I hate to throw a wet blanket on this party, but I don't think it's wise, using this spot for romance. You aren't breaking any laws, but you're real isolated. You'd be better off getting a room. At least the door locks."

"Point taken," Matt said.

The trooper drove away, and Matt put his arms around her again. "You afraid to be out here alone? With just me?"

"I have a feeling you could keep me safe."

He kissed her again. Long and wet and deep. "Ginger, I don't know whether to congratulate myself or apologize. I've been wanting to do that for a while now, but we both know I'm a mess."

She ran her fingers over his scruffy cheek. "Please don't apologize."

"I won't," he said. "I should get you home."

"Whenever you're ready."

They were quiet on the drive back, but held hands all the way. When he parked in front of Ray Anne's house, he leaned across the console to give her a brief kiss. And when he helped her out of the truck, he stood there with her for a moment, embracing her and kissing her deeply. She couldn't help it, she was melting into him and wanting him. Wanting him so much.

"I had a nice surprise today," she whispered against his lips. "Grace is giving up her little apartment over the shop. She offered it to me." She smiled at him. "I'm going to have my own place soon."

"How soon?" he asked, surprise in his voice.

"A couple of days, actually. Ray Anne has been so generous, but she's used to living alone. And she does have a boyfriend."

He lifted her hand and held it close between their bodies. "Do you have a boyfriend, miss?"

"Not sure," she said. "But I think I want one."

He gave her another quick kiss, then turned her toward the house. "I'll call you tomorrow."

CHAPTER TEN

He ran. He could've stayed overnight at his sister's house and had a more leisurely drive in the morning, maybe even a little more time with Ginger, but instead Matt hit the road and headed north, though it was almost nine. He was a little panicked. Most definitely conflicted. He was falling in love with Ginger and it was a bad idea for him to be in love. If he recalled, he had two gears—not in love and thinking straight or in love and a complete idiot.

He wanted to fall into Ginger and drown in her. She was going to let him. And now she was getting her own place. Where they would be alone.

It was dark and he didn't have the radio on, so he tried interviewing himself to see if he could figure out what was happening to him. Was he over Natalie? Most definitely. He might still find her beautiful but he didn't want her back. So then, what was the problem? Well, he thought he'd known Natalie. He had trusted her, more or less. What had he failed to see? He had known she wasn't perfect, and that was okay with him because he wasn't perfect, either, and damn, she seemed good enough for him. So she wasn't into the farm. He thought he'd been okay with that, but what if he wasn't? What if he'd secretly expected her to come around? So she wanted to have more fun? Didn't wives always want a little more than what they were getting? There wasn't any Achilles' heel he couldn't live with, or so he'd thought. He'd had no illusions—she wasn't going to wear overalls and rubber boots and dig in the ground. Ever. She would never share his passion. But he might've thought she'd eventually develop a grudging respect for it. He knew his brothers looked at him with a combination of envy and amusement. Natalie wasn't practical or earthy, but she was gorgeous and laughed at his jokes. She would always wear sexy, inconvenient clothes and ridiculous high heels. And the most amazing underwear... and when she wrapped those long legs around him, he'd leave the earth for a while.

Of course he now realized you can't build a real relationship on hot underwear and sexual abandon. There had to be more. A lot more.

He was falling in love with something more—a woman he could really talk to, a woman with values that matched more closely to his own, a woman who wanted a family. A quiet, gentle, loving woman with an inner strength so powerful it humbled him; a woman he respected. Admired. A woman who turned him on, made him so hot he wondered if he'd snap! He realized he was terrified of that, with good reason. Once he fell into Ginger and experienced her, he was not going to be able to go back. Ginger wanted a stable home life, a solid man to lean on, a grounded future. He wanted to be that man.

What if he was getting all the wrong signals? Again? She seemed so transparent, but...

It was pretty easy to look back at his brief marriage and realize Natalie hadn't really surprised him that much. She wasn't much of a giver, that Natalie. She might've done some selfish things that shocked him but when he looked back, they shouldn't have. He should've seen it coming. She was focused on herself, her needs. He always knew it was all about Natalie being happy, being entertained, being satisfied, having lots of attention heaped on her.

And there was the problem. When he fell for a woman all the blood drained from his brain and his eyes glazed over. He stopped thinking logically. He stopped being pragmatic.

What if he let go, let himself fall for Ginger? And what if it was a big mistake? What if there were some other things he couldn't see right now, lurking, that would keep them from having a successful long-term relationship? Like? Oh, hell, he didn't know. If he knew, he could check them out, examine them. Sometimes these things sneaked up on you.

He was going to have to be still and quiet for a little while. It would be a good time to dig, aerate, fertilize, trim and prune. He should be by himself and spend some time in his head. Thinking of all the possibilities, because Ginger was getting her own place. With a door that closed. With a bed in it.

If he was wrong about a woman he felt that strongly for again, it was going to be ugly.

Ginger hoped Matt had stayed over at his sister's house Saturday night and would call her on Sunday. She hoped he had because it had been far too late by the time he could have begun his four-hour drive north. But her phone didn't ring.

So she told herself a different story—he'd gotten up early and headed back to the farm, got caught up in the after-church family circus with twenty people at the table. So later, he would call her later.

She stayed busy, longing to talk to him. They'd just had that romance at the lookout, the kissing, the whispering, and she wanted to hear him talk about it. He was gentle but there was such a power there; she could feel the tension in his arms, his body, as he was reining it in, keeping all those runaway emotions under control.

She walked the beach in the early afternoon. She stopped off at Cooper's bar, which was hopping because it was a sunny Sunday. Even Troy was working, getting out kayaks and paddleboards for rent.

"I can't believe you're working," she said. "You just got married last night!"

"I know, but I was up early. We had a great breakfast with the family and now they're all headed home. Grace is exhausted and she's taking a nap. I think we wore out Winnie, too. The only person with energy to spare is Mikhail—he's looking for things to do. Last I saw him, he was headed into town on foot, determined to look around."

"You should be with Grace," she said.

"Shh, don't tell, but I got restless. I don't want a nap. I'm going to go over to the loft in a little while and clean it up for you. You do want it, right?"

"I do," she said excitedly. "I've only been in it a couple of times. Can I go, too? Help?"

"Sure," he said with a shrug. "I'm going to give Cooper a couple more hours. Should I call you?"

"You can. Or… I think I'll go to the shop and make sure everything is right for tomorrow morning. I'll be over there already."

So, back to town she went. There wasn't a lot to do in the shop, though the Saturday rush for the wedding had left it a little messy. The arch was standing in the alley beside the back door, as promised, and had to be dismantled and put away. There was the usual sweeping and wiping down to do. She listened to the work cell, but there were only congratulatory messages for Grace and no orders.

She looked at her own cell phone several times, wondering why Matt wasn't calling. There was a kernel of fear in her. She couldn't wait any longer. She texted him. Are you home safely?

Then she stared at the phone, waiting. He didn't reply. If she

didn't hear from him soon, she would call Peyton. In the mean-
time, she began to tidy the back room and office. The phone
that a couple of months ago she didn't even care to recharge
was now in her pocket. She was waiting for it to chime or ring.
And she hated that!

She went from tidying and wiping to scrubbing, putting a lot
of muscle into it, making that scarred old worktable shine. Waiting. It brought to mind how she waited to hear from Mick, to
hear he was nearby and could see her or out of town on some
gig but thinking of her. Waiting for his affection, waiting for
him to come to bed in the wee hours, waiting, always waiting
for some affirmation from him. Didn't he feel horrible about
leaving her alone and pregnant? Didn't he want to at least discuss
the divorce? Make a compromise? Didn't he wonder how she
was getting along? Wonder about the baby? She almost reached
out to him ten thousand times and it took a will of iron not to
but she could remember the agony of that waiting so clearly, it
might've been yesterday. And had that agony ever touched him?
Not in the slightest way. *This next song is going to be it, babe, it's
going to push me to the top.*

Her phone chimed, and she pulled it out. Twenty-five minutes had passed when Matt responded. Safe and sound.

She waited, staring at the phone screen. Was there nothing
more? No, talk to you later? Hope you weren't worried? Had a
good time last night?

Nothing.

She felt her eyes well with tears and told herself to stop! She
couldn't be that woman again, that woman in love and desperate to have her passions returned. She couldn't cry for attention from a man, hoping he'd call, hoping he'd notice, hoping
he'd care. It was too painful, living in a one-sided relationship.

She turned off her phone. She blew her nose.

It wasn't long before Troy arrived, knocked on the locked
back door of the shop and then took Ginger upstairs. It was

such a darling little apartment. One room, really, the bedroom separated from the living room by an arch. There was plenty of room for one person, a large bathroom, the linen closet, which held a stacked washer and dryer along with shelves, a galley kitchen with a few cupboards and a table for two. But there was a regular-size sectional and wall unit holding a TV. The bed was queen-size and there was a wall unit of drawers and closet space.

"This is adorable," she told Troy.

He was busy moving around the little apartment, checking the bathroom, bedroom, kitchen. "Well, I should have known. My mother wouldn't leave a speck of dust behind." He flipped open the lid of the washer. "I guess this means you even have clean sheets on the bed. I'll run this load of sheets, make sure the bathroom is clean and—"

"You'll do no such thing," she said. "I'll take care of that. I know you have your own apartment to clean up. Didn't I hear you say you're taking the living room furniture for your game room in the new house?"

"There will be no games in the game room," he said. "That will be our living room. It's a good apartment for us."

"What do you need from here?" Ginger asked.

"I think Grace took everything we could use when we moved to Winnie's house. I cleaned out the fridge before my folks came and since we don't have our own kitchen, Grace left some kitchen things here. I'm going to move out of my place this week now that I don't need the space for family."

"This is very thoughtful of you and Grace," Ginger said. "And if you ever have family coming to town, just say the word. I always have space at Ray Anne's house. I can give you back this guest room whenever you need it."

"Thanks, we'll try not to impose," he said. "I guess you can have it whenever you want. And here's the key."

"Is there anything else here you want to take with you?"

"Grace moved all her personal things out early last week. Ev-

erything left here is for your use. You shouldn't need too much."
He picked up the container of laundry detergent and gave it a
shake. "You only have a couple more loads in this," he said.

"You are a very good landlord," she told him with a smile.

"I imagine you'll be a perfect tenant." He looked around.
"She was really smart to do this, wasn't she? Right over the
store and all."

"She was smart about everything."

"I thought I'd have to do some cleaning but there are even
vacuum tracks. It's all yours—move in whenever you want. I'm
going back out to the beach to see if I can get Cooper to help
me move. With his truck." He grinned.

"And I'll walk back to Ray Anne's and give her the good
news—she can have her life back."

"I'm sure she loved having you."

"I'm sure she'll love having time with Al more. But no worries, I'm sure I'll see Ray Anne every day."

As she was walking back through town to Ray Anne's she
thought about her new life. *That was easy. I am not going to be
lonely; I am not pining over some man who wants me one minute, can't
remember my phone number the next. I'm a whole person. I have a
great job, a super loft to live in, good friends, a little family nearby…*

But she gave him forty-eight hours to remember he had kissed
her passionately and promised to call. Forty-eight hours to get
a text, a message, a call.

Then she'd changed her cell phone number.

"How do you like that little space upstairs?" Grace asked
Ginger.

"Oh, it's perfect," she said. "My mother is sending a couple
of boxes of things—my favorite books, DVDs, stuff I wouldn't
have thought to bring since I was only staying a couple of weeks.
The last time I was home I went through my closet and brought
all the clothes that still fit me. And there are a few boxes in my

closet, things packed up from my rental house when I moved out.
I worked in housewares and in bridal registries—I have some
of the prettiest wineglasses, earthenware, sheets and towels, and
small items that there will be plenty of room for.”

“I’ve always used the cooler to refrigerate things I didn’t have
room for in that little fridge,” Grace said.

“I’ve already figured that out,” she said. “Poor Ray Anne, she
didn’t know whether to jump for joy or cry when I told her I had
my own place. I’ve had to reassure her that we’re still close, we
can get together for dinner, for a glass of wine, for girls’ night…”

Grace wandered over to the front window and looked out.

“I think she’s convinced this will be better in the long run.
She needs personal space and I need to not hide in the bedroom with the door closed when Al is on the property,” she
said with a laugh.

Grace turned from the window. She wore a melancholy expression. “Mikhail,” she said. “He’s taken to long walks while
Winnie is having her morning washing and primping rituals
and again in the afternoon while she’s taking her nap. But he
gets her breakfast, makes sure she has lunch and, although he
doesn’t think I know this, he sleeps in the chair in her bedroom
at night.”

“Ohhh,” Ginger said. “That is so sweet.”

“I had no idea how devoted he is to my mother.”

“Are they in love?”

“I don’t think so, not the love we’d identify with. I don’t
know if they’re like best friends, brother and sister or an aging
couple. I think Mikhail is grateful to Winnie for all the years
they were a team, while I was in training. He became like a
father to me after my own father died. And of course, he took
direction from Winnie, who had hired him. And Winnie took
direction from Mikhail, who had great training instincts. I think
he’s going to hang in there till the end. I don’t want him to be
lonely.”

"And when you say 'the end'?"

"No one knows. There are odds—most people don't live many years after they're diagnosed and Winnie was diagnosed a few years ago. On the other hand, there are cases of people who live many years."

"How is she feeling?" Ginger asked.

"She feels pretty good. If it weren't for weakness, trembling and fatigue, you'd never know. Her mind—sharp as a tack." She chuckled. "They sure can throw the gibes back and forth, Winnie and Mikhail. They bicker like an old married couple."

"You have so much to deal with," Ginger said. "You're very strong."

"We all have so much to deal with," Grace said. "Haven't you figured this out yet? No one has it easy. I always thought the pressure I had on the circuit was the most extraordinary pressure in the world and no one would ever understand. Then I met others who had challenges entirely different from mine and even more difficult. Then I met *you*. You're one of the most amazing women I've ever known. And the most loving and giving."

"Aw," she said, blushing. *Maybe a little too loving and giving sometimes*, she thought.

"I've been meaning to ask—I heard a rumor that Matt Lacoumette showed up Saturday night."

"True," she said, busying herself with some receipts on the counter. "I ran into him on my way home from the wedding."

"And?" Grace asked, a twinkle in her eye.

"And what?" Ginger asked.

"Did you spend any time with him?"

"A little bit," she said. "In fact, we drove up the coast a few miles to a lookout where a lot of people enjoyed the sunset. It was beautiful. I have a picture," she said, taking out her cell phone and flipping through some pictures. There were lots of pictures of floral arrangements she'd created and then—two pictures of the sunset, texted from Matt's phone. And one selfie—Matt's arm around her, both of them smiling into the camera.

"Well now," Grace said. "There's a happy couple."

"Just friends," she said.

"But you've spent a lot of time on the phone, right? And you went to see him at the farm?"

"I was on my way back from Portland and it was on the way," Ginger said. "It's a wonderful farm."

"So, maybe this will turn into something a little more than friendship?" Grace suggested by way of a question.

Ginger only shrugged, looking back at her receipts.

"What does Matt say about that? After all, he drove all the way to Thunder Point to see you."

"I don't know. I haven't heard from Matt."

"Really? But you gave him your new cell number, right?"

Ginger gave Grace her full attention. "I didn't," she said.

"You don't like Matt?" Grace asked, looking a little surprised and confused.

"Sure, I like him. Ever been in love with the wrong guy, Grace?"

"Matt's the wrong guy?" Grace asked.

"I don't know, but I know what it's like to love the wrong guy. To stalk him, follow him, call him, wait for his calls and even when they're long overdue, melting into one big puddle because he finally deigned to go to the trouble of making a phone call. I did that already and I put that far behind me—I don't want to ever be that lonely, desperate girl again—it's just too painful and shameful. So, Matt and I talked almost every night. Then we went to see the sunset, talked and laughed and kissed. Truthfully, we made out like crazy—it was so nice. I haven't had that in my life for well over a year, over two years, maybe. It's been so long since I had strong feelings for a guy that weren't all gnarled up with regret. You know those feelings, right? Think about him all day, can't wait to talk to him at night..."

"Or in my case, can't wait for him to sneak up the back stairs…" Grace admitted, smiling devilishly.

"Oh, that must have been so romantic," Ginger said.

"It was so romantic. So, you had those feelings?"

She nodded. "And then I realized that once again, I was having those feelings all by myself."

"Are you sure about that?"

"You tell me. We told each other deeply personal things, kissed like romantic fools, he said he'd call and he didn't."

"Well, maybe—"

"Maybe he was in a car accident?" Ginger asked. "Worried, I texted, asking if he made it home safely. And he texted back three words. *Safe and sound.* There was nothing more. I waited for days."

Grace got a very naughty smile on her face. "And you changed your number."

"Well, that was really overdue. I told you my ex called, right? He shouldn't have my number…"

"You did this for a bigger reason than that. You can hang up on your ex."

She laughed softly. "Oh, I did. He's such an idiot—you know what he said? Something like, 'Gee, Ginger, you're a little hostile.'" She laughed harder. "Really? Me? Hostile? I wonder why?"

"You did this to show Matt."

"Show him what? If he wanted to find me, he'd know where to look, right? If he wanted my new number, he knows where I work. No, I'm not punishing Matt."

"You're not fooling me," Grace said. "And good for you! Ha! I did that to Troy, you know. Right before we got engaged. I told him I was pregnant and he said he had a lot to think about, to process, that he needed time to think before he could decide where we go from here. Before *he* decided? Like it was up to him and didn't really have much to do with me! I was only the pregnant one, but hey—Troy would figure it out and let me know what we would do next. I told him to take a hike, stay away from me and be sure to let me know when he'd 'processed.' I was so done putting up with indecisiveness from a man!"

"I didn't know you did that."

"Well, I probably don't look that stubborn. And you certainly don't."

"Oh, I'll be the first to admit I feel a little sad that it's been days and Matt hasn't tried to contact me."

"Maybe he has the flu. Or was finally put in jail and needs his phone calls to get a lawyer. Hopefully the latter."

"Grace, this isn't about him. I don't think Matt has any ulterior motives. This is about me. I'm never going to that place again—that insecure, lonely, desperate, unloved place. I'm not waiting and hoping. If I ever have a man in my life again, it's not going to be because I'm fantasizing, it's going to be because he's made sure I know it." She took a breath. "Very likely I will be alone. But with this new start of mine, with a good job, friends, family—I'm not going to be that sad, disappointed person. I don't want to be that person ever again."

Grace leaned a hip onto the front counter, half sitting. Her hands were folded across that raised thigh. "Fair enough—you should never be sad or lonely. You're too wonderful. But I want to tell you something. Coming from me, I don't know, you might want to get a second opinion since I have so little experience. Troy was my first real love. But there's something I learned. In love we're vulnerable, Ginger. It would be nice if it were more certain and immediate, but the truth is—we have our worries, doubts and fears. We have to inch our way along. We have to discover trust. Sometimes we have to just believe in someone. And sometimes we have to know when to let them go."

"I guess that's what I'm trying to learn," Ginger said. "It's possible Matt's just not ready. After all, he went through some heartache, too."

CHAPTER ELEVEN

Matt brought a cooler full of dead chickens into the kitchen for his mother. She was going to pluck, wash, butcher and freeze them. Since he'd been hanging around the farm, she snagged him for butcher duty.

"Help me with this," she said, throwing a headless hen in her work sink. "It won't take that long. And I wanted to ask you why you put in such long days and such silent nights."

He frowned. "Silent nights?"

"You're at my table every night. And you're back to being quiet and withdrawn. You think we don't see?"

"I have things on my mind, Mama. Nothing for you to worry about. I'm not depressed at all."

"Ah," she said, plucking away with hands that moved over that chicken carcass like greased lightning. "Maybe you think about that pretty friend of Peyton's, that Ginger. She looks like ginger, doesn't she? Kind of golden."

"I've been thinking about the farm, the house I'd like to build. It's a big step, building a house," he said.

"And how is that pretty Ginger?"

"I'm sure she's fine," he said. "I should call her."

"Oh, I thought you liked her."

"I do like her," he said.

Corinne laughed softly, feathers flying. She held up a naked, plump hen. "I'm behind the times, but usually when a man likes a woman, he pays attention to her."

"She lives in Thunder Point. I can't exactly carry her books home from school," Matt said irritably.

"I understand that. Just so you're not confusing her with Natalie," Corinne said. "They're not alike."

"I know that," he said. "I'm going to go clean the mess in the barn. Then I'm going out."

"Of course. Friday night," Corinne said. "No dinner tonight?"

"I'll take care of my own dinner."

"Have a nice time. I'll see you Sunday?"

"Maybe," he said. "I put in a long week." He wasn't going to share dinner if they were going to be watching him.

"You did. I think you worked harder than Paco, not easy to do. The farm is quiet for now. You should take advantage of it."

"I was catching up. I'll see you soon. And you're welcome for killing ten hens. Nasty work."

"You made a quick job of it."

Why couldn't she thank him? he wondered. All his parents could do was get in his business.

He scrubbed up in the barn, then got in his truck. He had a problem with "that pretty Ginger." First, he had granted himself a couple of days to think about things, about her. Then he realized he had ignored her, hadn't called when he said he would and probably either pissed her off or hurt her feelings, and that took a couple more days of silence. Here it was Friday and last Saturday night he had promised to call her the next day. When he was younger he'd have pretended that he'd forgotten or he'd have made up some excuse.

Ginger was too smart to fall for that. He'd been all knotted up inside because he was starting to need her, want her so much, maybe love her. He wanted to examine that for a little while, privately, with none of the confusion that came with having those long, quiet, intimate talks. Or the scent of her skin. Or the taste of her lips. Or her softness. Or the way she felt in his arms. He wanted to be sure he wasn't setting both of them up for disappointment before he went one step further.

Then his mother, who knew everything, said, "As long as you don't confuse her with Natalie." And he snapped out of it. Ginger had emotional sturdiness; she knew how she felt. She wasn't always thinking of herself first. In fact, how she could help others seemed very important to her. Whether they talked or kissed, she was so honest about her feelings, far more honest than he had been. This was a high-quality woman. And he'd been screwing around, wondering what to do next?

Before leaving the farm, sitting in his truck, he called her.

"This number is no longer in service."

He tried it five more times. Then he called Peyton, who was still at the clinic. "Hey, Peyton, Ginger's phone is disconnected. Something's wrong."

"Nothing's wrong. She got a new number."

"Huh? Okay, I need the number," he said.

"Why? You lose it?"

"Ah. Yeah. Lost it."

That hesitation ruined him. "You liar," she said. "She didn't give it to you. Why didn't she give it to you? Did she get a new number because of you?"

"No! No! I think it was her ex. She said he called her…or something."

"When did you talk to her last?" Peyton demanded.

"Come on, is this really your job, deciding who gets her phone number? Give me a break, will you? I want to talk to her. Right away."

"You screwed this up, didn't you?"

"Peyton," he said in a threatening tone. Then he calmed himself and took a breath. "Okay, listen, I might've done a stupid thing…"

"Shocker," Peyton said.

Matt wanted to reach through the phone and strangle her. "Okay, listen, we were together last Saturday night after the wedding. I took her out, we had a great time. I wanted to see her again right away, it was that great. But I thought maybe I should think this through since my track record is, you know—"

"Shitty?" Peyton filled in.

"I was going to say *spotty*. Jesus, could you be any less supportive? I took a little time to think it through, okay? I was starting to have those feelings, you know? I scared myself a little. I made a big mistake with Natalie. I didn't want to do that to Ginger. She's too sweet to have some idiot like me make a poor decision and get her into something not good for either one of us. So yeah, I shouldn't have waited to call her, but I had to think it through. So that's it. I know Ginger isn't like Natalie and I'm not like I was with Natalie and I thought about things and… I need that number now."

"Wow, that's kind of mature, Matt. Fessing up like that. Admitting you're wrong and everything."

"So? The number?"

"No," she said. And disconnected.

He looked at the phone and told his sister he hated her.

It took him a while to get the number for the flower shop because he couldn't remember Pretty Petals. Then when he called, Ginger didn't answer. He assumed it was Grace and he said, "Hi. Is Ginger there, please?"

"Sure. Can I tell her who's calling?"

The moment of truth, he thought. "It's Matt. Matt Lacoumette."

"Oh, hi, Matt. Hold on. She's pulling in displays."

He heard Grace summon Ginger, and then she came on the line. "Hi, Matt. How are you?"

"I don't know," he said. "You tell me. Did you change your number because of me? Because you're angry?"

"No, of course not. I changed it because it needed to be changed and no, I'm not angry. But I can't really talk right now—we're closing up the shop and it's busy."

"When can we talk?"

"Hmm, let's see. I have plans tonight, right after I get cleaned up. I'm going out to dinner with Ray Anne and some friends. Maybe I could give you a call later, if it's not too late."

"Ginger, I was calling you to tell you I know I screwed up. I didn't call when I said I would. I hardly answered your text. I ignored you. You really scared me when my call wouldn't go through. I should explain. I was thinking about us, about whether—"

"Matt! Matt! I can't wait to hear all about it but I really can't talk right now. It's a little busy here and I don't want to keep my friends waiting. I have to sign off. We'll catch up later."

She disconnected.

Matt sat there in shock. All confidence was gone. The Ginger he was falling in love with just announced it to the world. She would not be taken for granted. She wasn't going to put up with vague messages and broken promises. She'd already been there once. She was all done with that.

And like a shotgun blast he understood everything. The whole time he was getting closer to Ginger he'd been focused on Natalie and a relationship that hadn't worked from the start. That was mistake number one. Then he'd built a barrier of self-protection, aloofness. Distance from the woman he knew better after a couple of months than he'd known his own wife in a year. Mistake number two. So, mistake number three would be sitting there like a doofus, acting confused and licking his wounds.

A little fight replaced his sudden lack of confidence.

★ ★ ★

Ginger hung up and went back outside the shop. She rolled up the awning and dragged a big pot of colorful mums into the store. She stopped dragging when she ran smack into Grace.

"It's not as though I meant to eavesdrop," Grace said.

"Bull. You probably wanted me to put it on speaker."

"That would've been helpful. So—what did he want?"

"Apparently he wants to grovel. I wonder when he figured it out? I think about ten minutes ago. I have to say, I'm very relieved…"

"What's his story?"

"Well, obviously I don't have the whole story, but I think the gist is—Matt's a little gun-shy. He married the wrong girl. I think he sort of knew it all along and married her anyway, and of course it didn't work out. And he likes me, which I think scares him. My educated guess is he doesn't want to screw up again. You'd have to understand his family a little better to appreciate where he's coming from. I know you met them, but it's entirely different when you sit down to Sunday dinner with them. They're so enmeshed in each other's personal lives, it's hard to have a secret. I imagine they've all given multiple opinions about where Matt went wrong with his first wife. Matt pretends to be completely independent and to not really care what anyone thinks, but trust me—he doesn't want his family to see him make another mistake."

"And so? He didn't call for almost a week? What was he doing?"

"Brooding," Ginger said, going back outside to fetch a couple more displays.

"I guess you snapped him out of it," Grace said.

"Possibly," Ginger said. "But the important thing was to snap *me* out of it. There's nothing more pathetic than a girl with a ridiculous, moody crush, singing love songs to herself, kissing her own hand and fantasizing, checking the phone every five minutes to see if *he* called yet. I tried just turning off the phone, but then I'd turn it back on to check for messages every fifteen minutes. You want to make out with me in the bed of a pickup truck then string me along for a week? No, not going to happen."

Ginger went back outside, pulled in another pot of colorful summer flowers, stopped short just inside the door.

"All this happened in the bed of a pickup truck?" Grace asked. "Ginger, might you have left out some details before."

"It was so lovely. He had a sleeping bag to spread out, a cooler of soft drinks, a couple of blankets because it gets cold when the sun goes down. He said it was how his parents used to go to the drive-in movie and it was fun. And then all the other people who had driven to the lookout to watch the sunset were gone and it was just us—talking, laughing, kissing. A trooper pulled in to make sure we were all right." She laughed. "Good thing it hadn't gone any further, right?"

"Will you call him tonight?"

"Sure. If it isn't too late when I get home. I'm not playing games here. I don't mean to punish him. I just think guidelines are important."

"You could just give him your number," Grace said.

"I could have, couldn't I? When I talk to him next, I'll give it to him if he asks."

"You might not be playing games," Grace said. "But you were sending a message, don't bother to deny it. And he got it."

"I think we're done out here," Ginger said, speaking of the front walk in front of the shop. "Ready for the closed sign?"

"Ready. I'm just going to clean up my office and shut down the computer, then I'm headed home. I suppose you're going upstairs to wash off the flowers before dinner with the girls?"

"I am. By the way, have I told you how much I love it up there? It's like a little cocoon. It's just perfect for me. I nestle in at night, flip through the channels or listen to music, relax, read, check emails on my laptop, fall asleep in my little nest. It's so wonderful, Grace."

"I know," she said, grinning. "You tell me five times a day. Have I told you how wonderful it is having you in charge of the shop, opening and closing, taking orders, giving me so much freedom?"

"Five times a day," Ginger said.

Ginger went upstairs to shower and change. Tonight was dinner at a Greek restaurant in Bandon and she was looking forward to it very much. It would be Ray Anne, Lou, Carrie, Gina and Gina's daughter and stepdaughter, Ashley and Eve. Three generations, more or less. With the college girls home for the summer, their group had grown and become even more fun. Ginger got the biggest kick out of these college girls and their stories, even as their mother, grandmother and aunt cringed. She was feeling much better about herself since she started living independently and, in truth, since Matt had tracked her down and apologized. She looked good, felt good and didn't look at her watch even once.

She was home at a little after nine, kicked off her shoes, dropped onto the couch while still chuckling over one of the funny stories told over dinner. And she thought, *Look at me—I have a life.* She would not have believed a few short months ago, when she was mired in depression and hopelessness, that she could have this—laughter and enthusiasm and anticipation. She couldn't believe she'd ever look like she was among the living, much less look in the mirror and actually admire the reflection.

She heard tapping at her back door and wondered if Ray Anne needed something or if someone was looking for flowers. But she opened the door to Matt's frowning but so handsome face.

"If you don't want me in your life anymore, you have to tell me to my face," he said.

She laughed and stepped back so he could come in.

"That's funny?" he asked irritably.

"Well, yes. Not talking to a guy never worked for me before. Usually they could care less. I just got home, Matt. You came all this way? I was going to call you."

"You were?"

"I said I would," she told him. "And there is no reason I wouldn't. You came all this way because I got a new phone number?"

"I came all this way because I have to apologize," he said.

Again she smiled. Their first dinner together, the beginning of a most unexpectedly lovely relationship, had been about apology. "Since you really excel at apologies, I look forward to it."

He shut the door behind him, slid an arm around her waist and deftly brought her mouth up to his, kissing her. She was bent over his arm and hung on to his shoulders to keep from crumpling to the floor. His kiss was hot and demanding and delicious. Then he moved, his hands on her face, holding her against him, covering her mouth with an almost desperate heat. Her lips opened for him, and he swept the inside of her mouth with his tongue, and she not only allowed this but welcomed it. She held him close, moaning. Sighing. It was a very long time before he let her go even enough to speak. He panted eagerly.

"Well. You're pretty messed up," she said. "We really have to talk. Maybe a little later..." And she went back to his lips, her arms around his neck.

"I couldn't give you up if I wanted to," he whispered. "I don't want to." Then he sighed and put his lips against her neck, holding her close. "God, I thought you'd given up on me."

"But you're the one who disappeared, not me."

"I know. I know. I'm not good at this, haven't you figured that out yet?"

She laughed as she ran her fingers through his thick, black hair. "Oh, I don't know, you're pretty good..." She pulled back a little so she could look into those troubled, coal-black eyes. "I don't know what you're holding inside, but if you don't get it out pretty soon, you're going to start getting headaches."

"Worse headaches. How did you know?" he asked.

She shrugged. "I don't have headaches anymore." She kissed his cheek tenderly. "If you can't trust me with whatever it is, there must be someone you can talk to. A priest, maybe?"

He laughed. "Definitely not a priest." Then he kissed her neck, holding her against him. "I feel better already." He ran his hand down her back and over her butt. "Much better."

"Maybe we could sit down. Would you like something to drink?"

He looked down into her eyes. "Can I have something to drink later? Right now all I want is you. And I want you real damn bad."

"You should have given me a little notice…"

"For what? You feel like velvet and you taste like…hmm. Heaven. What is that smell in your hair? It's like dessert."

"Vanilla. I don't have any birth control…"

His laugh was deep and a little evil. He looked into her eyes again, and his were getting fiery. "I'll take care of you," he said. "I'm prepared."

She shook her head. "How does that not surprise me? Don't most men bring flowers or champagne or chocolates? Okay, forget the flowers…"

"I'll do that next time. This time—I was in a little panic."

She pressed herself against him. "I think the panic has passed."

"Are you ready for this? I'll be careful. I'll take good care of you."

"I trust you, Matt."

"Then why? Why the phone number thing?"

"After," she said. "We'll talk when there's less distraction."

"Good idea," he said, lifting her into his arms. He carried her into the tiny living room, eyed the couch and moved on past it to the bed. He set her down gently, sitting down beside her to kick off his shoes, get rid of his belt and shirt, then turned to take her into his arms again, delivering kisses that were hot and strong. He slid the straps of her dress down over her shoulders, pulled it down and kissed her breasts for a long time. She held his head there, his mouth sucking gently, then not so gently.

She turned into soup. She felt the hot and molten passion inside her flow through her until she was almost aching for him. And that made her squirm. She pulled him down on the bed and reached for his jeans, struggling to find the snap or button or zipper but after a moment of that, he stilled her hands. "Easy," he said. "I've got it."

"I thought it would be slow," she said with a shade of embarrassment.

He pulled condoms out of his pocket before tossing the jeans aside. "It'll be slow next time," he promised. "Right now I think I should take care of you. Orgasm." He laughed. "Great icebreaker."

Her dress came down to her waist, up to her waist, and there she was with a whole bunch of clothing around her waist while everything above and below lay bare to his hungry eyes. "Aw, Ginger, I love those little panties. I think I'll take them off. With my teeth."

"No teeth!" she said, laughing.

"Okay, no teeth," he said. They were white lace, fitting around her hips. He tugged them down and said, "Well now."

"Natural blonde," she confirmed.

He got out of his boxers fast. He suited up right away, leaving nothing to chance, then he lay down beside her, brought her into his arms and, kissing her, his hands explored her whole body from her knees to her neck. Finally, frustrated by the cumbersome folds of that discarded sundress, he tugged it lower, down her legs and off. He tossed it. His hands on her were much freer and deeper, and she pushed at him with her hips, so ready. But it was when she tried to close her legs against the pressure of his hand on her that he stopped. He looked into her eyes and said, "Uh-uh. No." He pushed her legs apart once more and put himself there. "Let's do this the old-fashioned way. You want to come, don't you, my love?"

She squeezed her eyes closed and just nodded.

"Good idea," he whispered. "You first."

He entered her slowly, watching her face the whole time. "Perfect," he said. "Perfect." Then he began to move, creatively at first, listening for the response that said he'd found the sweet spot. There was only the slightest whimper but she held his shoulders in a death grip and inhaled sharply. Her heels dug into the bed and she pushed against him. "There it is," he whispered against her lips. "There it is." And he slid down her neck to her breasts, licking them and sucking them while he pumped his hips.

Ginger wasn't sure what hit her—she was full of him. Full and aching and tingling and spiraling, hanging on for dear life, letting go of every other thought and focused only on one thing— let it go, let it go, let it go. And then it came, hot and hard and sweet and she pushed her pelvis against him suddenly, holding him there.

He slid a hand behind her, under her butt, and pressed himself deeply into her, his thrusts smaller and deeper, and she felt her insides grip him. Grip him, hold him tight, tremble, spasm. She heard him moan appreciatively and then it started to subside. She couldn't believe her own ears when she heard herself say, "More."

He chuckled. "We can do more." His mouth latched on a nipple and sucked hard while he pumped his hips anew, hard and deep, and in just a second she had another one—so deep and hot and heavenly she thought she might faint. She relaxed beneath him, still quivering. "More?" he asked, a smile in his voice.

"I'm good," she whispered.

"You are that," he said. "Hold me."

Her arms tightened around his torso, her legs came up to wrap around his hips, and she held on. For him. He rode her, thrusting deep and hard, groaning loudly, murmuring little victory shouts and calling her name. And then she felt him stiffen, harden inside her and spill in what seemed like a million short bursts. It went on longer than she was prepared for, long enough that she started to get turned on all over again while he throbbed inside of her.

Finally he quieted and just moaned, but it was a very happy moan. She stroked his back and loosened her legs. And he put soft kisses on her lips.

"You are not quiet," she finally said.

"I couldn't help it," he said. "It was that good."

"It was. I think you growled. Maybe barked."

"I didn't bark!" he said, laughing.

"You prayed," she said.

"Sort of," he admitted. He rolled to one side, trying to keep them together a while longer, but nature had its way and he slipped out of her. "Listen, probably this should have come first. I think I love you."

She was quiet a moment. "Do let me know when you're sure."

"I'm sure. I love you. Scared me a little. I can't think of any reason it should scare me, but all of a sudden I froze up and worried about ridiculous things. Like what if it couldn't last, what if I'm kidding myself, what if I just don't know what I'm doing and make the same mistakes over and over again? What if it's me? Do you understand? Am I just crazy?"

"I don't know, Matt. I won't know until you tell me your story."

CHAPTER TWELVE

Matt excused himself from the bed and returned a few minutes later with a couple of beers. He sat down on the bed and put the bottles on the bedside table. "I can drink one or even both of those if you're letting me stay."

She leaned against the headboard, the sheet covering her breasts. She looked down at herself. "I'm naked and just had wonderful sex. If you leave me now, I might change my number again."

"So, it *was* because of me," he said, handing her a beer.

"Only a little bit," she said, shaking her head. "Look, we hadn't professed our love, hadn't been intimate, hadn't made promises. If you got busy or sidetracked or just plain lost interest and decided not to call after all, that's your option. Right? I think I know how things work—women usually prefer to lay it on the line, say things like, 'I don't think this is going to work for me,' while men tend to say they'll call, then they just don't. Obviously I could've left my number just the same and if you didn't feel like going any further with me, you wouldn't call. But I wanted to hear from you. I reached out once and didn't get much of a response and it made me very sad and moody.

Not the end of the world, right? But I saw a reflection of what I once was. I was that way with Mick—so desperate for him to show me he cared. Obviously I don't feel that for Mick anymore but I was not going to get into an identical situation with you. I had to put a stop to it. So it wasn't really about you as much as about me. Do you see? I didn't have enough willpower to forget about you, so I cut myself off. I knew you could find me if you wanted to, but it helped me stop watching the phone." She touched his hand. "I'm sorry if I hurt you by doing that."

He shook his head a little guiltily. "I told myself it was because you heard from Mick and were cutting him off."

"A little of that," she said with a shrug. "But truthfully, Mick isn't that hard to get rid of. Just tell him you don't live for the chance to worship him and he's long gone. I'm sure I'll never hear from him again."

"Did he ever offer to support you and your child? Did he ever try to save it? The marriage?"

She shook her head. "It wasn't what he wanted. He wants to be a star. He's perfectly willing to take me along for the ride. He always said he made some of his best music with me."

"God," Matt said. "You must hate him so much!"

"No, I don't care about Mick. So—what's making you crazy, Matt?"

He instantly hung his head. Then he raised it slowly. "There are two things you have to know, Ginger. Number one, I haven't told anyone, especially not my family."

"I'm good at keeping confidences."

"And number two, I'm not as good at relationships as you are."

She smiled tenderly. "Oh, you might be just as good. It's okay to take your time."

He took a drink and shook his head. "I'm not sure where to start."

"Right where you think the beginning is," she said.

"Okay. I think I married Natalie because she's beautiful. And she's a playful little sex kitten. I think men make that mistake a lot."

"Well. How'd that work out for you?" she asked, smiling in spite of herself.

"Don't be sarcastic, because you're beautiful. And talk about sexy." He shuddered. "You almost killed me. In the best way. In the way I really want to die."

She frowned. "I'm sure there was a compliment in there somewhere…" She cleared her throat. "Back to business."

"Guys looked at me with envy. Some of them, like my brothers, their eyes glowed right before they shook their heads like I was the dumbest ox. I wanted it to work—it made me happy. She wanted to get married and I said, 'Okay. Why not?' I wanted a wife. What I'm only starting to understand is that Natalie had an agenda from the beginning—she was going to become my wife and we would begin to do everything her way, starting with getting me off that farm and into a suit. I swear to God, we talked about everything before we got married. We lived together for almost a year and there was a little grumbling about my hours, about the family being overwhelming, but nothing like after we got married. The second we were married we started to argue about how little we had in common, how disparate our lives were. So from the beginning we fought. And my family said, 'Could have told you that wasn't going to work.' They all saw how she grimaced at the goat shit on her designer heels, picked at her food, wrinkled her nose at the smells, screeched if a dog or chicken got close to her, cried for hours before and after we spent some time at the farm."

"Wow," Ginger said. "That must have been awful. Even I didn't cry for hours before and after Mick's all-night jam sessions or concerts. And I grew to hate them."

"It just wasn't going to work, we both knew it. I wouldn't change, she wouldn't change. But something happened that finished it. No one knows about this. Natalie had an abortion. She was planning to keep it a secret, sell it to me as a heavy period, but it got bad, she got scared and I had to take her to the emergency room. I left her right after that, as soon as I was sure she was okay. She had gone too far. I was angry and I was through."

Ginger was speechless. She noticed that Matt had to look away to compose himself. She said nothing for a little while. "Your baby," she finally whispered.

"Ours. And it meant nothing to her."

"Oh, Matt. I'm so sorry. How did you find out?"

He took a breath. "I came home one day and found her in bed, gripping her belly with cramps, crying. She was white as a ghost. She said her period was so bad she was scared she was bleeding to death. It was a lot of blood, staining the sheets and a towel and her clothes. I took her straight to the emergency room. I hear a buzzing in my ears when I remember her telling the doctor she'd had a procedure that day and told him who performed that procedure, and heard the doctor say that he'd examine her but a routine D&C for an abortion was often followed by heavy bleeding for several hours. And for a while I just shut down."

"Dear God."

"They looked at her, said it had already slowed down, suggested she stay off her feet for a day and if it didn't get considerably better to come back. They gave her instructions—watch for fever, severe cramping, hemorrhage… I helped her get dressed and took her home but I couldn't even look at her. I couldn't speak. She cried and yelled all the way home about how miserable her life was, how unhappy she was and how she felt trapped by getting pregnant. She didn't know what else to do. I left her the next day, as soon as I was sure she was not going to die." He gave a lame shrug. "That's pretty much it. It was already terrible and then it got worse. And these were things I should have known. I should have known how bad it could get."

"Or she should have," Ginger said.

"My family can't ever know about that. They'd hate her."

"Is there a reason they should still hold her dear? I mean, are they going to run into her at the State Fair livestock show or something?"

"No, it's just…"

"It's not just on her. You're afraid they'll blame you."

"Maybe I am," he said. "It blindsided me, that's for sure. I felt like a failure and a fool. And of course I knew in five minutes, you're nothing like Natalie. There was no reason for me to be afraid of getting close to you."

"Oh, I don't think you were, Matt. You just weren't quite done with the last relationship. It's understandable if you need a little time to be sure you're ready. You've been through a rough time. And with no one to talk to."

"I couldn't talk about it. I was too angry. I'm still angry. That was wrong, what she did. And I hate her for it."

"I can imagine. It must hurt so much. I think you were right in the first place—you and Natalie married the wrong people. No one understands that better than I do—I did that, too. I should have known better. I wish I could explain what makes us blind and deaf to reality."

"Let me ask you something. Are you afraid of what your life could become with me?" he asked, reaching out and tucking her hair behind her ear.

"Of course not. But see, I wasn't afraid of what I'd become with Mick, either. I wanted a different life when I married a man who said he would never go that route. Oh, we have so much in common, Matt," she said, shaking her head sadly. "I wanted Mick to turn into a domesticated husband and father when he promised me from the start that was never going to happen. You wanted Natalie to do the same thing when all she wanted was to get you off the farm."

"And how is that my fault?"

"Oh, Matt, my sweet, sweet Matt. It's not about fault. It's

just about understanding. We're all part of the equation, we're complicit. Not to blame, but participants. I told Mick I wanted a family and he said, 'Knock yourself out, but you know that guy in the supermarket with the baby strapped to his chest? I am never going to be that guy.' He meant it and I didn't hear him. What the hell was I thinking, being married to him, having a baby with him? What right did I have to expect things of him that weren't possible? I had to forgive him. It's kind of freeing."

"I'll never forgive her. I hate her. That was underhanded and selfish and cruel."

She smiled at him. "It was, I agree. I love you, Matt," she said. "I've been honest with you. I swear." She couldn't resist— she reached out and ran her fingers through that glorious hair.

"How could you forgive him?" he asked.

"Oh, he can still make me furious—for about twenty minutes. When he called me I was outraged by his self-centered idiocy. And then I just laughed at how predictable he is. I don't have room in my life for hate. I tried it for a while. It didn't work. And now I want to be with you and I don't want hate to be part of what we have."

"Then it isn't going to drive you away knowing I'm still a little fucked up over my failed marriage?"

"You'd hardly be the first. It takes time to heal. And I think you're going to figure it out real soon. At least you can finally talk about it."

"I'm not sure talking about it got rid of the headache," he said. "Might've been something else," he said, grinning playfully, pulling down the sheet to expose her. He fondled her breast.

"Done talking, Matt?" she asked, humor in her voice.

"For now, I think. Are you? Done talking?"

"Depends. What's the alternative?"

He took the beer from her hand and put it aside. He grabbed her around the waist and said, "Come over here and find out." He pulled her close and just held her tight, held her like he was afraid to let go. After a little while he covered her body with his and smothered her with hungry kisses.

Ginger wasn't sure what time it was, but she heard the back door open and close and smelled coffee brewing. Matt came into the bedroom with a small satchel in one hand, his phone in the other. "Your reputation is completely ruined," he said.

"Is that so?"

"I went to my truck to get my phone and this bag. I went in my shorts, barefoot. There was a gray-haired woman a few doors down tossing trash in the Dumpster and she eyeballed me. I gave her a wave."

"Carrie," Ginger said. "She owns the deli. She's close with Ray Anne."

"So, that means she'll call Ray Anne? Will that get Ray Anne upset, that I spent the night?"

"Are you kidding? Ray Anne thinks getting laid is a cure for almost anything."

"I knew I liked her," Matt said, dropping the bag and putting the phone down. He shed his boxers and climbed in. "Let's cure a few things while the coffee perks."

"You're insatiable…" she murmured, acquiescing immediately.

"I'm not the one who keeps saying *more*!"

"It turns out you're up to the job. Are we going to get up?"

"In case you hadn't noticed, I am up. Can you get in the mood again?"

"Maybe. How long are you planning to stay?"

"Until the last possible moment. God, why didn't I think of this weeks ago…?"

He finally stopped talking, and Ginger just relaxed and enjoyed him. He was a powerful lover, but also sweet and sensitive. His hands were a little rough and he apologized for them, but the roughness that came from hard work felt good on her skin. He couldn't be quiet, always whispering sweet things, always asking her how she felt and serving her needs. His one goal seemed to be making her happy, pleasing her. And when she said *more*! he laughed and seemed thrilled by it.

Ginger hadn't had a lot of partners in her life. There were a couple of men before Mick when she was right around twenty, guys she knew immediately weren't right for her. Then there was Mick who, to his credit, was very romantic when he felt like it, but their time together wasn't a priority for him. And while it wouldn't be ladylike to say so, Matt's skill made Mick look like a bumbling lad.

She didn't even want to know where he came by all this experience and skill. She was a little afraid of the answer.

Limp and satisfied once more, she lay in the bed while he went to get them coffee.

"I have to go to work," she said. "We don't open early on Saturdays and there's no wedding today, but I'm needed in the shop."

"When do you open it?"

"We're open ten till four on Saturdays, unless it's the day before a holiday like Valentine's or Mother's Day—then we stay open till six. Today is a short day. I might be able to sneak away early. But I really should shower and get down there. Will you go back to the farm? Is this the last possible moment now?"

"Hell, no, sweetheart! I'm hanging around unless you want me to leave. If I'd known your work schedule I'd have taken you out for breakfast."

"I'll grab a bowl of cereal or power bar."

"Maybe you should have both. How about we plan a nice dinner out tonight," he asked. "Maybe we'll drive over to Bandon or Coos Bay. Just tell me what you'd like and I'll find a nice restaurant for us."

"If I let you stay, let you sleep with me, is there any chance something is going to go all wonky in your head and you'll turn into Mad Matt again?"

"God, I hope not," he said. "Here's what I think we should do. We should talk, like we already do. We should spend time together. We should take it easy and slow and make sure we understand each other. Right? If there are things about me you don't like, don't want to be stuck with, you have to promise to speak up. And vice versa. I'm not going to try to change you, but I want to really know you. So far, you'd have trouble convincing me you're not perfect."

She laughed at him. "Well, I guarantee you, I'm not!"

"Let's do it, Ginger. Let's check this out—us. I've been alone over a year and no one ever shook me up like you. I'm not walking away without a real good reason. But if you tell me to go…" He shrugged. "Just be honest with me, that's all. I'm sure I'll make mistakes but I'm not going to force myself on a woman."

"And yet, you packed an overnight bag," she pointed out.

"I am the eternal optimist."

"I'm going to get in the shower. What will you do today while I work?"

"Well, with your permission, I'm going to go see Peyton, tell her we're together and ask her to butt out."

"Oh, Matt," she said.

"Seriously, she's been hell to bear ever since she first saw the way I looked at you. I love my sister but she's a bossy pain in the ass. Sisters should *always* be younger. She's not the boss of me."

Ginger laughed. "You be nice to her or I'll dump you."

"Sure. Right. So then I might check and see if I can bring you lunch. I'll walk around town a little, maybe head down the beach if the weather holds. And there are some organic farms east of here. I like looking at farms, talking to farmers." He lay back on the bed, lacing his fingers together behind his head. He crossed one long, hairy leg over the other. "Right now I'm going to watch you do your morning things. And enjoy it."

She took her coffee into the bathroom. "No," she said. "You're not." And she slammed the door.

★ ★ ★

"Well, good morning," Grace chirped when Ginger came in the back door of the shop. Grace was making a centerpiece, and Ginger marveled at how fast her hands moved, how perfectly symmetrically every stem and blossom fell into place. "How was dinner last night?"

"Hilarious—Ashley and Eve joined us. They tell these riotous stories of college life, the older women get the vapors and we all laugh until we have to stop and take a bathroom break. And the food was out of this world. Zorba's. Have you been?"

"I don't think so. I'll have to talk Troy into that some night when we need a break from Winnie."

"And how is dear Winnie?" Ginger asked.

"Dear Winnie is in fine form. You know, I brought her here because it was practical—that big old house in San Francisco wasn't going to work for an invalid. And selfishly, I thought the only way I could spend time with her without killing myself flying back and forth to the Bay Area was if I could get her up here. But I didn't realize how perfectly it would work out. First of all, Lin Su is a dream come true. She's there almost every day in spite of the fact we hired her for a forty-hour week. As long as she can slip away to take care of her own personal business while Winnie rests or is tended by Mikhail, she's happy to check on Winnie almost every day. And Winnie loves her. Whew, huh? And when Winnie is outside on the deck enjoying the activity on the beach and bay, people drop by to visit with her. I'll go out on a limb and say she's never had this in her life—she's been too isolated by *position*. No one in Thunder Point knows or cares that Winnie is important." She laughed almost gaily. "Mikhail is developing a routine and making friends—he's off to the diner, the neighbors', Cooper's, he's even driven up to the rink in North Bend to check out the skating and he let it slip the other night that he's thinking of retirement. Now, I don't know if that's true but I bet it means he's not leaving anytime soon."

"He must like this little town," Ginger said.

"Kind of sounds like it." Grace stopped working and looked at Ginger. "I brewed coffee for you even though I am staying off caffeine."

"Apparently you don't need it," Ginger said. "You're pretty energetic."

"And you look fantastic this morning. You must have slept better than usual or something."

"I think so, yes," she said, getting herself some coffee. While dressing her coffee, without looking at Grace, she said, "I had a surprise visitor last night."

"Oh? And who might that be?"

"Matt," she said quietly. "He came knocking…"

Grace gasped. "Oh! Did you talk?"

"Of course we talked," she said with a laugh. "He freaked out that I was out of reach."

"And drove all the way down here!" Grace said. "And back? That's about eight hours round trip!"

"He didn't go back," Ginger said. "I think he's showering right now."

Grace gasped again. "Oh, my God, get out of here! Go back upstairs. I can handle this—there's not much going on. You should have just called me! You could have had the day. After all you've done for me—"

"It's okay, Grace," Ginger said. "I'm not changing my schedule for Matt. And he has things to do today. I'll see him later. In fact, I might suggest we go to Zorba's for dinner. There are tons of things on the menu I want to try."

"If you don't mind me asking—what does he have to do today?"

"I think he's starting with a visit to Peyton to tell her he's here to see me. I hope that goes well—to hear Matt tell it, she's been trying to spare me Matt's pursuit."

"I take it you'd rather not be spared?"

"He's a wonderful man, Grace. He's kind and generous and very strong in principle. I think I'm falling in love with him."

"Think?"

"Okay, I'm sure, but don't tell, okay? We're both a little wounded—a couple of painful relationships, a hard time getting back on our feet, all that baggage. We'll be okay, I think. But we shouldn't have to deal with pressure from loving friends and family."

Grace was grinning. "No pressure. Check. But if I were you, I'd go right back upstairs."

"No," Ginger said, laughing.

"I used to hate leaving Troy up there in my bed. He was so cute…"

Matt is beyond cute, Ginger thought, laughing. Still, it took great discipline to keep her work schedule knowing he was right up there. "I'm here to work," she said.

"Okay then," Grace said. "But I bet you're not worth a damn with that love hangover glowing all over you."

Matt decided to walk to Peyton's house. When she opened the door, his sister was dressed for cleaning with a feather-duster thing in one hand. She had a babushka-type scarf covering her head, wore yoga pants with an oversize T-shirt and had bare feet.

"What are you doing here?" she asked.

"You and I have to get a few things straight," he said. "Can you take a break from whatever you're doing there?"

"I guess. Is this going to lead to a fight?" she asked.

"I hope so," he said. "I'm pretty pissed off at you. Where are Scott and the kids?"

"He took them fishing for a while so I could clean house. Why are you pissed off at me?" she asked, holding the door open for him.

He entered. "Gimme a break, Peyton. You've been bossy and controlling, deciding things that are not for you to decide, and you know it. I mean, you could've offered to call Ginger and deliver a message for me."

"Because I didn't give out Ginger's phone number? I didn't feel it was my right to do that. She had a new phone number for a reason, after all."

"Yeah, and it wasn't me! You could have been helpful instead of mean. As it turns out, she wasn't upset with me. And I had to go to some trouble to track her down."

"I didn't know," she said stubbornly. "It's not my business. And besides, I see you got down here bright and early to check it out."

"I came last night," he said, trying not to act smug about it.

She raised one dark brow and suddenly Matt saw his mother in her face. *Oh, boy.*

"Really?" she said.

"Now, I want you to listen," he said. "We're together. I love her. We've both been through some stuff and we've had a couple of rocky situations, and we'll probably have a couple more rocky moments while we try to get beyond our stuff, but we want to hammer it out because we both happen to think we're good together. I don't know if this is going the distance. I want it to, but it's possible we're not perfect together or it's not the right time or one of us isn't ready, but you gotta butt out. Really, you'd fuck up a wet dream."

"Nice, Matt," she said, curling her lip.

"I'm serious here, Peyton. I'd never hurt Ginger. I'm sorry I'm not coming to her all perfect, but I'm trying and I'd never hurt her. She's a good person. She's a beautiful person. Talking to her really helps me and if I can believe her, it helps her, too. We seem to really care about each other and we're working the kinks out. You have to back away slowly, let us be. Or I swear..."

"Come in, Matt," she said almost cheerfully. "Let's have a cup of coffee."

He hesitated. "Sounds like a trap," he said.

"Don't be ridiculous," she said, walking to the kitchen and leaving him to follow. "I'd just like to sit down and hear what you have to say."

A little reluctantly, he followed. She put a cup of coffee in front of him and sipped herbal tea from her mug. She made a face, which made him laugh. "You feeling all right, Peyton?" he asked.

"Well, I have moments," she said. "I'm tired, get nauseous, can't have anything good to drink. I think when the baby moves, I'll feel lots better about giving up coffee and wine. Now, tell me about you and Ginger."

"In your dreams, Peyton. I'm not here to discuss my personal life, just to get some boundaries in place."

"Well, what kind of rocky stuff are you working through?" she asked.

"Like you don't know? We're just out of tough, unsuccessful relationships. She's had losses and so have I. I know you didn't like Natalie but that doesn't make it easier to know I failed at marriage. You know how the men in our family feel about marriage."

In a miraculous moment of compassion, she tilted her head and the look on her face was contrite. "I know, Matt. I'm sorry that didn't work out."

"But you're not all that sorry," he said.

"Sorry for you," she insisted. "I'm sorry you were hurt. I knew you would be, but—"

"See, that knowing everything? That's going to get between you and me. So you were right, good for you. But I did my best with Natalie and guess what? If you tell me right now that you don't think I'm good enough for Ginger, that there's no way it's going to work, I'm not listening to that, either. See, I didn't see it working out with that asshole Ted you were with for three years but it was what you wanted at the time and I kept my mouth shut. And when you settled in with Scott, I thought that was great, but I never said anything like, 'Hey, great re-covery, Peyton.'"

"Wow," she said. "You didn't like Ted?"

"Who did?" he asked. "I know you think Ginger is too good for me. You're probably right. I know you think it would be great if I could somehow deserve her and make a decent life with a decent person—I get that. The bottom line is—we didn't hire a matchmaker. That's no good, Peyton. We have to find out if we work, not get together because someone as smart as you endorses it. You have to let it be up to us."

"You love her?"

"I do. She's amazing. I admire her so much."

"What about all those other women?" she asked.

"I don't know." He shrugged. The question quieted him, made him think. "Spinning my wheels. Marking time. Look-ing and making mistakes and... Look, I'm not proud of that, all right? I didn't break laws. I was careful with their feelings. It didn't always work but I was. There hasn't been anyone in a while now. And if it makes you feel better, it didn't do anything to make me happy. In fact, it made me miserable.

"But I'm happy right now," he went on. "That doesn't mean I'm diving in too fast, but for God's sake, let me try being happy. Will you?"

Peyton got tears in her eyes. "Aw, Matt..."

"Jesus, don't cry! Don't! I want to smack you so don't cry!"

"I'm pregnant," she said, and tears ran down her cheeks. "I hate that you ever thought I didn't want you to be happy."

"Awww... I'm not mad at you, Peyton. Well, a little bit be-cause I thought you wanted to keep me away from Ginger. I just thought you wanted me to be happy *your way*," he said. He got up from the kitchen table and found the box of tissues. He tossed it at her and it accidentally hit her in the head before she caught it. He winced.

"I did," she said. "I wanted you to be happy my way. I have

a little issue with that being-right thing. But I didn't know you knew so much about yourself. About Ted. About rocky situations. About working through things with an amazing woman. About looking for love in all the wrong places. I just thought…"

"That I was a big dumb lummox."

"Well…"

"Save it," he said. And he waited while she mopped her eyes and blew her nose. He tried keeping a scowl on his face while she sniveled. He crossed his arms stubbornly over his chest. It was all an act. He wanted to hug her.

"Really," she said with a sniff. "Nothing could make me happier than to think of you in a healthy relationship with a nice woman like Ginger."

"All evidence to the contrary," he said.

"If I say sorry can that be the end of it?"

"I don't know, Peyton," he said. "Can you mind your own business?"

She narrowed her eyes at him. "You might want to go a little easy on me."

"That's the price of forgiveness," he said. "Your word. Then you stand by it and mind your own business."

"All right," she said irritably. "I can't believe you made me cry."

"Those were fetal tears and you know it. I can't remember when you've ever cried over one of us boys."

"I might cry a little easier these days," she relented. "So. You're going to be around awhile?"

"I'm going to leave for the farm Sunday night. We might bump into each other but let's be clear, I'm here to be with Ginger. I need to spend time with her."

"All *right*, jeez."

He softened. He smiled warmly. "Maybe next week or the week after we can get together."

"Well, don't go to any trouble," she shot back.

"So. We understand each other?" he asked.

"We understand each other, *mutiko*," she said, meaning *little boy*.

That made him frown. "Don't push it," he warned. "I have things to do." He stood to leave. After taking a couple of steps toward the door he turned back to her. He put a small kiss on her forehead. He hugged her gently. "Behave," he warned.

CHAPTER THIRTEEN

Grace had never wished illness on her mother but it was true that the relationship she had with her now was better than ever. Their routine was calming. When Grace rose in the morning she would go upstairs to Winnie's room. She would usually knock softly, not just to be sure Winnie was awake but also to be certain she wouldn't wake or disturb Mikhail, who never admitted to spending nights in the chair beside Winnie's bed. Grace would go into her mother's room to find Winnie sitting up, wearing her favorite bed jacket. This particular morning she'd seen Mikhail out on the deck with coffee.

Winnie's trembling had worsened and she could no longer fluff her hair or paint on her rose-colored lips—two things she hated to be seen without accomplishing. Grace actually enjoyed helping her mother with these small tasks. It made her feel useful, indispensable even.

"Time for that silly wench from the town to come out and give us a fix-up," Winnie said of the local hairdresser who had obliged them by making regular house calls.

"As long as you promise not to call her *that silly wench*," Grace said with a laugh.

"I know better than that, for God's sake. It's like insulting the chef—he might spit in the soup."

"You could end up with red hair. Or bald," Grace pointed out. "Would you like to have your tea on the deck?"

"Only if I don't look like the wrath of God," Winnie said. "First the ladies' room, please."

"The fog hasn't lifted, but the sun is over the mountains already. You can watch it rise and chase the fog out to sea," Grace told her. "You'll need your shawl. Troy and Mikhail are already out there with their coffee. It's a lovely, dewy morning."

Winnie didn't say so often but she liked this place. It was like a vacation, like a chilly and wintry Cabo San Lucas. When she was on the deck, which was a couple of times a day in good weather, there were regular visitors. Sarah Cooper liked to have a morning run with her Great Dane, Ham, and she would stop by some mornings to say hello to Winnie, leaving the dog at the foot of the stairs. Seth Sileski, on the other hand, enjoyed an early-evening jog and would then meet friends at Cooper's, but he'd frequently stop by for a little report on the town first. Winnie really enjoyed the local news from Seth even if she didn't know half the people. Grace liked a walk on the beach now and then and she always walked to and from the flower shop if it wasn't raining. Dr. Grant took his little ones fishing off the dock sometimes and he used that opportunity to ask after Winnie's health, and their next-door neighbors—the Lawsons—checked in frequently if they saw Winnie enjoying the sunshine.

This was actually new for Winnie—friends and neighbors who weren't intimidated by her, who cared if she was well or ill.

Mikhail was often about, but he had his own routines. He now donned board shorts that were extralong on his short body, a hat, white socks in his brown German walking shoes. He walked on and off all day long. He went into town, had a meal at the diner almost every day, visited with Waylan at his bar, sometimes helped Grace and Ginger pull in their sidewalk displays at closing time. Even though he didn't drive he made regular visits to the service station having struck up friendships with the owner, Eric, and his right-hand man, Al. These days he talked a lot about buying a car. And weirdly unsurprisingly, he had many female fans who honked their horns and waved as they drove by. He frequently walked out of town to the nearest farm stand and brought home fresh vegetables. Grace said he must log twenty miles some days.

As July warmed the beach there was a new development that warmed Grace's heart. She waved to a couple on the beach, and Winnie said, "Who is it, Grace?"

"Ginger and Matt. Holding hands and strolling." She sighed. "They're in love and together every weekend."

"Do I know this Matt?"

"I don't think so, Mother. We could have them to dinner some weekend if you like. He's very nice. He's a farmer from north of here—the Portland area."

"A farmer? That sounds tedious."

Grace laughed. "It's Peyton's brother. They're not very showy people but that farm is enormous and very successful. Peyton tells me Matt is a scientist with an advanced degree, science applied to farming. He's very smart."

As the couple stopped on the beach and kissed, Winnie made a sound. "Well, there's what your generation calls something... public displays of something."

"Is called PDA," Mikhail informed her. "Public displays of affection, Babushka. Something you have never been accused of."

Winnie leaned toward him. "I'm not agile and I'm not strong anymore, but if you call me that again I'm going to hurt you."

That made Mikhail grin. "Is adorable name for you, my dove. Is sweet Russian name for grandmother."

"I'd rather be a dove than a sweet Russian grandmother."

The sound of the front door opening and closing announced the arrival of Winnie's nurse. She yelled, "Good morning," from the foyer. Then she migrated to the deck. "How is every-one this morning?"

"Very well," Winnie said. "All things considered. Now, Grace, who is that boy down there by the dock?"

"I don't think I know him, Mama. A kid from town, no doubt."

"That's my son, Charlie," Lin Su said. "I've brought him to the beach before. Don't worry, he's just going to hang out while I'm with you."

"Can't we meet him?" Grace asked.

"I didn't want to bring him to work, exactly. But I don't want him to sit in front of the computer or TV all summer while he's out of school. So on nice days I bring him along, and he gets some fresh air."

"No, you shouldn't allow all that TV and computer non-sense," Winnie said. "He'll go blind and his brain will rot. But what will he do? Sit there all day?"

"He has the run of the town. If he makes the slightest effort, he could actually meet people."

"Oh, Lin Su, you shouldn't let a child that young loose all day without your supervision."

"He's not as young as he looks," she said. "He's fourteen, just kind of small for his age. And when he was little he had health problems—I suppose he's still catching up. He won't be any trou-ble for you, I promise. He has money for lunch. And sunscreen and stuff in the car, like his laptop, which he can only use for an hour or two. And we have our cell phones for texting so we can keep tabs on each other."

Winnie turned and looked up at Lin Su. "I want you to go down there and tell him he's welcome here anytime as long as he's not too wild or loud because sometimes I have to rest or I'm useless. Tell him you'll make him lunch here—there's an abundance of food, and Troy keeps buying more. He can even watch TV, just not all day—he needs air and sunshine."

"That's very sweet, Winnie, but—"

"I'm done talking about it. Be a good little nurse and go talk to your son."

Lin Su turned desperate eyes to Grace. "We don't want to be any trouble… This is my job. I'll leave him home if—"

"You don't have to leave him home if he's no trouble," Winnie said. "I didn't know you had a son. You never mentioned it."

"Lin Su, you must have been pretty young. You don't look much over thirty yourself," Grace said. "Oh, I'm sorry—that was rude. I didn't mean to pry!"

"Maybe I'm catching up, too," she said. "I'm not married. We make a pretty good team, me and Charlie. And now that he doesn't need babysitting or after-school programs, we do very well. But Charlie is kind of shy…"

"My specialty," Troy said, jumping up from his spot on the deck. "I'll go invite him up."

"Oh, Troy," Lin Su said, embarrassed.

"Let him," Grace said. "Troy needs a playmate."

"As do I," Mikhail said, rising a bit more slowly to follow.

Grace looked at Lin Su's almost pleading expression and laughed. "Try not to worry, Lin Su. We're not exactly a traditional family. Charlie might fit right in. After all, you have."

Matt's world had changed because of Ginger. He was experiencing life in a whole new way, in a way he hadn't even been smart enough to long for, to hope for. Because the farm was stable, no drought, no damaging storms, no infestations or illnesses, he was sneaking away for at least three nights every week. He drove to Thunder Point on Thursday afternoon and home either Sunday night or Monday morning. Because his eyes were bright and his smile quick, Paco kept telling him to take time while he could.

"Come August, things will be crazy again," he warned Ginger. "First the grapes—Uncle Sal's grapes. I could probably get out of it, but I shouldn't. Those early grapes have to be brought in and we depend on his people when the pears are ready. It's steady for a couple of months. It's hard work."

"I could come to you," Ginger said. "I could help a little. If you showed me what to do."

"Peyton will spend a couple of weekends at the farm, she hardly ever misses it. But Grace needs you," he said.

"Grace and I can job share a little bit. I'm good at running the front of the store and I'm getting better at creating the arrangements. I've had days on my own with only delivery help from Justin. I can give her a couple of days off every week if she can give me a couple of days. You don't care when I come, do you?"

"I just can't think about not having you next to me for more than a week," he said. "It's torture."

"You might be getting a little spoiled," she said.

"And you're not?" he asked, an evil little gleam in his eye.

Matt couldn't remember ever feeling this way. He was a little embarrassed by that, though he wasn't sure how he was supposed to know the difference between a good thing and the real thing. There was no question that when he was deciding to marry Natalie his life had seemed good. If she wasn't having some wedding meltdown or issue with having Sunday dinner with his family, he was feeling pretty damn satisfied.

But Ginger took that to a whole new level. Just being herself, she made him feel like the richest man on earth. He had never before felt this secure with a woman; he never felt even a second of doubt. He'd heard those ridiculous love songs about being willing to die for someone and he always found himself thinking, *I'd be willing to give up a few things—bowling, shaving, driving a truck, cutting my hair. But die for someone? A little extreme…*

But here in his arms was a woman he would do anything for. Would he leave the farm for Ginger? He just might, except she wouldn't ask him to. If he was wrong about her he was going to retire to a mountaintop and live a completely celibate life, but if there was one thing that seemed real it was what Ginger said to him. She liked his farm. She *loved* him. And when someone loves you, they let you know your happiness is paramount to them. He'd never had that before.

They had a few blissful weeks together that brought them to July; long phone conversations at night, long weekends filled with plenty of time in each other's arms and also enjoyable time with Thunder Point friends. And with his sister.

"I have to admit, I never saw this coming," Peyton said to him. "My brother, Mad Matt, all soft and cuddly."

"I told you if you'd just get out of my way, I knew what I was doing," he said.

"Except, did you? Know what you were doing?"

"Not really, but fortunately Ginger did."

"Really? And are you a man to be led around by the nose?" Peyton teased.

"Yes. I am."

There was a moment of doubt and worry in the middle of July when Ginger became a little quiet. It was sudden. He was getting ready to go back to the farm when she seemed very tired, a little down in the dumps. He wasn't used to seeing her eyes downcast. She wasn't as talkative on the phone that night or the next night; she didn't seem to have much to say. She complained of having a headache and being tired.

"I thought I drove away the headaches," he teased.

"It's very unusual for me and it'll pass. Thanks for understanding."

Of course Matt didn't understand at all. But he just kept telling her he loved her. He didn't know what else to do.

Al Michel climbed the back stairs to Ginger's little apartment and tapped on the door. When she answered, it was obvious she'd been crying. "Hi," he said. "Got a minute?"

"Is it important?" she asked.

"It is. I think it's important. Could I just have a few minutes?"

"Is Ray Anne all right?"

"She's excellent, but I wanted to talk to you," Al said. "I won't take too much of your time."

"Okay, I guess," she said, opening the door. "I'm a little under the weather, though."

"Sure you are, honey," he said. "Let's just sit down in there."

She shrugged and let him follow her to the sofa, where they sat.

"I know what tomorrow is," Al said.

Immediately, tears began to run down Ginger's cheeks. "Ray Anne told you," she murmured.

"Sort of. She told me a long time ago but it's possible she doesn't even remember. I remembered. I stopped by the shop late today and you'd already left, not feeling so good, Grace said. And she mentioned you were taking tomorrow off. She didn't think you were real sick, though."

"I'm not so sure about that," she said.

"What you're feeling, it's okay," Al said. "I've felt it myself. Felt it deep. Do you have a plan for how you're going to spend the day tomorrow?"

"Driving," she said, letting a slightly embarrassed laugh squeak through the tears.

"I figured as much. How about I take you?"

"You?" she asked, shocked.

"I have experience with this. Ray told you, I'm sure. I lost a son to SIDS. We think it was SIDS—it was a real long time ago. Doctors know a lot more about it now. I was a young husband, only about twenty. Just a kid. I didn't go to his grave on the anniversary of his death. I went on his birthday every year. Every summer for over thirty years. You and me—we have some things in common."

"I don't know anyone else who lost a baby to SIDS," she said.

"There aren't that many, thank God. My wife and I didn't

stay together. She went on to have a good marriage and a couple of healthy kids. It took me a long time to give up going to that grave in absolute agony every year."

"Can you still feel him?" she asked, fresh tears escaping.

"Not anymore, honey. For a long time I could feel him against my shoulder, his little head lying against me right here," he said, demonstrating by positioning his hands. "I finally let the kid rest. I know you're going to do what you have to do, Ginger. I hope there's some way I can help. And I hope you don't dedicate as many years to grief as I did. Remembering is good. Agonizing is useless."

"It's the first year," she said, sniffing.

"Let me take you so you don't have to drive. I can manage not to talk. I won't ask questions."

She shook her head. "I just want to have a day alone to remember, that's all."

"You can talk about it if you want to, you know."

She gave her head a little shake.

"You can talk to Matt. He seems a real good man. And I can tell, he cares about you."

"I just don't want to put this on Matt."

"Aw, he's a big tough guy, he can handle it..."

"I want it to be *mine*," she said. "Do you understand that?"

He laughed a little, a small laugh that said he knew *exactly*. "Ginger, I left my wife—I couldn't even talk to her and it was her baby. Sweetheart, I know you're in pain right now. I just hope you don't do that to yourself. Don't waste the years like I did. Remember him sweetly. Let him rest. Go forward and have his brothers and sisters."

She nodded, looking down, tears falling on her hands.

"Let me drive you. I've arranged for a day off. No one knows why, not even Ray. Just let me drive you, keep you safe."

She looked up. "Please," she said softly. "This is mine to do. I promise you I'll be all right."

He gave her a look of acquiescence. "Come here, angel," he said, pulling her against his big hard chest. She leaned against him and cried for a little while, but not for too long. He just stroked her back until the tears passed.

"I'm okay, Al. Just a tough day, that's all. And I will—let it pass, let him rest. I have a lot ahead that's good." She sniffed and reached for a tissue.

"Yes, you do," he said, running her pretty hair behind her ear. "Would it be all right if I called you tomorrow night? Just to be sure you're okay?"

"Yes. Sure. But I promise you… I might need a couple of days to be done with this but I promise you, I'm not going back to that dark place I was in when Ray Anne rescued me. That wouldn't exactly do my baby proud, would it?"

Matt had to get a map from the mortuary office so that he could find the right grave. The security patrol had no trouble finding the location and handed a copy to Matt.

He was not at all surprised to see Ginger's car parked along the road. And there she was, sitting on the cool grass about forty feet from the road.

He took the flowers from his mother's garden to the spot, walking past Ginger to put them on the grave. There were lots of flowers already there. She looked up at him.

"Did someone tell you? Call you?"

He shook his head, then crouched to her level, sitting on the heel of his boot. "No one called. No one told me."

"Then why are you here?" she asked, wiping a tear.

Matt sighed and sat on the ground. "You've been blue and I thought I might find you here. If you weren't here I would have just left these flowers from our garden to mark the day of his death. I'm not surprised to see you but you could've told me. You can tell me anything, you know."

"You just…came? You just… How did you know?"

"You went inside yourself," he said, wiping a tear from her cheek. "I could think of a few possibilities. So I went to the newspaper archives online and found the obit. I wanted to pay my respects."

"I wasn't hiding it from you."

"I know, baby. Come here," he said, stretching out his long legs and pulling her onto his lap. "I know it'll take a little time for us to know everything about each other but that's okay. I think we've got the important stuff covered for now."

"Like what?" she said, laying her head on his shoulder. "What's important?"

"You love me," he said. "I don't have the best instincts with women but with you I feel different—like I know what you say is absolutely true. And I know I meant it when I said it to you. And I trust you. When you got quiet and wouldn't tell me why I figured it was something you were still working out. You don't have to say anything. But I'm listening when you're talking. Okay?"

"Okay," she said. "It was the worst day of my life."

"I can believe that…"

"I called the paramedics. I tried to breathe for him, but it was too late. Sometimes I pulled him into bed with me but not that night. That night I put him in his crib where he died without my warmth close by. Part of me wishes I had him in bed with me, but then I would forever worry that I rolled over on him, suffocated him. And part of me is relieved he wasn't in bed be-cause then I didn't hurt him… So the paramedics came and didn't even try anything because he was gone, he'd been gone for a while. They let me hold him and we went to the hospital. I think they were breaking rules. I saw one of them crying; he was trying to hide it, but he had wet eyes and kept wiping them. At the hospital they asked for him and I wouldn't give him up and I *wailed*. I went to the hospital in pajamas and not just any pajamas, the worst pajamas ever worn by the lowest vagrant—

and I saved them, the pajamas. I saved his little onesie. And I wailed like a wounded animal and they had to give me a shot to get me to let go of the baby, of Josh."

Matt started to rock her slightly, holding on tight, his lips against her hair.

"It was terrifying how crazed I was. And when they took him I couldn't really believe he was dead. They did an autopsy, did you know? Because they had to make sure it wasn't a disease or a homicide and oh, God..." She shook her head. "When I was able to see him again I didn't believe it was him but I didn't say anything because I knew they were this close to locking me up for being a lunatic."

He kissed her temple. "Do you believe it now?" he asked in a whisper.

She nodded. "Yes. My baby died. There it is. It was no one's fault. He wasn't even a high-risk baby or in a high-risk lifestyle. Our pediatrician had two SIDS cases in his entire career and he was no kid." She turned to look up at him. "Sometimes I wish I could just die like that."

Matt shook his head. "No, sweetheart, no. We're going to go forward. We have things to live for, I'm sure of it."

"That's what Al said," she said. "Go forward and have his brothers and sisters."

"That's a good idea."

"You'd do that? With me?" she asked him.

"Sure. When we're ready. There's plenty of time. Make sure it's what you want. Make sure I'm what you want."

She put her fingers on his lips. "Matt, I never thought I'd have a man like you in my life." She smiled weakly. "I sure didn't think so at Peyton's wedding when you went for my boob."

"Ah, a defining moment. Impressive, wasn't I?"

"Drunk and clumsy," she said.

"Yeah, but I'm persistent. I'm with you now. What do you

want to do, sweetheart? Stay here awhile? Go to my place and rest a little bit?"

"I just want to go home," she said. "I need to go back to my life. Will I see you this weekend?"

"I'm taking you home, honey."

"You're following me?"

"No. Driving you. You follow me to U-Haul. It's not far. I'm going to rent a half trailer, hook your car up and tow you. We'll ride together. We can hold hands and talk. Or not talk, if you're feeling quiet. You can sleep a little—grieving wears a person out. We'll stop for a good meal because I bet you didn't eat..."

"Al's going to be jealous. He wanted to drive me."

"He needs to watch it," Matt said teasingly. "This is my territory now."

"It is, isn't it? I should mind being called territory, but I don't. You'll be missed on the farm..."

"No, it's all good. No one's expecting me, but I'll make a call, let Mama know I'm busy. She'll tell Paco and George."

"Do they know about me? That I'm damaged? That my baby died and I'm so damaged?"

"I haven't told them the particulars, just that you needed me today. You can tell them someday if you feel like it." He stood up and held out a hand to help her to her feet. "You ready or do you want more time here?"

"I'm ready," she said.

Matt hated to put her in the car to drive even a short distance. Ginger never mentioned him, not even once, but Matt thought about him—that loser, Mick. He probably changed his name to Mick to be like Jagger. He should have been with her when that baby died. And even though Matt didn't want him anywhere near her ever again, he should be here now, propping her up, supporting her. He should cry that his son died.

Matt hated him.

★ ★ ★

Ginger did sleep a little on the way back to Thunder Point. They stopped just outside Eugene at a homey little country restaurant that also sold hams and pies. Ginger had a bowl of soup with crackers and half a sandwich while Matt, no doubt concerned about getting enough to eat when they got back to that little loft, indulged in a large meat loaf and potato dinner. She called her parents, explaining she'd been to the cemetery and her suspicions were right—they'd made a visit early that morning and left a bouquet. She had planned to visit Josh's grave alone, spend a couple of hours and leave, not feeling like seeing people.

Then she explained Matt being there, taking her back home. "I didn't tell him I'd be there and if he'd asked to come with me I would've said I wanted to be alone," she said to her mother. "But I'm so glad he was there. And it turned out to be the right thing for me."

Then she slept a little more. He unhooked the tow bar and parked her car behind the flower shop while she went upstairs. Once she was in her secure little loft apartment, she called Ray Anne and asked her to relay to Al that she was fine.

"I went to the cemetery today to put flowers on his little grave, and Matt came. He guessed I might be there. He brought his own flowers. It was so lovely that he'd do that without being asked, without being needed."

"Oh, baby," Ray Anne singsonged. "And now? Feeling all right?"

"Feeling a little wrung out, honestly. But I'll sleep tonight and tomorrow I'll be so happy to get back to my flowers and friends." Unbelievably, that was the truth. She needed that pilgrimage to Portland. She wished there was more by way of closure, but that was as good as it was going to get. She was beginning to understand that there was nothing she could do, no ritual that could make the feelings go away. The sadness would just have to leave her with time as replaced by new feelings. Remembering him, his sweet little face, that belonged to her.

Matt said he had no instincts where women were concerned, but she was amazed by them. He seemed to give her plenty of space while staying near. At about eight that night he went out for ice cream, which they ate in bed, then they talked a little while about ordinary things—she wanted to know about the grapes and pears. He wanted to know about her flowers and Grace's mother. He told her they'd be breeding sheep at George's in the late fall. He was slated to teach a few classes as a visiting professor in the fall after the harvest. She was looking forward to the harvest celebrations and food.

At the first light of dawn Ginger woke to the gentle stroke of Matt's rough hand on her upper arm. She turned to him and smiled.

"How do you feel?" he asked.

"Okay. You?"

He just nodded. "If you think you'll be all right, I should get back to the farm."

"Of course. Thank you."

"I'm glad I was there."

"I meant, thank you for going to his grave even though I might not have been there. He wasn't part of your life. That was one of the nicest things anyone has done for me."

"*You're* part of my life," he said. "I'll talk to you tonight."

He pulled on his clothes and slid out the door quietly.

CHAPTER FOURTEEN

Lin Su got into the car to go to Winnie's house. Her son was already in the passenger seat, his backpack in the back. "I brought you a clean shirt," she told Charlie. "After you knock around the beach and town all day, we're having dinner with Winnie and her family because I'm taking a turn at cooking. They'd like you to come, too."

-"You're right, I don't. But this is a very unusual job. I'm the nursing help but the whole family is around. Usually when I'm the nursing help, it's just me and the patient with maybe one or two other relatives checking in."

"And then when I came with you, I could just watch TV," he said.

True enough, she thought. Her patient would usually be in the bedroom and as long as Charlie didn't mess up the house, kept the volume very low and didn't eat their food, he could tag along and no one knew the difference.

"Troy said you can watch the TV in their game room downstairs as long as you don't mess up the house. You can use your computer just about anywhere, upstairs or down—you can jump on their Wi-Fi. Not too much computer or TV, though. We have to stay out of the way of these people or I'll lose my job."

Actually, Troy had not been specific about the messy house or about the amount of time Charlie spent watching TV. He had said Charlie was welcome in the house whenever he wanted or needed to be.

"I'm an expert at staying out of the way…"

"And do I have to tell you how bad it would be if I lost my job?"

"No," he said. "I think I get it." His tone was sarcastic as they'd been over this a thousand times.

She went over it once more. Money was tight. Very tight. A nurse didn't earn enough to support a family. A single parent had a lot of trouble making ends meet. She never said it aloud but the truth was, they lived on the edge of poverty in an old rented trailer in a crappy mobile-home park. She hated leaving Charlie at home; their neighborhood was rough. Having him around Thunder Point so she could check on him now and then was much better.

"So, there's a clean shirt. You can wash up and put on a clean shirt for dinner. Be sure to wipe up the bathroom behind yourself…"

"Why are you cooking?" he asked.

"I offered. Everyone was choosing a night to cook, even Mikhail, the old Russian. God knows what that will be…"

"Maybe borscht," he offered.

Lin Su laughed. He was so funny sometimes. She looked over at him. So small, so nerdy. So adorable.

"What are you doing today? Any plans?"

He shrugged. "I'll be busy on and off. Troy and Spencer don't mind having me around. Troy said he might put me to work. When it's not busy in Cooper's it's okay if I get a table inside and use my laptop. I get out of there if a lot of people come in. And if I'm charged up, I can always use it in the car. Don't worry, okay? No one knows how to stay out of the way like me."

Her vision blurred slightly. "Charlie…"

"Don't get emotional, okay? Because we're fine. Everything is temporary."

"Not too temporary, I hope. Mrs. Banks is holding her own and with any luck she'll be with us a good long while. It's a nice place to work. You have money?"

"Never used the money you gave me two days ago."

"How'd you buy lunch?"

"Didn't have to," he said. "I was hanging out at the dock and Troy made us sandwiches. I told him I had money for lunch and he said it wasn't necessary."

"I could have made you lunch," she said. "I could have made something while I was fixing Mrs. Banks's lunch. Or while she napped."

Charlie sighed. "He made it in the same kitchen, Mom. We're good."

"Did you ask what was in it?"

"I checked, Mom. It wasn't peanut butter or anything like that. You have to relax."

She took a breath. "You have your inhaler? EpiPen? Sunscreen? Vitamins? Power bars and fruit drinks?"

He glanced at her. He pushed his glasses up on his nose again.

"Yeah, I guess you have everything," she said.

"I think Troy or Landon might take me out on the paddleboard today."

"Oh, Charlie…"

"It's okay so don't freak. I'm not falling in or anything."

She appreciated that he wasn't paranoid about his fragile health but she thought one plunge into the cold Pacific could bring on an asthma attack or bronchitis or pneumonia.

"I haven't been sick," he reminded her, reading her mind.

"Last winter," she said.

"I didn't go to the hospital and I haven't had asthma attacks or allergic reactions. Not too many, anyway. I had a doctor who said there was a good chance I'd grow out of it and even though I haven't grown that much, I'm leaving all that shit behind."

"Your language," she said.

"Is entirely appropriate," he argued. "It's all a lot of shit and you know it."

She completely understood the attitude. It wasn't just his disgust with chronic illness, it was also his impatience with a mother who watched every bite he took, every move he made, listening to every breath. In fact, those days she started out tired were usually caused by her inability to sleep, listening to him snoring or wheezing or the whistling of his sinuses.

There had been times during the first ten years of his life that he'd been so sick, so weak and fragile, that she feared losing him. Complicated allergies, a weak immune system and asthma conspired against him, leaving him vulnerable to infections and viruses.

It was true—in the past few years he'd gotten stronger. It was also true that she hadn't relaxed enough yet. But what mother wouldn't understand sitting vigil at the bedside of a small boy in an oxygen tent? She'd lost years of her life every time he was hospitalized. She'd felt so alone.

That wasn't fair, she reminded herself. In the fourteen years since Charlie had been born there had been good friends here and there, coworkers or neighbors. They'd had to move around too much for a lot for reasons ranging from rent to changes in work, but she'd always known good people along her way. She'd been working in the small hospital in Bandon when they moved into the trailer park. When the hospital downsized, laying off a few nurses and staff, Dr. Grant suggested this job to her if she was willing to make the drive. Ha! Willing? She'd be willing to walk it! She was interviewed by Dr. Grant and his wife, Peyton, but then it was the patient herself who chose her, with Grace sitting in on the interview.

"When I do a background check, what will I learn about you?" Winnie had asked her.

She wasn't surprised by the question. People who could afford a private nurse were usually well-off, worried about having their property plundered. So she answered, "I prefer private home health care when there's a need for me. When there's no job in the private sector I work in hospitals or clinics. I'm good at what I do and have an excellent job record."

"And why don't you work for an agency?"

She shook her head. "They don't pay well. The patient will pay the agency a substantial amount of money for the luxury of having a bonded health-care worker but pay the actual professional very poorly. And then they'll move the nurses around—not good for the nurse or the patient. The irony is—the bond won't get you much. Who cares about bond? Find a professional who checks out instead. After a dozen years, I have references you can call. They'll tell you if I did my job well. They'll tell you I'm trustworthy. And I'm not limited to a shift or specific number of hours. I can be your primary caregiver. Provided you want me to be."

Winnie had agreed to give her a month on trial but within two weeks she was established as permanent. And now Charlie was a part of the family, as well.

Lin Su didn't know if that made her happy or scared to death.

Charlie liked the beach area, even if he did stay out of the sun—his own preference because he didn't want his laptop to overheat. And he stayed sheltered if there was a wind. It wasn't easy for him to make friends as a rule, but the area around Mrs. Banks's house where his mom was working was populated with kids younger than he was and their parents. That made it easier. On this morning, there was a pretty brisk breeze and not too many people around. He sat on the steps right off Troy's patio where he was out of the wind. He got his laptop out of his backpack and, holding it on his knees, fired it up. He logged onto Troy's Wi-Fi and brought up a TED Talk on astronomy that he'd listened to about ten times. *Can astronomers help doctors?*

He loved TED Talks. It broke everything down into under-standable terms. He was particularly interested in medicine but he didn't dare tell his mom that. She'd start to freak out about the cost of college or something.

He was a little lost in the video when a shadow crossed in front of him. He looked up to see a guy two steps up moving toward him, grinning. "Well, I'll be damned," the guy said.

If you're just going to kick sand in my face, get it over with, Charlie thought.

The guy was big. He had a little sandy-colored whisker growth on his chin and cheeks and hairy legs sticking out of his board shorts. He did wear glasses, at least. "I wouldn't have believed it if I hadn't seen it with my own eyes. A computer nerd on the beach."

Charlie slowly lowered the screen. "What's wrong with that?"

The guy let his backpack drop off his shoulder, lifted the flap and pulled out a shiny silver laptop. "Not a thing, my man. I just thought I was the only one. Come on, let's go to Cooper's."

"I'm okay here," he said, embarrassed by his shyness.

"Come on," he said again. "I'm meeting some people. We'll get a drink. Juice or something. We'll open up the computers for a few minutes till they get here." And then he walked off, stuff-ing his computer into his backpack, willing Charlie to follow.

Which he did. He figured if the guy was going to kidnap him or beat him up, he wouldn't do it in front of Cooper. At least he was reasonably sure.

By the time he got up the beach stairs the guy's stuff was all set up at a corner table out of the breeze on the deck but he wasn't there. Charlie stood there in indecision. Then the guy appeared from inside, still smiling, a bottled juice in each hand. He handed one to Charlie and indicated he should sit down.

"What's your name, kid?"

"Charlie," he said.

"I'm Frank," the guy said, sticking out his hand for a shake. "New in town?"

"I…uh… My mom works for Mrs. Banks…"

"Oh—the new lady? ALS, I heard."

Charlie nodded.

Frank clicked away at his keyboard while Charlie just sat there. Then he pushed up his glasses and read the label on the plastic bottle.

"Allergies?" Frank asked.

"Peanuts, shellfish and insect bites."

"You carry an Epi?"

"Uh-huh."

"That juice is okay. No additives. No MSG, no artificial sweetners, no gluten or corn syrup."

"Oh," Charlie said. "Thanks."

"So—what are you doing on the computer? Games?"

"I have a few games, yeah. You?"

"I have some papers to read."

"You're a teacher?"

He laughed. "No, a student. I'm reading some published papers for research—physics, mainly. And astronomy. Have you heard the term 'astrophysics'?"

Charlie nodded, feeling a little better about everything. The guy didn't look like a nerd even if he was wearing glasses. Kind of thick ones. "The study of physics as it applies to heavenly bodies." He opened up his laptop, clicked it back to life and turned the screen toward Frank, showing him the TED Talk.

Frank grinned and said, "You are my brother. I've seen that one. How old are you?"

"Fourteen," he answered, fighting the blush. "I'm short for my age." He had rejected the word *small*, even if it was accurate.

"So was I," Frank said.

"You're not anymore. I guess you grew."

Frank chuckled. "I have an older brother, big jock. He got all the testosterone in the family. I think he was shaving in the sixth grade. I started shaving two or three weeks ago. I was small, skinny, nerdy."

"No way."

"Way."

"You get beat up a lot?" Charlie asked.

Frank frowned at the question. "I had a couple of secret weapons. There was my brother, for one thing. But also I helped kids with their homework all the time. Kept me safe. Why are you listening to that video? You like astronomy?"

"Yeah. I like science. Where are you a student?"

"MIT," he said.

"To be an astrophysicist?" he asked, in awe.

"Physics is my study but I love astronomy so I'm looking at it, but who knows? I'm not even two years in yet."

"You live here when you're not at MIT?" Charlie asked.

"I'm home for a visit—just a few weeks. I'm getting ready for fall. How about you? What are you headed for?"

I'm headed for being a freshman if I live that long and no one beats me senseless for being a nerd, Charlie thought. "I start high school in the fall. So I don't know."

"You know what you like, though, right?"

"Science. Math. *Star Trek* and *House*."

He laughed. "A Trekkie doctor, I like it."

Troy came outside with a cup of coffee. "Oh, God, there are two of you!"

Frank laughed and looked back at his screen. "You have your laptop out half the time," he accused Troy.

"Schoolwork, young man."

There was the sound of whooping and laughter wafting across the bay. "And here come the women," Frank said. Two young women were approaching on paddleboards from the marina side of the bay. "Do you know when Landon and Cooper are going to get here?"

"Soon," Troy said. "But there's not enough wind on the bay yet."

"There will be," Frank said. "Stick around, Charlie. We're going to have some fun today. Windsurfing."

"Really?" he asked a little excitedly.

"Well, I'll be windsurfing. No one else has done it yet. Cooper's renting us some equipment."

"I don't know how you talked him into that," Troy said with a laugh.

"He said if it works he might turn it into a business opportunity."

"That explains it. By the way, I've been windsurfing. Badly, but I've done it," Troy said.

As the women got closer to the shore in front of Cooper's, Frank put away his laptop, got up and went down the steps to greet them. He left the backpack on the deck by his chair. The women were wearing wet suits with long sleeves and were covered down to their knees. And they were gorgeous. They pulled their paddleboards up onto the sand, Frank lending a hand.

"Those are not women," Troy advised.

Frank kissed the redhead.

"On their way to becoming women. On their way fast, I'd say. But they're still girls. They never had girls like that when I was his age," Troy muttered.

Landon's truck came across the sand to Cooper's. The bed was full of equipment. And as if Frank commanded the heavens, the wind immediately picked up. And the beach became a swarm of activity. Equipment was unloaded. Landon pulled on a wet suit. There seemed to be some assembling required.

Troy locked the back door of the bar and wandered down to the beach. Charlie could see that the windsurfing boards were slightly lighter and trimmer than the paddleboards.

Frank pushed off, Landon close behind him, and they paddled out into the bay. Frank, on his knees, raised his sail and it sat for a moment, then a small gust took it and he stood tentatively, turning the sail into the wind and he was off, skidding across the bay. The girls screeched and whooped happily.

Charlie stood up to watch from Cooper's deck.

Landon was struggling to get up, to adjust his sail, and in he went. He got himself back on the board, tried again, went into the ocean again. Every time he got dunked the girls howled with laughter. On his fourth try he got up and the cheers were wild. He turned his sail into the wind and blew across the bay. Where he fell again and everyone laughed.

Spencer came outside; Mikhail wandered down the beach. Spencer's son and daughter were at the water's edge, waving and splashing with their feet. The girls with the paddleboards pushed off the shore and paddled out into the water just to get a closer view. Landon and Frank were gliding all around the bay, leaning into turns, leaning away, shifting their sails into the wind. For a little while they sailed in tandem, like twins.

God, that must feel good, Charlie thought.

Cooper was beside him. "Go on down there, Charlie," he said.

Charlie was on his way instantly. Then he stopped. "I should take my backpack and laptop to my mom's car or something..."

"Forget it—I'll put your backpack and Frank's behind the bar where it won't get overheated or...lost."

"Thanks," he said, racing down the stairs to watch.

Watching Frank and Landon out there was amazing, and made Charlie long for things he had no business longing for. Impossible things—like an active life filled with people like these crazy people. He looked over his shoulder once and noticed that his mom had Mrs. Banks out on the deck, watching.

As interesting as what happened out on the water was, what was happening on the beach was even cooler. More and more people were walking down the beach to watch. Sarah Cooper came down in a wet suit and demanded her time on Landon's board and that woman knew what she was doing—she got way out on the bay and that sail was putty in her hands. She was whipping it all over the place, leaping out of the water a few times. As if watching a circus performance, the voices in the crowd rose in excitement.

One of the guys Charlie had seen around town, a guy named Al, was down there with a couple of his sons, grumbling that another new sport was going to cost him while the boys begged to try it. Pretty soon there were six paddleboards on the water, some of them sitting idle to watch the windsurfing, some pad-dling around the inner bay while the surfers were flying around the outer bay. The sheriff's deputy drove his cruiser out on the beach; there were a few folks there in all-terrain vehicles like Rhinos and RZRs.

The windsurfer boards changed passengers—everyone wanted a turn. Sarah Cooper turned from surfer into instructor along with Frank, and the girls finally got their turn. Then Troy and Spencer had a chance; Troy didn't embarrass himself too badly but Spencer was great entertainment. A group of cyclists rode onto the beach from the town and stood watching for a while. There were ten of them. They looked like serious cyclists, their gear expensive, their team patches flashy. They looked like such studs to Charlie—legs like tree trunks, leather gloves, fancy hel-mets and Ray-Bans. Those bikes—they were amazing, sleek, mega-expensive cycles. These were either long-distance riders or racers. He decided to read about it later.

The beach grew crowded, Cooper's was full, hours flew by.

Charlie wondered if half the town had shut their businesses down to see what was going on.

"Want to go out on the paddleboard?" Landon said to Charlie.

"Huh? Yeah, can we?"

"You a good swimmer?"

He didn't swim at all, as a matter of fact. "Not that good," he said, shaking his head.

"That's okay—we'll get a jacket. And we won't go out too far. Your mom say it was okay?"

"Sure," he lied.

"Lose the shoes and socks," Landon said. Then he jogged off to the beach level under the bar where they stored kayaks, boards and equipment. He jogged back with a jacket for Charlie, helped him suit up. "Sorry I don't have a wet suit that'll fit you. My advice? Don't fall in. And don't lose your glasses, okay?"

"Gotcha," he said.

Landon pushed out the board just a little bit, got Charlie kneeling in the right spot then got on his knees behind Charlie, then up to a standing position. "You good?" he asked.

"Good!" Charlie said.

It wasn't a wild ride by any means, but it was exhilarating. He watched the windsurfers—now it was Ashley and Frank, and Ashley was struggling to stay on the upside of the water. He saw the beach full of people as he glided by. Troy was talking with the cyclists, checking out their bikes. Eve, Landon's girlfriend, paddled out to glide alongside Landon and she had Austin, Spencer's boy, sitting on her board. Austin wore a life jacket, as well, and Charlie decided right then and there, he was somehow going to learn to swim. He wasn't sure how, but he was going to.

"Can I stand up?" he asked Landon.

"I don't know, can you?" Landon asked.

"I think I can. I'll be careful."

"Don't fall in. That water's cold."

"I'm not planning to," Charlie said. And he got to his feet awkwardly, standing against Landon for balance.

"Problem is, I can't paddle with you standing in front of me," Landon said.

"I could try."

"Okay, but just for a second. Okay?"

Charlie took the paddle and clumsily dipped it into the water on the right side, then the left, and after about four strokes his arms ached. And shook.

"Okay, that's all of that," Landon said. "You're not quite ready for that, but I'm sure you'll get there. Get back down so I can get us in."

"Not yet, okay?" Charlie begged.

Landon laughed. "Okay, champ, we'll take a couple more turns."

It was the best day of his life. Troy called him to go inside and wash up for dinner. He had to fetch his backpack and his clean shirt. His mother made that eggplant thing that people loved, but Charlie didn't love it. He ate a lot, however. He'd completely forgotten lunch and was starving. Everyone at the table seemed completely charmed by his appetite except his mother, who was a little put out.

So to make up for it, he helped with cleanup while his mom settled Winnie in her room for the night. He didn't mind. He and Troy talked about the day, about all the things that went on at the beach in the summer when the weather was good. And in the fall during football season when most of the teenagers gathered on the beach for their parties and bonfires.

Then he had to struggle to stay awake, waiting in the great room for his mom. Finally at about eight, she was finished. Troy and Grace were out on the deck so Lin Su said goodbye to them, then locked the front door behind them when they went to the car.

They had driven a little while when she said, "You had a very big day. I'm not sure you were careful of your health."

"I was totally careful," Charlie said. Then he yawned. "You ever think about moving here? To Thunder Point?"

She laughed softly. "We can't afford to live in Thunder Point."

"Well, we can be poor anywhere. And you said Mrs. Banks is doing good."

"Well," she corrected. "She's doing well."

"We should think about it. Troy said it's a good high school." He yawned. Then moments later his mother woke him to go inside to bed. He'd slept the whole way home.

CHAPTER FIFTEEN

Ginger blossomed with the flush of true love. She had Matt on the weekends and because of that fact Grace was more than willing to work by herself on Saturdays. But with the onset of August the days of summer were fast coming to a close for farmers. She cherished every second she could lie in his arms because she knew that soon his time would be at a premium.

"I have an important question," he said to her.

It was Saturday morning and there was no reason to get up early, except to eat. Soon they might starve, she thought. "You have me in a very vulnerable position. I'll probably say yes to anything now."

"It's a serious question," he said.

"Sounds grim."

"Will you stick with me through the harvest?" he asked.

How she loved looking into those black eyes when he was serious. "It sounds like I'm not going to see very much of you. We'll manage somehow. I'll come to Portland and if you can't get away I might come to Portland a lot."

"You understand we work seven days a week…"

"Do you work after dark?" she asked with a twinkle in her eye.

"We sleep the sleep of the dead after dark," he told her.

"I'll still feel your body close to mine." She ran her hand over his chest and down. Then she laughed and stopped her hand.

"Something's funny, miss?"

"Not so much funny as remarkable. If I keep touching you I'll never get breakfast! Yes, Matt, I'll still be your girl when all the pears are in."

"Weekend after next we go to Sal's vineyard. At least it's closer to you than the farm, but I won't have very much time. I'll try to spend a night or two with you."

"Do you need my help with the grapes?" she asked. "I'm sure I'd be good with them—I do specialize in flowers."

"I'd like to say yes but in fact it might be a distraction. Not because I'd keep touching you when we should be picking grapes but because these early grapes are fragile and only trained hands can deal with them. The later grapes, the ones that come after the pears, they're heartier."

"Grapes, pears, grapes again..." She kissed him. "A girl hardly stands a chance."

"Throw the potatoes in there, too. But we hire harvesters for those—they're not as tender. But then come the cold, silent days of winter. I'm really good in the sack in winter," he said.

"You're not that bad in summer..."

"Will you stick with me through the harvest? Even when I seem unavailable and distant and tired?"

"I don't know why you even have to ask. Of course I'm yours through the harvest. Through many harvests if you want it."

"That's exactly what I want, Ginger," he said, solemn. "I want to marry you."

She was a little surprised. "I didn't think you were quite ready to chance it again."

"It doesn't feel like I'd be taking a chance. How about you?"

She ran her hands through his hair, his glorious hair. She looked forward to being with him when the first strands of silver appeared. She smiled tenderly. "It doesn't seem a risk for me, either."

"One thing I think you'll like about the harvest. I never have time for a haircut."

"Yes," she said, laughing. "I think I'll like that part the most."

"Will you? Marry me? Be mine forever?"

"That means you'll have to be mine right back, you know. No kidding around."

"I've been yours since last April. The second you coldcocked me, I knew."

"I didn't do that, you know. I only shoved you. I didn't even shove hard."

"Let's say you decked me. A better story for our grandchildren."

She sobered a little, glancing down.

"Ginger, there will be grandchildren. Are you afraid? Too afraid?"

"Oh, the thought terrifies me. But I'm not going to let that keep me from trying. It's all I've ever wanted—a family."

"We'll be careful," he said. "Good medical support. The best pediatric support available. We have Peyton and Scott to help hook us up. There isn't any rush about it. We won't take any chances and we'll be sure you're ready. Emotionally ready. As ready as possible."

"Are you? Doesn't it make you a little nervous? Counting on grandchildren through me?"

He shook his head. "If it had been me, I'd probably feel just like you do. But things will be different, Ginger. This time you won't be alone. This time your man will be with you every step."

Such a good man, always looking for ways to reassure her.

"Are you going to say yes?" he asked. "I love you. I want to be with you forever."

"Yes, of course I'm going to say yes."

"Where do you want to live?"

"Do you think that house on the farm will have room for me?"

That made him smile. "You'd do that?"

She nodded. "This can't happen too fast, Matt. I'm not going to abandon Grace. Her mother is sick and she's pregnant. It's going to take planning."

"I want to sweep you away," he said.

"That would be fun but I won't run out on her. Until I'm sure she's taken care of we'll have to make do like this." She smiled. "The anticipation has been great. When you speed into town on the weekend… Tell me, Mr. Lacoumette, when I'm just a farm wife, will you speed home from the orchard to be with me?"

He laughed. "Have you seen my parents? Married almost forty years and still hot for each other. You and Grace have to talk about it, okay? Think about a plan. I need you. I love you."

"First we have to take care of something important. My family. If I understand you, we have one more weekend before the harvest is in full swing. I know you know some of my family through the business, but I want to bring you home. I'll see if I can gather the troops for next weekend. A barbecue or something with my brothers and their families, with my mom and dad. But if it's okay with you, I'll stay with you at night."

"They know about me, right?" he asked.

"I've talked to my mom the most but she's told the family I have a man in my life. And of course, they know your family."

"Paco will be pleased," he said, scratching his chest. "I'm marrying a trucking company."

"I don't know who to tell first. My mother? Ray Anne? Grace? Peyton?"

"Tell everyone. We need a ring, Ginger. A nice one."

"If I can get my family together for next weekend, will we stay in your apartment?"

"If I can't think of a good alternative. My mother was right, I only stayed there so I could have privacy. I can't wait to live on the farm. You'll help me build the house. It has to be your house."

"You're committing to an awful lot, Matt."

"I'd do anything for you. Don't you know that?"

Peyton was first, as it turned out. They walked down to her house and found the whole family home. Ginger thought she knew Matt very well yet she'd never seen him quite so puffed up and proud as he was when he said, "We're getting married, Peyton."

"Oh, my God! When?"

"We don't exactly know," Ginger said. "We have a couple of things to work out—first the harvest and then I want to make sure Grace is covered. I mean covered very well. Her life is complicated right now. And need I even say it? She's been so good to me. I think between Ray Anne, Grace and some of my new friends I have a whole new life." She grabbed Matt's hand. "And it led me to another new life."

Next they found Ray Anne at Al's house with Al's family of boys, where Ray Anne was helping Al construct a Sunday dinner for the whole crew. There was a loud celebration of congratulations with all the same questions so far impossible to answer.

"I don't know why anyone wants to get married," said thirteen-year-old Kevin.

"And that's how we like it—you not understanding that urge," Al said. "I have enough worry that Justin's starting to get it."

"What? Me?" he asked.

"We know there's a girl," Ray Anne said.

"Yeah, but that's all there is. A girl. Not marriage. How would I ever manage that?"

"Good. We're on the same page," Al said.

Then they walked down the beach. They had already decided

not to impose on Grace. It was good enough for Ginger to tell her on Monday when they worked together. But Troy was on the beach throwing a Frisbee with Charlie, the nurse's son, and Austin, the kid next door.

"You're not imposing," Troy said. "She's on the deck with her mother, I think. Everything okay at the shop?"

"As far as I know," Ginger said. "I'm planning to open to-morrow morning. I just wanted to talk to her for a minute."

"Go on up," he said.

"Knock, knock," Ginger said as they neared the top of the stairs.

"Come up!" Grace said. "Out for a little walk?"

"We have news," Ginger said. "We wanted to tell you to-gether. Now, don't worry about anything..."

"We're getting married," Matt said, pulling the trigger on it.

Grace flew to her feet and hugged Ginger in a ferocious, excited embrace, shrieking happily. It took a while for her to calm down. Troy, Charlie and Austin came flying up the stairs from the beach to see what was happening. Grace threw her-self at Matt, hugging him fiercely. And then, inevitably, there was crying.

"Oh, that makes me so happy!" Grace cried. "This is perfect! It couldn't be more perfect!"

Ginger was a little stunned. "We were going to be careful to reassure you—I won't leave you without making sure you have the help you need in the shop."

Grace burst into laughter. "You mean Matt's not giving up that huge farm to live off you and your florist's salary in Thun-der Point? I couldn't be any more thrilled about this. Ginger, all I want in this world is to see you happy!"

"But we do have to find someone to take my place," Gin-ger said. "Someone good. Someone you can trust. But don't worry—we're certainly not getting married while there's a har-vest going on."

"We'll get to work on help in the shop, but first let's enjoy the excitement of this. This is wonderful! I knew this would happen! I knew last April when you knocked him out!"

"See?" Matt said, his arm around Ginger's shoulders. "Good story."

It took a while for the excitement to die down among Grace, her family and her friends. There was so much hugging and well-wishing it almost wore Grace out. But finally Troy and his playmates went back to the beach with their Frisbee, and Ginger and Matt walked back to town where they would have a couple of hours together before he had to head back to his farm in the north.

That left Winnie, Grace and Lin Su on the warm deck. Lin Su asked Winnie if she'd like a manicure. Winnie loved manicures and pedicures and Lin Su was more than happy to oblige. Lin Su knew that even if Winnie's hands didn't work as well as they once had, she wanted them to look good. "You should get a raise," Winnie said.

"You should," Grace agreed.

Lin Su laughed. "If you're comfortable, I'm happy." She brought a tray to the deck. Placing it between herself and Winnie, she began working on her nails.

"You're worth a king's ransom," Winnie said. "I'd never have requested a nurse who could double as a manicurist. I don't suppose you do hair and facials?"

"I'm afraid not," she said. "I learned to do nails before I attended nursing college. I thought I'd be a beautician one day but then Charlie came along and I needed a more dependable income. Doing nails has come in really handy during those tough times when nursing jobs aren't in good supply."

"It can't be easy," Grace said. "Being a single mother with a demanding nursing career. And I know nursing is a good field, but it's expensive raising a child."

"There have been challenging times, but this particular job, bringing Charlie along to be entertained by all the people around here, this is like a paid vacation." She massaged Winnie's hands. "It's true, there isn't a lot left over at the end of the month but we do fine."

"Do forgive the intrusion, but do you have a man in your life?" Winnie asked.

"Yes, ma'am. Mr. Charlie Simmons. All the man I can handle," she added.

"May I ask…?"

"You may ask me anything at all, Winnie. I'm in your employ and I want you to be comfortable that I'm completely honest with you."

"Charlie's father?" she asked.

"Unfortunately, he was killed in an accident before Charlie was born. We hadn't yet married. Charlie carries my name for that reason. I try not to make too much an issue of the fact that I hadn't been married to his father…but of course, he knows."

"And your family?"

"Well…" She stopped massaging for a moment. "We're estranged. They didn't approve of Charlie's father. And they didn't exactly approve of my decision to have and raise my son."

"Damn fools," Winnie said.

"Mama, don't pass judgment," Grace said. "We've had our issues, you can't deny that."

"I can't deny it but I sure as hell lived to regret it!"

Grace grabbed her heart. "Holy shit, get the Bible. It's got to be the end of the world!"

"Serpent's tooth," Winnie muttered.

Lin Su laughed at them. "Now, ladies," she admonished, "no need to feel sorry for us, really. We're a very good team. I've been so lucky—everywhere I go with Charlie people like him. Admire him. He had a lot of illnesses and look at him—smart as a whip, polite, handsome."

"You said that a couple of times," Grace said. "What kind of illnesses?"

"Luckily nothing we couldn't survive. But it was terrifying at the time. Asthma, a lot of allergies, a weak immune system, winter colds that turned into bronchitis and pneumonia. When he was three he spent two weeks in the hospital, most of that on oxygen. I don't think a camel could carry the weight of antibiotics he's had in his lifetime. And that's its own worry—too many antibiotics."

Grace glanced at the boy running along the beach below the deck. "He seems awfully healthy now."

"He's much better, but he has to carry an inhaler and an EpiPen. He's a little undersize—I know that frustrates him. He hates his glasses but he's nearly blind without them. When he's older, when contacts work or maybe even surgery... Well, I'm a nurse. I've seen young parents through far worse situations—cerebral palsy, muscular dystrophy, cancer..."

"How is the asthma?" Winnie asked.

"Well, it depends who you ask. If you ask Charlie it's much better and he hardly ever uses his inhaler, but he still takes daily medication for it. Charlie is determined it's going to go away and I'm determined he learns to manage it without telling himself fairy stories that it will disappear. If he eats peanuts or shrimp or gets stung by a bee—we could be rushing to the emergency room. That's why he carries an EpiPen and so do I."

"You're a superwoman," Grace said after a moment of silence. "I can't imagine the stress of that."

"You're having a baby," Lin Su said. "You'll soon realize you have many difficult and stressful moments to deal with and deal with them you will. If there's anything that can make a woman strong, it's taking care of her child."

"Amen," Winnie said.

"Are you getting by all right now?" she asked Lin Su.

"We don't have a surplus but where is the shame in that? We

do fine. Better than ever since we've been taking so many meals with you!" She laughed a little, then grew more serious. "We're doing very well, thank you for asking," she said.

Ginger felt there was an almost magical quality to her life. She put Matt in his truck and sent him on his way home before calling her mother. Sue Dysart cried, she was that happy at the news. Or maybe she was relieved that her only daughter wasn't going to rot on the vine, after all. Or choose another deadbeat like Mick.

It was true, Ginger had a new hope—a second chance. "I hope you never know the agony of watching your daughter suffer through such terrible heartache," Sue said. "I don't think there's any pain worse than the pain of watching your own flesh and blood struggle. I was so afraid you'd be alone forever. Not because you'd never find the right man to build a life with but because you wouldn't let yourself find him."

"You're going to love Matt," Ginger said. "He's the sweetest, most loving man I've ever known and he's so unselfish. I honestly don't know how I found him."

"Tell me every detail," Sue begged.

"I can only tell you the details of our courtship, which has been so romantic even if it hasn't been very long—just three months. But three of the most lovely months I've ever had. From the time the lambs were born and the sheep sheared until now, the onset of the harvest, we've had almost every weekend together. Long weekends. And soon the chaos of the harvest begins with the gathering of extended families every moment they have to spare, helping each other bring in the crops."

"My goodness, you sound like a farm wife already!" Sue laughed.

"I'm already starting to feel like one."

She gave her mother all the details she knew of a big farming empire. It would be such a busy few weeks she and Matt weren't sure there would be enough time to shop for and buy a proper ring, but he promised her she would have a beautiful one before they were wed.

Sue wanted to know what kind of wedding Ginger hoped for.

"Are you a little afraid I'm going to ask you to get me married a half dozen times?" Ginger asked.

"I expect you're looking for entirely different things in a man this time around," Sue said.

"I know I already apologized to you and Dad for the debacle of Mick," she said. "I don't know what to blame that failure of good sense on. I was young, but not that young. Not young enough to be that blind and foolish."

"I guess love isn't always brilliant even though it seems so at the time."

"You have no idea how I wish I'd been smarter," Ginger said. "I guess once you cast your lot with a partner you hang in there until it's entirely hopeless." And as she said that she couldn't help but think about Matt and his brief marriage. It wasn't dissimilar, only shorter. "Since we've both been married and divorced, we don't really feel like a huge celebration. Just something meaningful and modest, something to match how we feel about moving forward, that's all. It feels very safe and solid."

"Just safe?" her mother asked.

"Oh, Mom, I'm not settling for Matt, please never think that. Matt is like a dream come true, a man and husband I was never wise enough to long for."

"Just tell me you're completely over Mick," Sue begged in a tense whisper.

Poor Mom, Ginger thought. The whole family thought she'd lost her mind when she brought home this musician, this wannabe star. "I don't blame you for having doubts about my ability to make a sane decision after what I put all of you through. I'd love to explain it—it was all the glitter that he promised me day after bloody day. The irony is—I don't even like a lot of glitter!

I wanted it for him. If he fulfilled all those dreams, it would mean I'd been right to believe in him. But I wasn't," she said. "He lived in such a crazy dream world. It took me too long to realize it was nothing but pipe dreams, nothing but smoke and mirrors. Am I over him? Mom, the shock of reality is not only permanent, it's a little hard to live with. I wish I'd been wide-awake much sooner."

She was not only over Mick, she was certain he was completely over her. By now he had certainly found someone to share his fantasies. "You'll see, Matt is nothing like that. He comes from a large, hardworking family that values commitment and loyalty, fidelity and sound judgment. They're steadfast. Genuine and completely sincere." She laughed. "Also loud, a little crazy and noble."

Ginger went down the list of Matt's siblings, each one she had met and those she only knew about, all so different, from medical practitioner to public relations specialist to vintner to PhD candidate. "I think only his youngest sister married in the culture. Her husband is a Basque chef in San Francisco."

"They're not the easiest people to negotiate with," Sue said. "But they're good to their word. Maybe you'll end up with some good Basque recipes."

"Maybe so. But I bet not a day before we're married," Ginger said.

Her brother Richard had the largest home in the family and wanted to host the barbecue to officially introduce Matt to everyone. It almost rivaled a Lacoumette family gathering, it was that busy and loud. Ginger's sisters-in-law, Beth and Melissa, provided almost all the food with Dick buying excellent meat for the grill and Sue providing dessert that she bought because she was not into cooking or baking at all. The men all knew Matt and had dealt with Matt, George and Paco when negotiating trucking contracts for their crops but they were meeting a social Lacoumette this time, not a shrewd businessman.

The conversation was reduced to jests about business associates socializing together as in-laws.

"I suppose the elder Lacoumette will begin to take into consideration that we're now family when we write our next contract," Dick Dysart said. "Or maybe he'll hire an agent to do his negotiating."

"I think you'll be lucky if Paco doesn't insist on driving the trucks," Matt said. "He's a very hands-on businessman. My advice? Look at his own truck before you even consider the idea. It's a hundred years old."

"We know he has plenty of money, Matt," Richard said. "He's getting it from us and our low prices!"

"Is that a fact? Paco said you robbed him blind!"

Ginger, who had never been a part of the trucking business, learned something. These men were happy to have come to terms that satisfied them and allowed them to call each other thieves. It was an old and time-honored system.

There were four kids, still enjoying the backyard pool, ranging in age from five to twelve. Her brothers each had a boy and a girl. The food was wonderful, the day passed with everyone in great spirits and the proposed union of Dysart and Lacoumette was heartily and genuinely approved.

It was late in the day when everyone was cleaning up and packing up to say their goodbyes that Sue took Ginger aside. She pulled her around the corner of the family room of Richard's large house. They stood in a dimly lit hallway and Sue said, "I don't want to do this but I won't keep secrets from you. Mick got in touch with me. He doesn't know where you are, which I believe is what you want. He says he's in a crisis and needs to talk to you. It's urgent, he says, and you're the only person who will understand, who can help him, and he asked me to have you call him."

"What kind of crisis?" she asked.

Sue shook her head. "I don't know, he wouldn't tell me another thing."

"Is he sick?"

"He wouldn't say. Your father is angry—he told me not to tell you anything about it. But I won't lie. What if he just wants money?"

"Mom, I'm not going to give Mick money. I'm a slow learner but I'm not that slow."

"Thank God," Sue said. "Then you won't call him?"

"Of course I'll call him. Nothing is ever urgent with him—unless he wants to tell someone that he just got a personal call from Bruce Springsteen. But you know Mick would've told you that. I'll find out what he wants. I'm sure it'll be a simple matter to tell him to go away, that I don't care about his plans or his concerts, that I'm not giving him anything, that I'm no longer in any way attached to him."

"Don't call him, Ginger!" Sue said. "Don't even tempt fate."

"Mom, I'm not the simple idiot I was when I was with Mick. He can't threaten me or manipulate me anymore. Maybe he wants to make amends. That would be positive. Closure would be good. But I'll make sure he's not dying."

"What if he is dying?" Sue asked.

"Still," Ginger said. "I would be sorry to hear that but we're not together and we haven't been for a long time."

"Don't, Ginger. Don't talk to him."

"I'm not afraid of him, Mom. I'll call him. I'll give him as much as ten minutes."

Suddenly there was Matt, standing in the hallway. Looming in the hallway, bigger somehow. Broader. His face scowling. It was Mad Matt.

"No," he said. "No."

CHAPTER SIXTEEN

Ginger wouldn't let Matt say any more while in her brother's house. Once they were in his truck she turned in her seat to stare at him. He was still frowning.

"What was *that* about?" she asked.

"What?" he asked, but his expression was angry. He knew. Damn it, he knew!

"You tell me no? No, I can't return a call if I choose to? Seriously?"

"To your ex-husband? The man who ripped your heart out without a second thought?" he asked. "Yes, I'm serious!"

She thought maybe he was driving a little faster, his hands gripping the wheel. "We'll talk about this when we get back to your apartment," she said.

It was a quick trip back to Matt's home. It was a perfectly adequate one-bedroom apartment but there were obvious reasons why he wasn't comfortable there. For one thing, once his wife had taken what she wanted, he hadn't bothered to replace much. The bedroom set, a very masculine and heavy bed and dressers, he had purchased for himself after the apartment was nearly emptied of furniture. He had a TV and sectional but all the things that made a house a home were missing. There was one picture on one wall, the other walls blank but sporting the nails pictures had hung on. There was one bedroom lamp, one living room lamp, there were no accents or throws or plants or baskets of papers or magazines. There was a bookshelf filled with only the books he might care about—agriculture and science-related textbooks. They hadn't spent much time there, hadn't prepared any real meals there, but she'd been there long enough to notice dishes and glassware were not in great supply.

It was a home that had been abandoned and he had done nothing to make it his. He hadn't really tried to wipe out the past and start from scratch.

She tossed her purse on the sofa and sat down. "Tell me why you're so angry," she said.

"Do you really have to ask me?" he said. "You're going to get in touch with the slimeball who put you through so much!"

"You're pacing," she said. "Please stop. Please sit down and talk to me."

He sat, but he wasn't happy about it. "Ginger, he's not worth your time."

"I completely agree," she said. "There's absolutely no threat in asking him what's so urgent. I don't love him, Matt. I don't even like him very much anymore. Do you trust me? Do you believe I won't lie to you? Because I won't lie to you. I love you."

He reached for her hand. "I want you to hate him," he said. Simple and straightforward.

"There's a part of me that does hate him. At least I resent what he did."

"He used you!"

"I think you're right. And I let him. In fact, I nearly invited him to use me. I'm never going to let that happen to me again. What are you afraid of? That I'll give him a kidney?"

"I wouldn't be surprised…"

"Oh, Matt," she said, a slight chuckle coming out of her in

spite of it all. "If you like, I'd be happy for you to listen to the conversation. I'll call him from your phone and you can listen in."

"Why? Just tell me why? You don't owe him anything!"

"Not for him," she said. "For me! Matt, I want to be finished with Mick but not bitter. We were wrong for each other and that might've been more my fault than his."

"You excuse him! Over and over!"

"No!" she said. "No, I don't excuse his behavior! I don't know how he lives with himself. But I'm not going to carry hate into our future. I made quite a few misjudgments with Mick. I shouldn't have married him in the first place and I never should have tricked myself into thinking an innocent baby would change our relationship."

"How do you accept all that so calmly?" he nearly raged. "Oh, I made a little mistake, let's all just let it go and forget about it!"

"Matt, stop that. I don't know who you're really angry with. Is it your ex-wife that makes you so furious? Is it me? Is it Mick, who you've never met?"

"I hate my ex-wife," he said, looking away.

"I can't help you with that," she said. "But I can tell you it won't help anything. And it probably won't be good for us."

"Why?" he said. "They're not going to be a part of *us*!"

"You're turning that anger on me," she said. "You're having trouble trusting me because you couldn't trust Natalie. I'm not talking about a little anger that burns out quickly. It's like a cancer, eating away at you. It's not good."

"How would you feel if I wanted to get together with Natalie?" he shouted.

"Maybe you should because you're not at peace with your decision to get a divorce. Are you going to build your life around hating her? And being bitter about her?" She could see this was going nowhere. Matt didn't realize most of his anger was with himself. He, like Ginger, was starting to realize he was a participant in whatever had gone wrong. He wasn't at fault, but he was a part of it even if the only thing he was guilty of was marrying her in the first place.

"Before we can make a new start you have to come to terms with your divorce. You did the right thing—it wasn't going to work. You don't have to see her if you don't want to. You don't have to be mad at her anymore—it's over. And you don't have to distrust me.

"If you don't want me to talk to Mick, I won't," she said quietly. "But it won't be about me talking to Mick. It'll be about you. You and your pain and anger."

"Do whatever you want," he said. "I'm going to bed."

Ginger stayed on the couch. She looked at his sparsely furnished apartment with the naked walls. This wasn't just because he was a guy and couldn't be bothered. He'd been talking about the house he wanted to build in great detail and he wanted it to be beautiful and welcoming. He described a nurturing place, a family place filled with love and comfort. This apartment was to Matt what a tombstone was to a cemetery.

She tried to imagine him bringing women here. It didn't seem particularly satisfying. He must have felt he was trying to fill an empty spot.

She gave him plenty of time before she went to the bedroom. She slipped off her summer dress, brushed her teeth and slid in beside him. He took her instantly into his big, strong arms.

"I'm sorry, sweetheart. I was angry. I hate that bastard."

"I know. And not just a little angry."

"I don't like it. I won't talk to you that way again."

She snuggled closer. "I hope not, Matt. It hurts. I haven't done anything to warrant that kind of anger. But maybe I will someday. Then what?"

"You won't," he said. "I know you won't. We love each other."

"Oh, I won't do what Natalie did," she said. "I won't do what

Mick did. But I might defy you in some way and you'll turn into Mad Matt. I don't want to be with Mad Matt."

"Never again, I promise."

She turned in his arms, kissed his bristly chin and said, "Can you listen to me without getting angry? Because there's something I want to say to you. And I don't want to ever be afraid you're going to flip out."

"Say it. You can say anything."

"I'm glad we have the harvest, my love," she said. "We need the time, you and I. I'll do anything I can to help but I think it's important to get beyond these people from our pasts that hurt us."

"I am beyond it," he said. "I haven't said I want to see Natalie."

"I want you to see her," she said.

He actually jumped a little in surprise. "You can't want that!"

"I do. I think it would be good if you talked with her for a while. See if you can understand rather than blame her."

"But Ginger, it's her fault!" he said. "I was good to her. I tried, for God's sake."

"And now you have to try to forgive her," she said. "I don't want to bring that hate and anger into our future."

"I promise I won't let that happen to us," he said.

"It'll happen. I'm not going to be a perfect wife, sweetheart. I'm already failing you as a fiancée—just the threat of talking to Mick made you wild with anger. I'm sure there will be things I do or say that you hate, that make you so angry."

"Everyone gets a little pissed sometimes…"

She shook her head. "I'm not talking about a little grumpy or upset. I know what it is to be mad—I hung up on Mick the last time I talked to him. I'm talking about that rage you feel when you think you're not in control anymore. I don't want to take that forward. I want to go forward with joy. I want the past to be really in the past. I can't tell you how to feel but I think the person you really need to forgive is yourself. We're not perfect human beings. We all make terrible mistakes. Forgive her, Matt. If you ever figure out your part in it, forgive yourself. Then we can move on."

He was silent for a moment. Then he growled and turned away from her.

She stroked his back. "I don't want you to hurt over it anymore, that's all." *Because*, she thought, *we can't make a good marriage on the foundation of all that rage and pain.* "Maybe I don't know anything, but it seems if you were over it then being with me now would bring you more contentment. Peace of mind. And this doesn't feel like contentment and peace of mind."

Even though he had presented his back to her, she curled up to him and eventually went to sleep. Deep in the night she felt his hands on her, his lips on her neck and breast. His touch was so precious to her; she responded to him so naturally. She opened up to him immediately, returned his kisses, held him close, moved with him, took him into her and experienced all the rapture their intimacy always provided. He was slow and gentle until she encouraged him to be a little more urgent and he did what he did best, brought her the ultimate pleasure.

Then he held her close and gently stroked her naked body.

She was almost back to sleep when his gravelly voice came in the night. "I think you have to stop reading psychology or self-help books. We're fine."

In the morning Ginger was getting ready to leave while Matt scrambled them some eggs. They sat side by side on the sofa, holding their breakfast on trays on their knees. There was tension most obvious by their pleasantness to each other. After helping to wash up the dishes she said, "I know you're itching to get out to the farm and I have a long drive."

He nodded and pulled her close. "Let's not fight," he whispered into her hair. "Please."

"Let's not," she said. "Matt, think about getting out of here. This apartment. You hate it and it's not a home to you. It's a couple of rooms. And it eats at you."

"Where do you suggest I go?" he said, and she could see that dark look coming into his eyes again.

"I don't know. Go home. I think you stay there half the time anyway."

"Where will we go when you come to the farm?" he asked. "You know for the next several weeks I can't get to Thunder Point. You said you'd come up here. I need you beside me."

"It doesn't matter about me," she said. "We could get a room somewhere. We could camp in the hayloft or even stay with my parents. It's just that… Listen, you eat at your mother's table because there's comfort there. You stay at the farm because it's warm with allies, with family. This apartment is functional but I think it's like nettles in your underwear. Could be time for a fresh start."

"I'll have a fresh start when my house is ready."

"That's a long time for you to be itchy and cranky."

"If we don't talk about all the difficult stuff, starting with our exes…"

"It wouldn't have worked for me," she said, shaking her head. "I couldn't have stayed in my little rented house and just kicked Mick out. I had my marriage in that house and even though I wanted to end it and ending it was the right thing to do, if I'd stayed there I think it would've been harder for me to move on. You're not happy here. This isn't your home anymore. And I'm not ever going to live here with you. There's a barrier."

He glanced away from her. She could see his jaw tense.

"Just think about it, Matt," she said. "I'll still come to the farm to help during the harvest. I'm excited about it. You have family sleeping in every nook when they come to help—I can, too. I'll bed down with you in the back of your truck! We'll find a way to be together."

"Then we'll get married," he said.

"You won't have time to think about anything but grapes and pears and potatoes for a while. Let's resolve a few things after the harvest. I love you very much."

When Ginger was back in Thunder Point people were very anxious to know how her weekend with Matt and the family went. She put on a smiling face and said it was great. But then she looked for a time Peyton might be able to sneak away for a talk. "How about an ice cream sundae at the diner?" she asked.

"Sure. Things are quiet at about two and Scott's in the clinic. Want to meet then?"

Once they had a booth and their sundaes in front of them, they could talk. "So, did Matt win the Dysart seal of approval?"

"Oh, absolutely. But remember, he knew my dad and at least one of my brothers. Apparently they've done business together over the years. We had a nice time."

Peyton tilted her head and peered at Ginger. "Why do I sense something's wrong?"

"Well, something might be wrong. Maybe we'll just get beyond it easily. Matt lost his temper while we were there. Over something stupid."

"Uh-oh. Mad Matt?"

"One and the same," Ginger said.

"Mind if I ask what stupid thing?"

"My mother passed on a message that my ex-husband, who doesn't have my number anymore, wanted to talk to me. He said it was urgent and I said I'd give him a call. Matt went ballistic."

Peyton shook her head sympathetically. "Would you believe I've been there?"

"Really? But you and Scott have been together forever!" Ginger said.

"Not exactly," Peyton said. "I had just broken up with someone when I took the job in his clinic. I fell for Scott pretty quick.

But then the ex called to say he needed my help and sweet, gentle Scott threw a hissy." She whistled. "It was impressive."

"Hard to imagine Scott in a temper..."

"I know. But trust me—he went over the top."

"And what did you do?"

"Well, as it turned out, it wasn't my ex but his daughter who needed help. Scott was in no frame of mind to listen or understand so I cut him out of the loop."

Ginger shook her head. "I don't understand."

"Oh, Scott was throwing around ultimatums and acting like an ass so I just did what I had to do. I did try to patiently explain to Scott that he was going to feel like an ass when he finally understood my situation. I drove to Portland, helped the girl the best I could, told the ex to get his shit together before he lost his whole family, came back to Thunder Point and duked it out with Scott. And I was right—he felt like a fool. He hasn't acted like that big an idiot since."

"Let me ask you something," Ginger said. "Is Matt known for that? A temper?"

Peyton shook her head. "He's always been the sweetest-natured guy in the family. George is very silent and steady. Sal is a little like Paco—melodramatic and interfering. I'm like Mama—serious and sometimes quietly controlling, Mikie is a comedian who seems like he doesn't take anything seriously and yet he's close to a PhD in biochem, but Matt has always been a happy guy. Pretty laid-back and easygoing. Until his divorce. That seemed to take a lot out of him."

"He's not real happy right now. And he's going to be less happy. He basically told me to get over it but he's in for a surprise. I'm not going to set a date until we're beyond the harvest and I can see whether he's going to be sweet Matt or Mad Matt. I'm sure it's still about his divorce. I understand, I really do. And I'm sympathetic—I have some of that baggage myself. I was married to an idiot myself and it's not easy letting go of it. But he has to deal with his ex, bring it to a close. I refuse to bring her into our relationship, even if it's just in the form of Matt's emotional baggage."

"I thought he was past that!"

"You did? Weren't you at your own wedding when Matt was drunk as a skunk? When I shoved him and nearly knocked him out?" Ginger asked with a lift of one brow.

"So," Peyton said, dipping her spoon into her sundae. "What's wrong with him now?"

"I suspect a long list, all having to do with our ex-spouses. He blew a gasket when I suggested he talk to Natalie and see if he can lay some ghosts to rest before we try to start a new life together."

"You suggested that?" Peyton asked.

She nodded. "I understand being crazy mad at your ex," Ginger said. "Mick has the ability to make me want to choke him! I called him an asshole and hung up on him the last time we talked, and that wasn't very long ago! I can't recall that anger lasting and I never turned it on Matt. I think he has stuff to deal with. I wish he'd do so." She sighed and said, "Instead, he told me to stop reading self-help books because we're fine. Peyton, I love him very much, but we're not fine. I'm not going to marry a man who lays down laws for me. Whereas my ex didn't care what I did as long as he had no responsibility, Matt has decided what I can and can't do. That's not going to work. He has to make peace with that failed marriage before he has another one."

"This could be a challenge," Peyton said. She took another spoonful of ice cream. "He is a man. Not exactly the best at introspection, men."

"Peyton, I know you and Matt have a very loyal and loving relationship, but please let me deal with this without confronting him," Ginger said. "Yet, I have to ask, if you have any advice for me based on the fact that you know him better than almost anyone, I'll take it. Happily. I want it to work. But I'm not going to make another mistake by refusing to see the real man."

"I have some advice," she said immediately. "Stand your ground." She took another spoonful of ice cream. "Don't let him bully you. Don't take any shit."

"I won't."

"What are you going to do about your ex?" Peyton asked.

"Oh, I'm going to call him. I'm going to find out what he wants. I might hang up on him again. I might even call him a very bad name first. But the best way for me to be free of him, of the mistakes we made, is to be honest with him and with myself. If he doesn't hear me, not my problem."

"How long are you going to let this go on?" Peyton asked. "Because I let my ex suck me back in over and over. The new guy didn't stand a chance because I was still trying to figure out how to make an old relationship right."

"Nah," Ginger said. "When I call him it will only be the second time we've talked since the divorce almost two years ago. It'll probably be the last—I don't expect Mick to have changed in any way."

"How'd you let go so easily?" Peyton asked.

"Easily?" Ginger repeated. "Peyton, I stayed with a man who completely neglected me for three years longer than I should have. I left pregnant and alone, dependent on my parents at the age of twenty-eight. My baby died and had no father to grieve for him. There was hardly one more thing life could throw at me to convince me. It definitely wasn't quick."

"It wasn't for me, either," Peyton said.

"I had to acknowledge that I let Mick take advantage of me. That might've been the hardest part."

"Again, me, too," Peyton said.

"I'm not doing that again," she said. "I'll wait for Matt because I do love him. I don't love some ridiculous fantasy man like Mick. I love Matt, the real man. But I'm not going to always play by his rules. If he wants a new life with a new wife, he's going to have to assure me he's completely done with the old one."

Peyton took a last spoonful of her ice cream. "Have I mentioned Matt is incredibly stubborn?"

"And have I mentioned, so am I?"

Lin Su served lunch on the deck to Winnie and Charlie. Winnie had some small, bite-size sandwiches—easy for her to manage if she had coordination or trembling issues. For Charlie, a nice big one with chips. For both of them—fruit. On cool days Winnie liked soup, but that could be chaotic and if she spilled, it turned her mood foul. Of course she'd have no part of a bib or even a linen napkin tucked into her collar.

One of the most interesting developments was Winnie's fascination with Charlie. They had formed an unusual friendship. They had lunch together almost every day and sometimes Charlie showed her TED Talks on his laptop, after which they would have a discussion. Not surprisingly, Winnie had become interested in some of the more spiritual and inspirational videos. She had watched the video of Jimmy Valvano's last speech at the ESPY Awards several times until Charlie said, "You might have to start watching this in private from now on. It's too sad."

"You seem to be doing fine," she said. "It's inspiring."

"Maybe if you're dying."

"Charlie!" Lin Su admonished.

"What?" Winnie said. "He's right. It's more meaningful to me for obvious reasons." She looked at Charlie. "I haven't noticed you crying or anything..."

"Of course I'm not crying," he said. "It makes my throat hurt though. How about this TED Talk on the power of vulnerability? Sounds like the kind of thing you'd like."

"But what would you like?"

"There's one on the most important key to success—grit. And

there's one I like about a woman who survived a brain hemor-rhage and had to rebuild her life, learning to talk and walk all over again."

"When did you get so smart?" she asked him.

"When I couldn't go outside. Or to school."

"And when was that?"

"Before allergy shots, mostly. I was allergic to everything—grass, pollen, dust, animals, everything. Someone gave me a little computer and showed me how to look things up."

"No Facebook," Lin Su said. "The computer is for reading, learning, exploring, not for making jokes or picking on people."

"I don't think making jokes should be excluded," Winnie said. "I don't know this Facebook thing everyone talks about."

"You might be too old," Charlie said.

"Charlie!" his mother scolded. She shook her head. "I'm not going to be able to let you two hang out together if you're just going to make trouble for me!"

"A computer was a good idea," Winnie said.

Charlie was looking down the beach. A cyclist was riding down the beach road. He was bent low over his handlebars and was moving fast. He was sleek and muscular. "I'd rather have a bike," he said, watching the rider.

The rider stopped right in front of the house next door, the house that was only recently finished except for the interior. He balanced on the bike without putting a foot down; he looked up.

Cooper appeared on the deck next door and waved at the cyclist.

The man dismounted, picked up his bike and jogged up two flights to the deck.

"What the hell?" Winnie said.

"Why didn't he just lock it to the stair rail or something?" Lin Su said.

"Mom, I think he's a pro. He's wearing logos and Nike stuff. That bike probably cost a lot. Bet he sleeps with it."

"He ran with it," Winnie said.

"He's an athlete," Charlie said.

"And a show-off," Lin Su said.

The man did leave the bike on the deck, however. He shook hands with Cooper, then they talked. Cooper was pointing, gesturing with his hand, explaining things. Then they went inside together.

"Hmm, interesting," Winnie said. "New neighbor maybe?"

"That would be cool," Charlie said. "Let's look up that bike. I bet it's worth a billion dollars."

CHAPTER SEVENTEEN

Ginger talked to Matt at least once every day, despite the tension they'd had while she was in Portland. He was with his father and a couple of brothers and as many cousins as could be rounded up at Sal's vineyard to deal with harvesting early grapes. He could have ridden with Paco and George but he drove himself so he could spend one night with her before going home. He was so tired, she could hear it in his voice. This was the hardest yet most fulfilling time of year.

She tried to imagine being his wife through weeks like this. Not surprisingly, she could, and she saw it as a very satisfying job. What a monumental achievement it must be to bring in a year's worth of healthy crops, do it with your own hands, with your family's support. She not only envied him, she longed to be a part of it. Every night after talking to him she prayed he would resolve his issues soon so they could work together, so they could be together.

And then there was Mick. She called him from Grace's cell phone—a blocked number. "My mother delivered a message that you need to speak to me."

"Ginger. I do. Where are you?"

"I'm not in Portland, Mick, and we're divorced so there's no need for you to have a phone number or an address. What's the emergency?"

His voice was kind of weak. It even cracked. "I really have to talk to you face-to-face. I'll go wherever you are."

"Mick, just tell me what you need. I probably can't help you anyway…"

"Ginger, I had the worst news I've ever had and you're the only person who could ever make sense of things for me."

That certainly wasn't part of her memory. "Are you sick?"

"Oh, I'm worse than that, I'm not kidding. I'll fly to Houston if you'll just talk to me for—"

That's right, she thought. She'd told him she was in Houston. It had been sarcasm, but of course he wouldn't have realized that. "Listen, Mick, I can't be helping my ex-husband. I have someone in my life now, someone I love."

"Yeah, no surprise. It's not about romance, Ginger. It's bigger and more important than that."

"And you can't tell me on the phone?" she pushed.

"No. No, I can't. One time, that's all. I need your advice. It's life-or-death."

She sighed heavily. "How much time is this going to take?"

"I don't know. An hour or two, give or take," he said. "I'll come to you, it's that important."

"It must be," she said. He was coming to her for advice. She suspected a brain tumor or something equally terrifying. Perhaps he wanted her advice about treatment options. "There's a casino in North Bend. They have a coffee shop inside. I'll meet you there at three tomorrow afternoon and you can have a half an hour."

"Jesus, Ginger, what's happened to you?"

She nearly laughed but stopped herself…in case it *was* a brain tumor. "You have to ask?" she said. "Three o'clock. That's the best I can do. I have a job, I have an important man in my life. Take it or leave it."

She talked it over with Grace and while Grace couldn't even begin to understand why Ginger would accommodate him at all, she agreed to cover for her.

Mick was already in the coffee shop, staring into a cup of coffee when she arrived. When she got to his table, he stood. He was peaked, his features drawn, and he appeared thinner. She thought, *Oh, God, it is cancer! I have to make my peace with him so I'll have no regrets when he dies!*

"Ginger," he said, reaching toward her.

She withdrew slightly. "Come on, Mick. This isn't a happy reunion. Just tell me what's wrong."

"Let's get you some coffee. Okay?"

"Sure," she said, sitting down. "Is it your health? What's this about? If you don't mind me saying so, you don't look so good."

He lifted a hand to the waitress and when she came, he ordered another coffee. "I don't feel so good, either. My life is falling apart. I'm at the bottom. This is the end. I'm forty-two. I'm bottomed out."

"Explain," she said. Her coffee arrived immediately.

"Remember Buster Kleinman?" he asked.

She frowned. "Why does the name sound familiar?"

"Why? I talked about him all the time! He's one of the biggest agent/managers in the music business. He's tight with every recording studio in the country. He's represented some of the biggest names in the industry."

"So?" she said. "You already have an agent."

"Not a big agent. I need some power behind me. Mort's small-time. But I got an in to see Buster, to take a meeting and play for him. I sent him CDs all the time but finally Rory Denison, six Grammys, number one on the charts, he forwarded one of my CDs to Buster and I got an appointment. We really hit it off, me and Buster. We had some drinks, some dinner, talked for hours and the next day I went to his private studio and played for him."

No, she thought. *This is why I drove to North Bend?* She told herself not to throw hot coffee on him. It would be poor form, especially after her stand-off with Matt about anger. "Congratulations," she said. "And this concerns me how?"

"You know me better than anyone, Ginger. We were together for years. You know as much about my music as I do. We talked about my playlist after every performance. You told me which songs were my best. You listened to my backup musicians and singers. Your ear is almost as good as mine."

"This is about your music?" she asked, astonished.

"He said I just wouldn't work for him, that I have a good voice but no magic. He said I don't have what he's looking for, that he needs to see more passion, more emotional instinct. I lack passion? Have you ever known anyone in the business with more passion? Do you know anyone who wants it more, anyone who would do more to get to the top? He said my desire isn't translating, isn't tracking. He said I was a perfectly good entertainer but good isn't enough. How am I supposed to deal with that? What's he talking about? I've been taking every gig I can get for twenty years, jamming whenever I can, traveling, pouring every minute and every dime into it, reaching out to every famous musician in the business, sending every person with any clout sample CDs. No one has more passion than I do! And he wouldn't even talk about it."

Ginger felt a little numb around the ears and neck. She was completely flabbergasted. "What in the name of God do you want from me?" she asked, keeping her voice level.

"Tell me what I did wrong because I know my sound is good. I know my performance is at the top of my game—people follow me, just to hear me play. They stand in line! I know a hundred singer/songwriters in the business who aren't as good as I am who are getting more breaks!"

"This isn't happening to me," she said, her fingers on her temples, slowly massaging.

"You've always leveled with me, Ginger. What the hell could he mean? I think if I figure it out, I'll get one more shot with him because he liked me. If I give the right impression, he'll listen to me once more. I won't rush back—I'll make sure he thinks I really put some time and thought into it, but I know he's wrong. I have *presence*. I've been told I could be number one. Probably I didn't take the right music, didn't choose the right songs. I should probably include some more Lynyrd Sky-nyrd. And believe it or not, Neil Diamond works pretty well in auditions. Maybe I should beef up my own music, some of the stuff I sold, but that stuff didn't really score on the charts. Still, I think it was the way it was performed, not the music..."

"Oh. My. God," she said. She stood up and turned to walk away. She was about three feet from the table when he cried out for her.

"Ginger! Please! I know you can tell me what to do! This could be the chance of a lifetime."

She stopped walking and just stood there for a second. "I really am too nice," she said softly. "Maybe Matt is too angry and I'm too nice."

"Ginger, come on, baby..."

She whirled on him. How dare he call her *baby*!

Her eyes must have flashed in rage. "Whoa, Ginger," he said. "Just want your thoughts. I mean, who else would I ask? I want to give him what he wants. He says I don't bring enough emo-tion to the music."

She'd driven an hour. She had her pregnant boss covering for her. There was very little hope that she could get anywhere with Mick, but...

She went back to the table and sat down. She looked into her cup for a moment and when she looked up, he was staring at her expectantly, his eyes huge, waiting for some magic formula that would change everything.

"It's not your sound. It's not your choice of music. It's you."

"Huh?" he asked, thrown back in his seat.

"It's just you."

He was silent for a long moment. "You're still really pissed, I guess," he finally said. "Thanks for nothing."

"No, I'm not pissed," she said. "It's the truth. It's you. You have nothing to give. You have a lovely voice and you're very entertaining. I bet you'll play for people your whole life. In fact, you'll always work, always. But you don't have that incredible, indescribable ecstasy when you play, just pulling the wonder out of the music, because the music is less important to you than being a star. You don't create relationships with the people you play for, you play *at* them. You get ecstasy from schmoozing with stars, from your big dreams. You don't work at getting better—"

"I practice all the time," he argued, cutting her off.

She held up a hand, her eyes closing gently. "You *perform* all the time. You run in a crowd of fans who live to hear you play, hear your stories, praise you, worship you. You name-drop. You've sent out so many CDs to superstars begging for help to make *you* a superstar, the number is probably too high to count. Every time you hear of a new producer, you shoot off your CD before you even find out if it's a good match. You carry them with you everywhere you go. You don't ask people how they are, you tell them all about how great you are. I mean, here you called me all the way to North Bend and you don't even care how I am!"

"Course I do… I just…"

"You don't feel the music in your bones. I bet The Boss has a closet full of your CDs and has never listened to one. You never ask how you can make your music better. And let me guess— when you were at dinner with this Buster character—I bet you mentioned every famous musician you've ever known even if you just ran into them once in the men's room."

"Hell, a lot of that is résumé material, you know... I've played with some of those famous musicians, you know!"

"Not *with*, Mick! You opened for a few! You don't get happiness from your art, you want money and fame. The agent is probably looking for someone who's pouring love out, not sucking it in. A singer who gets so much satisfaction from his music he doesn't care if he ever gets paid. All you want is to be a star. Instead of telling this Buster guy how grateful you were for an opportunity to play for him, you tried to show off."

He was speechless for a moment. "It's important, you know, who in the business you've met, who you've jammed with. And if I'm a star won't that mean I'm memorable and satisfying?"

"You have your cart before your horse. Your priorities are all wrong. You can't infuse your music with love until you've loved, deeply and unselfishly. You can't bring joy to the music until you've poured it into life. Same with grief, agony, ecstasy, fierce desire, loss... It's like method acting—drawing on your own life experience to relate as closely as possible to the music, to the lyrics. You have to have those feelings in your life before you can have them in your music. Instead of sacrificing for the sake of a good life, life you can bring to your art, you've been sacrificing for the sake of fame. As you get older you get more desperate, more arrogant. You're looking for your break, not your insight. There's no question in my mind you would do anything to be number one. You'd sell your soul for it. I think you have! And from all I hear, fame isn't that much fun."

"Yeah," he said with a hollow laugh. "Right."

"Well, I promise you money and fame won't hug you on cold, lonely winter nights... Buster saw it. Your passion is for notoriety, not for art. It's empty, Mick. It's not real. But great music and feeling joy from creating it, conveying authentic feelings, that's real. You should learn to pull up the emotions of an experience, like meeting or losing the love of your life, and it should be so real you cry! The best sound, the most unique voice, the beauty of your instrument. Emotions you've experienced. That's real." She shook her head. "If you start with your life and your art you won't have to talk about all the great singers you met in the men's room or how many stars have your CDs because it won't matter. Hard, hard work, focus on real living and real emotion, not on the stature you want. It's not just marketing, it's talent. You're not authentic, Mick, that's the problem. You have a good voice and a lot of arrogance. And you're selfish. That doesn't translate well."

He was silent, mouth open slightly. He mulled this over. "You have a great strategy there, Ginger. If he thinks I don't care about success but just want to share my great music…"

She rolled her eyes.

"I think you're really onto something there, Ginger. I think Buster will go for it."

"Good luck," she said, making to rise again.

"Ginger," he said. "You've always been there for me."

"I know. I did my best. But that's in the past, Mick. I have a man in my life and I don't want you to ask for my help again."

"Who is this man?" he asked.

"His name is Matt," she said with a smile. "He's a farmer."

"Seriously? A *farmer*? Wow, I would've never seen that coming!"

"The smartest, sexiest man I've ever known."

"Ever?" he asked.

She leaned toward him. "Ever."

"But hey. We were happy once, weren't we? I mean, I was happy and I thought you were happy. You loved me. You loved my music."

"Uh-huh. And you loved you. It was very compact. I was almost superfluous. You always had very big dreams. They didn't leave much room for anything or anybody else."

He frowned. "What are you saying? That you loved who you thought I'd become?"

"Not really. But I think I might've loved who *you* thought you would become. And I was pretty young—it might've been the way you moved your hips when you sauntered on stage with all that confidence. In the end, it was very lonely. I wish you the best but I'm glad not to be in that relationship anymore. It really wasn't good for either one of us. I'm going now. Don't call my mother again—it gets everyone all riled up. My brothers want to beat you up and gee, if one of them broke your jaw, think how inconvenient..."

"Very funny," he said. "You came, Ginger. Thanks for that. I think your ideas really helped."

"Right," she said. *Strategy. Not hard work or sincerity or honesty, but strategy to get ahead faster, to make money more quickly, to be the top dog. Not to live a fulfilling life and also make good music.*

"And Ginger," he said, causing her to turn back to him. "I'm really sorry about the way things turned out. You were great. I'm sorry about your baby."

Your baby.

It was tempting to correct him, remind him it was his baby. Except really, it wasn't.

"I gotta remember that," he said. "I'm creating relationships with the people I play for. I'm *feeling* the emotion. Like method acting, that'll work."

She just nodded once and left. When she got to the door of the café she turned to look at him and he was already on his cell phone. He was no doubt calling one of his many contacts to explain how he was now putting all his passion and energy into his music without worrying about fame...

It surprised Ginger how tired she was after a meeting with Mick that didn't even last an hour. She was back in Thunder Point before five, just in time to help Grace bring in the sidewalk displays. It took quite a bit longer than usual because Grace was bristling with curiosity about Ginger's meeting with Mick. Throughout the tale Grace let her indignation fly with comments like, "You've got to be kidding me!" and "Unbelievable!" and finally, "Man, you're lucky you escaped!"

"True," Ginger said. "Mick and I have nothing in common. But Grace, who knows—he might really take to fame and fortune. He's pretty shallow. A lot of attention works for Mick."

"He'll never know," Grace said. "Trust me. I've been in the trials where being first is everything. You know what? People think it's luck. And they're right. It's down to luck *after* you've done everything humanly possible to sharpen your skill, *after* you've put in more work and time than anyone else, *after* you've established you have the greatest talent and sacrificed everything else for that one goal. Then it's luck and timing. And then you'll know if it makes you happy."

"I already know it wouldn't make me happy," Ginger said.

"Didn't for me, either. I'm happier in this little shop with my hottie schoolteacher than I ever was in competition. And that's why there's chocolate and vanilla. Because we all need different things."

Ginger grabbed herself a to-go burger from the diner, opened a bottle of red wine and looked forward to an evening in her little hideaway—alone. After half a burger and one glass of wine, she just reclined on the couch and let her eyes close.

She awoke to the twittering of her phone and sat up with a start. *Matt*, she thought. He called every night even though he was so tired. It was pitch-black out. She grabbed for the phone and checked the time. It was so late for him to call; it was after ten. He must be exhausted.

"Matt," she said, answering.

"Ginger, are you out this evening?"

"Huh? Out? No, I'm home. I fell asleep on the couch. I must've been—"

"I knocked. I called and I knocked."

"You…?" It took her a second and then with a cry she jumped off the couch and ran to her back door, throwing it open. And then she threw herself into his arms. "Oh, God, it's so late! It's not the weekend! What are you doing here?"

"I stole a night," he said, burying his face in her neck. "Let's not talk too much. Let's just make love."

"Good idea. We've had enough talks for a while."

"I need a shower," he said. "Then I need you."

She ran her fingers through his hair. It was getting too long and it made her smile. "Then let's not waste a minute."

In the end she shared his shower, helped dry him off while he dried her and then fell into bed with him. Oh, how she'd missed him! They hadn't been together since Portland and even though they had talked, they had both needed this—love that was kind and happy and filled with tenderness. His touch was gentle yet fiery and she responded as though this man was made for her. He whispered words of love that brought tears to her eyes. As she lay satisfied in his arms, gently touching his stubbled cheeks, she whispered, "The grapes let you go?"

"For a little while. I'm going home to check on a few things at the farm, then right back to the vineyard. Another few days and our work with Sal will be done and we'll start picking in the orchard. On the weekends, in most cases three-day week-ends, our cousins will help. Dysart trucks will be parked on our land for three weeks, loaded with pears."

"Can I come?"

"If you want to, if you feel up to it. It's hard work."

"But you have women helping?"

"A few sisters, sisters-in-law and quite a few teenagers who look at it as a way to earn extra money. The temperatures are dropping. Dad and I will stand watch, in case we have to put out smudge pots, but the forecast is good."

"Will I be in the way? Tell the truth…"

"I'll take care of you," he said. "I'll make sure you know what you're doing, that you don't feel awkward. Maybe you want to ask Peyton if she's coming?"

"I will. I can't believe you snuck away!"

He kissed her temple. "In a couple of days, when I leave the farm to go back to the vineyard, I'll be back. I'd rather spend the night with you than some hairy-legged cousin who snores and farts in his sleep. The only problem is, I have to leave so early. Before sunrise."

"I'll take anything I can get."

He squeezed her. He didn't ask about the phone call, about Mick. She had already decided she would never lie to him. But on that night, so rare and unexpected, she didn't bring it up. She only loved him with every fiber of her being.

Two nights later when he snuck back into her bed during the hours of darkness, he did ask. They lay naked, tangled in each other's arms and legs, and she hoped he didn't feel her grow tense. If he became angry or upset, it would spoil everything and all she wanted was to be like this with him, trusting and confident of his love.

"I talked to him. He was so pathetic and wimpy on the phone I started to worry he might be sick. Maybe dying! I agreed to meet him for coffee in North Bend. I thought I'd better, just for my peace of mind, in case he died or something and my last words were hateful. But he's fine. He wanted my opinion on his career strategy."

Matt rose up on an elbow and looked down at her. "You're making this up."

She shook her head.

"And did you give him advice?"

"I did. I told him that as long as he applied all his attention to being a huge success and none to being a good musician, a good man, he wasn't likely to ever make it. And I suggested that all his bragging and name-dropping could be counterproductive. I also told him never to call my mother again because my brothers really want to beat him up and maybe break his jaw and that could impede his meteoric rise to fame and fortune."

To her great relief, he grinned. "Meteoric, huh?"

"I said it with a great deal of kindness," she said, smiling at him.

"I'm sure you did." He brushed her pretty hair away from her face. "I take it he didn't upset you."

She shrugged. "Only in the usual way. Those regrets, you know."

"You have nothing to regret," he said.

"Oh, I didn't do bad things. I just wish I'd never been so foolish, so naive. I really have nothing in common with him. I could've started picking pears instead and found the man of my dreams long before now."

"You have things in common with me then?" he asked, twirling a little hair around his finger.

"Everything, though it's hard to think about practical things when we're naked together. When we're naked all I can think about is how well we come together, like I was born for this, to be with you. But when I have my clothes on and can think straight, I realize we like the same things, want the same things. I have no trouble imagining why you love your work, why you love all that dirt and manure..."

"That interfering family?" he asked.

"I get the impression from George's wife that she makes sure she gives them plenty of respect and attention but she runs her own home," Ginger said. "She has a career." She looked away. "I won't ever have a career, you know. I have some regrets about that, too."

He kissed her nose. "Be yourself, Ginger. You're perfect the way you are."

She smiled at him. "I *am* good with the flowers."

"So I've noticed." He rolled with her until she was on top of him. "And you're good with me."

"You think so, do you?"

"Oh, yes. You get right into my head and won't leave."

"Oh, dear—I'm a nag."

He slapped her on the rump. "I like it, I think." He pulled her mouth down to his. He moved his hips beneath her. "Nag me a little more now. Before I have to leave you again."

She played with his hair, which had grown and begun to curl. "Something's different about you."

"I'm tired," he said with a laugh. "Nothing's different. Especially the way you rejuvenate me."

In the predawn when he was leaving her, she clung to him. "I hope we can make things work, Matt. I love you so."

"Don't worry about anything. We're going to make it perfect."

Something was different with Matt. Thank the grapes—hours of hard work with very little interaction gave a man time to think things through. He'd been there before. In fact, it wasn't that long ago when he was trying to figure out if it would be safe to let himself fall in love with Ginger. He'd gathered his answers while he worked, silent and introspective.

But while he was communing with the grapes, he was careful not to withdraw from *her*. That had been his mistake the first time he'd sought insight in his crops. This time he had called her at the end of every day. He was going to remember that— your woman needs to be talked to and touched every day. When your woman feels you're moving away, she feels abandoned and alone. And she changes her phone number.

She wanted to marry him but couldn't be wed to his anger. Well, Basque men were a little on the passionate and possessive side and if they got mad, look out. Even sweet old Paco, who had held ten grandchildren on his lap, had his days. He'd had one yesterday, as Matt remembered with a smile. Something had gone wrong with Sal's grape harvester and holy shit, Paco was livid.

It passed pretty quickly. That was the other thing about men in their family. That flame would go up fast and hot and then it was over. Doused. Reference an ice bucket on Matt's head at Peyton's wedding. And aside from some occasional grumbling over the years, Paco had never turned his anger on his wife. His grown sons had been the recipients here and there, but again, once the anger was expressed Paco could move on.

Matt made a resolution. He would go outside, turn on the hose and drench his head before he would ever again turn that black mood he was capable of on his woman. She must never fear or hate him. Ginger was the kindest, most selfless woman he'd ever known. She was so beautiful in her heart. If his words ever touched her with anything less than the purest love, he would be completely ashamed.

They could start with love and trust and go from there. In the spirit of trust, he would do those things Ginger asked him to do. He wasn't sure they would work worth a damn, but if it showed her he was really making every effort, maybe she would be more patient with him. And if he could bite off that temper and she could be more patient, he couldn't think of anything standing in their way. Therefore, he was not going home to dig out the smudge pots or check the fruit, although he would, since he was there. He was going home to work through Ginger's checklist.

CHAPTER EIGHTEEN

"What has your interest so completely?" Winnie asked Lin Su.

She turned toward Winnie. "Come and see," she said. "Here, let me help you up. You should take a few steps anyway."

They made their way together, clumsily but efficiently, to the deck rail. Below them on the beach were two beach chairs under a beach umbrella. Frank sat in one, Charlie in the other, each holding their laptops on their knees.

"Dueling computers," Lin Su said.

"What do you suppose they're doing?" Winnie asked.

"Lord only knows. Charting solar systems for all I know. Charlie's laptop is far less sophisticated than Frank's, but when they sit side by side like that, Frank turns his screen to show Charlie everything interesting he's looking at. He's researching for a paper he has to write when he gets back to MIT. He's a genius."

"I think Charlie might be a genius, as well," Winnie said.

"Nah," Lin Su said. "He's very smart, though. Much of that comes from the fact that he was housebound so much as a little kid. We found all kinds of educational programs for him. It took his mind off not being able to run and play with the other kids."

"We?" Winnie asked.

"Huh? Oh, me and anyone interested, friends or babysitters. Sometimes other nurses or doctors where I was working. A couple of times I had home healthcare patients who encouraged him. He got that laptop from one of my patients when he upgraded his own and gave Charlie the castoff. It's been a lifesaver."

"We've been looking at new models together," Winnie informed her.

"You mustn't do that, Winnie. That computer works very well. It's got a couple more years in it, for sure."

"It's purely selfish, I assure you," she said, turning from the rail to go back to her chair. "I have my assistant, Virginia, still managing my affairs in San Francisco. I've accustomed myself to giving her instructions and projects and then she reports to me. The only thing I've ever bothered with is opening her attachments and looking at what she's done. But Charlie has me going all over the internet, looking at things. I've had to borrow Grace's laptop a few times—it's more sophisticated than mine. I want to sit with Charlie, our computers in front of us."

Lin Su helped her into her chair. "You're not going to see quite as much of him when school starts in a few weeks."

"I have a few ideas about that, as well. Are you satisfied with his educational program?"

"In what way?"

"Do you like his school?"

"It's a perfectly good public school," she said. "Charlie started there last year."

"Was he satisfied?"

"With his studies, I believe so. He didn't complain about the work and he had a lot of homework. He got straight As, of course. He always has."

"Was the rest of his experience good?"

"What do you mean?" Lin Su asked.

"You know perfectly well what I mean. He's not as robust

as other boys his age, though I have to say, a month or so on the beach seems to have given him more color, more stamina. I think we may be in for a growth spurt. So, back to the subject. Does Charlie have good friends at school?"

"He has a few. And if you're asking if he has conflict from time to time, the answer is yes. I think all small boys in thick glasses have those struggles, which is why I won't allow things like Facebook. I've heard too many horror stories."

"I think it makes sense for him to consider a change. You should discuss it with him. His opinion counts the most, I think. But—you come to work here every morning and leave every evening. It's convenient. More important—if Thunder Point can produce an MIT scholarship student they deserve more credit than I've given them."

"But Winnie—I work here. I don't live here."

"I've spoken with Troy. Charlie would be allowed to attend based on that fact. Now, before you want to discuss that this employment is at best temporary let me suggest that my time might not be as short as people think. That's my expert opinion."

Lin Su smiled at her. "And would you mind explaining your wonderful theory?"

"Not at all. I'm trying to catch up with my daughter after years of bossing her around and making her do everything that was important to me rather than what was important to her. I'm making great progress—I think she's starting to actually like me, hard as I make it sometimes. That's one reason. Another reason—she's carrying my grandchild. I'm not giving up a chance to know that baby without a fight. I might die, but it'll be heel marks all the way. And three, I might miss my old body and find the handicaps that come with ALS to be perfectly terrible, but I can cope as long as I have my mind. And by God, I have it. I think the lot of you should be warned—I might hang around for the next two grandchildren. And Charlie's graduation from Harvard."

Lin Su smiled at her. "I agree, stubbornness has played a crucial role in life expectancy."

There was the sound of footsteps on the stairs and the women stopped talking. Charlie came onto the deck first, Frank right behind him. Charlie plopped his backpack on a deck chair. "I gotta get my Nikes," he said, running through the house and out to the car where he kept extra clothes and necessities.

"Hi, Frank," Lin Su said with a smile. "How are you?"

"Good. Excellent. I'm going to take Charlie up on that ridge and show him the flora and where we go to watch whales. I won't be here when they migrate in a couple of months, but I can show him the spot."

"The ridge?" Lin Su said. "The flora? The whales?"

"Yes, ma'am," Frank replied.

"There are bugs up there. Pollen. Bees and plants he hasn't been around. He has a lot of allergies. And asthma."

Charlie was back, sitting down to put his shoes on. "We'll go slow. If I get out of breath, we'll stop," he said.

"But is this a good idea? You've been doing so well! Why tempt fate?" Lin Su said.

"Because tempting fate is fun," Charlie replied.

"Do you have your—"

"Inhaler and EpiPen? Do you ever get tired of asking me that? You think I want to blow up like a blowfish right before I die?"

"If he has to even pull the inhaler or EpiPen out of his pocket, I'll bring him back off the ridge. But insect life is dying off up there with the cooler temperatures and the bloom has died down. But there are still some great species to see. Plus it's a good steady hike and an amazing view."

"I'll be fine," Charlie said.

"Of course you will," Winnie agreed. "Have your cell phone?"

"What am I going to do if I wheeze up there? Call home?"

"I just wanted you to take a few pictures if you see anything interesting. It could be a while till I get up on that ridge to see for myself."

"Right," Charlie said, grinning. Then without any further conversation, he was scrambling down the stairs.

"Don't worry," Frank said. He put his backpack on the chair beside Charlie's. "Can I leave this here?"

"Sure," Lin Su said. "Please be careful."

"We will, but it's not dangerous. It's a path, that's all. He gets shots, he said. He shouldn't have any problems."

When Lin Su was alone with Winnie again, she sat down a little weakly.

"You should have that conversation with Charlie about going to school out here. He needs a little more freedom, a little challenge."

"He has plenty of freedom!" Lin Su snapped. "I've been leaving him alone while I work for the last two years."

"And I bet it's driven you crazy. It would be better if he had a little more freedom while you're nearby to nag him constantly."

Lin Su scowled. "I think it might be time for your nap, Mrs. Banks."

Winnie laughed. "Not on your life."

Grace was amused by the amount of entertainment Winnie was getting out of her new friend Charlie. Any other daughter might've been jealous, but Grace was pleased. Charlie took some of the heat off her, absorbing all of Winnie's opinions and objections and interfering. And because Winnie wasn't his mother, he could take them in stride and dismiss them.

So, the dinner table was occupied with animated conversation about Charlie's trek up on the ridge with Frank. He took a lot of pictures with his cell phone and, he announced triumphantly, he had not wheezed or had any allergic reactions.

Grace had brought home a pan of Carrie's lasagna, garlic bread and salad, what she called a perfect Winnie dinner. Anything

Winnie could stab with a fork or lift with her trembling fingers worked very well for her.

"I used to have a chef, you know," Winnie said to Charlie. "And guess what? It wasn't any better than this."

"Isn't having a chef kind of like someone else's mother making dinner?" Charlie asked.

"Not quite as good as that," Grace said. "Chefs are more in love with the art of their flavors and their presentation than what you really like. I asked for mashed potatoes for years but they didn't come into fashion until a few years ago."

"I love mashed potatoes," Charlie said.

"Then the next time Carrie has meat loaf and mashed, it's yours," Grace said. "I love mashed potatoes, too! What's your favorite, Lin Su?"

"Oh, this is amazing," she said, taking a bite.

"Mom doesn't like dinner that much," Charlie said. "She usually isn't hungry and maybe has a bowl of cereal before bed."

"You cook just for Charlie?" Grace asked.

"Sure. He is always hungry. I make all his favorites and I freeze meal-size portions. Sometimes I have what he's having, but he's right, sometimes I just want a snack."

"Do mashed potatoes freeze?" Grace asked.

"They sure do. You'd be surprised the things you can freeze."

"Mom will freeze one asparagus spear," Charlie said, shoveling lasagna in his mouth.

"That's not so," Lin Su said with a laugh. "But I don't waste. And when I'm cleaning up your kitchen, neither do you!" she said. Then she stood and started picking up plates. "Charlie, when you're done there, will you help?"

"Sure," he said, gobbling two last bites.

"I'll help," Troy said. "Charlie looks like he might need a second helping. Hiking up to the ridge is hard work."

"And I think I'll get ready for bed," Winnie said. "Somehow I missed my nap."

"Yes, I wonder how," Lin Su said, letting Troy take on kitchen duties so she could take Winnie to her bedroom.

Once Winnie had washed up, changed and was settled in bed with the TV on, Lin Su made sure her few evening chores were done. There was a little laundry to fold but she would put it away the next day. She gave the bathroom a quick clean, checked to make sure the extra lasagna and bread were properly stowed and gave the kitchen floor a once-over. The rest of the family was out on the deck with Charlie, watching the sunset over the bay.

"I'm ready to leave, unless anyone needs anything," Lin Su announced to the gathering.

"I'm taking walk on beach before bed," Mikhail said, rising from his chair.

"No one needs anything more, Lin Su," Grace said. "Thank you for everything and I'll probably see you when I get home from the shop tomorrow."

"Good. Let me know if you want me to come up with dinner."

"I'll text you in the morning after I check out Carrie's specials. Have a good evening."

Charlie dragged himself up from his chair and followed his mother out to the car. He slumped back in the seat, worn out from yet another busy day filled with fresh air, sun and exercise.

"I want to ask you something," Lin Su said. "Would you like to go to Thunder Point High when school starts?"

He straightened instantly. "Could I?"

"Troy seems to think you could, based on my work location and schedule. But Charlie, I don't know that it'll be better. You could have issues there, as well."

"I could, but I know people there. I wouldn't be the nerdy strange kid who popped in from out of town. Troy and Spencer are friends. Iris and Seth are friends. Um, I mean Mr. Headly, Mr. Lawson, Mrs. Sileski and Deputy Sileski." Then he grinned.

She laughed. He might not be big but he sure was good-look-ing. "So—you like that idea?"

"I love that idea. Can you do that? Does it cost anything?"

"It's public school. And they have a chess club."

"Cool. Yeah, I'd do that in a heartbeat. But what about…you know… Winnie?"

"She thinks she's going to last a long time and I wouldn't be surprised, but we know the reality—her disease doesn't promise long-term survival. We could have to make another change."

"I get that. But I'd do anything to live in Thunder Point!"

"I know it's nice, Charlie. But there isn't anything I can af-ford in that town."

"But I could go to school there for a while."

"You could, I guess. But you'd have to remember, it could be temporary."

"Mom. Everything could be temporary."

Grace was just about to close the doors to the deck when she noticed something. She went over to one of the chairs and lifted Charlie's backpack. "Uh-oh," she said. "Look what he forgot."

"He might make his mother come back for it. I'm going to run over to Spencer's. He's hooking up the automatic garage door and I said I'd help," Troy said.

"And you think you're the man for that job?"

"Try not to damage my manhood. I do many manly things. I have my own tool belt."

She laughed, but then she kissed him. "All right, then. I'm going to run this over to Lin Su's. She said she lives about fif-teen minutes away. I'll get the address from Winnie and take the Jeep. By the time you're done with Spencer I'll be back."

Grace put the address in her phone before leaving the garage and watched as the directions were calculated. It was calculated as farther than a fifteen-minute drive, but she dismissed that.

She'd beat the GPS at its own game in the past with some clever shortcuts. In fact, she enjoyed that challenge. She wouldn't try it tonight, however. She'd play it safe.

She drove through the south part of Bandon and then east toward Coquille. She passed a barbed-wire-encircled industrial lot where construction equipment seemed to be stored. Guard dogs patrolled inside the fence, an eerie sight. Nearby, there were storage lockers of the large, commercial capacity. A convenience store and bar were on the corner across the street from a run-down apartment complex. Customers were spilling out onto the street with their drinks in front of the bar. A bunch of teenagers were hanging out in the parking lot and a police car was parked nearby, an officer in the front seat. On the other side of the convenience store was a motel. The vacancy sign was flashing, missing the *V.* She passed through a sparse neighborhood comprised of old houses, crossed some railroad tracks, made a few turns and assumed she was leaving the populated area for the more rural area. Then the nice GPS lady informed her that her destination was on the right and she noticed the entrance to a trailer park. There was an outdoor lavatory attached to a small Laundromat. There were exactly two security lights shining down on maybe twenty trailers of various models. Among the mobile homes was an old Airstream, a few fifth wheels, a couple of abandoned trailers. The ground was dirt and a couple of trailers seemed to be well lit with outdoor lights for the purposes of beer-drinking gatherings or home auto and motorcycle mechanics. There was a police car at the far end of the one-street park. Two officers were cuffing a couple of men who wore jeans and leather jackets and looked dangerous to Grace.

She spotted Lin Su's car sitting next to a very small fifth wheel with one dim light shining inside. It was more of a little camper. The car was parked very close to the single door. And in the yard between Lin Su's trailer and a mobile home a man and woman who appeared to be drunk were having a very loud, very angry argument. The man—who, Grace noted the irony—wore a wife-beater T-shirt and was gesturing at the woman with his beer bottle. The woman wore a bathrobe. And the only vehicle at that residence was an old truck up on blocks.

The squad car was now moving toward Grace. There were two officers in the front and two passengers in the back. The driver pulled up next to her and rolled down his window. "You looking for someone, ma'am?"

"I guess I'm lost," she said with a nervous giggle. "I'm going to turn around and reset my GPS."

"Well, if you're coming to buy something, the drug store is closed."

Grace's eyes grew round. She swallowed.

She drove to the next wide space in the road and maneuvered the Jeep into a U-turn. She drove out of the park, slowly. An elderly man was taking a bag of trash out to a silver garbage can that was chained to a post. She noticed that his mobile home had a screened porch and some patio stones forming a walkway to an ancient Oldsmobile.

The place wasn't a complete ghetto and drug haven. But it was poor. Very poor. And there was no place for a boy to play; no beach or park. She had no idea where the school was but if Charlie had to walk there, he would be crossing railroad tracks, industrial parks, storage lockers and passing the convenience store, bar and seedy motel.

She stopped at the entrance of the trailer park, made sure her doors were locked and turned on the dome light to program her GPS to take her home, though she was certain she could remember the way. Then she got out of there.

She was sure it looked a lot better by the light of day. After all, not having a lot of money was no crime. She even thought about taking a drive out this way the next day to see if her worst instincts were confirmed or if she was just scared of the dark. There was one reality she was certain of—Thunder Point didn't look like that after dark. And if there were drug dealers in town, they were very well hidden. And domestic disputes? Seth hated them, but he took action—no one was waving beer bottles around, yelling at each other in their yards.

When she got home, she dropped Charlie's backpack on one of the dining room chairs.

"Grace?" her mother called.

She went to her mother's bedroom.

"Lin Su phoned," Winnie said. "She wanted me to know Charlie left his backpack behind and that they'd catch up with it in the morning. I told her you were taking it to him."

"I got lost," Grace said. "Rather than hunting in the dark, I just gave up. Would you like me to call her and tell her not to watch for me?"

"I can do it," Winnie said.

"Good. His backpack is on the dining room chair. Tell her I'm sorry she was waiting for me. I made a couple of wrong turns and got frustrated, not knowing where I was going, so I just came home. I figured by the time I got straightened out Charlie would be in bed anyway." She faked a yawn. "Which is where I'm going. Is Mikhail going to watch television with you tonight?"

"I imagine so. He's gone upstairs to get into his comfortable pants and slippers."

"I'm going to lock up and go to bed."

"I thought we never locked anything," Winnie said.

"Tonight I'm locking up. Because...uh, because I usually forget but tonight I remembered. Good night, Mama."

Downstairs in the quarters she shared with her husband she told him about her little adventure. "It's probably not nearly as bad as it looked, but my first thought was—they're very vulnerable living in a seedy neighborhood in a trailer that can barely keep the wind out. I don't know how to handle that. I can't stand to think they might be at risk. Either of them. Lin Su's a single woman and Charlie is a small boy."

"Why don't you give me that address. I'll drive over that way and look around, see where the schools are, what the neighborhoods look like in the light of day, just kind of see if I'd live there. My apartment wasn't exactly high-rent."

"We live in a million-dollar house," she reminded him. "We might not be the most objective."

"Well, Winnie lives in a house that cost a million plus and we live with Winnie. I grew up the son of a teacher and a city maintenance worker. Our neighborhood was safe and clean but it wasn't exactly chi-chi." Then he laughed.

The next day at about noon Troy wandered into the flower shop. He said hello to Ginger then invited Grace to walk down to the deli with him to check out the day's specials. "Then I'll know if I have to make a store run before dinner."

Once they were outside he fessed up. "I went to look around Lin Su's neighborhood. It was pretty well balanced between little old people on fixed incomes without a lot to spare, some unemployed, some down on their luck and some real badasses. I don't know how it looked in the dark but it was pretty tame in the light of day. I'd live there, but I'd have a baseball bat under my bed."

"Oh, Troy."

"I even talked to a couple of folks. They were elderly. I said I was looking for something for my sister to rent and asked if a single woman would feel safe there. One old guy said there was a single nurse in the park and he looked out for her. He'd be just as willing to look out for my sister. That was nice. Not that he could, however. Look after anyone. This old guy was no Rawley, if you get my drift."

"They sell drugs in that trailer park!" Grace said in a heated whisper. "And what is this business about her eating cereal at night? She's always had a perfectly good appetite around here. I think she's saving real food for Charlie."

"Maybe she has debt," Troy said with a shrug. "I'm no stranger to debt. Listen, I think this can be remedied," he said. "I think it would be best if you'd be chairman of this project. Winnie would just offend Lin Su by not approving of her residence and try to give her something. Hell, I'm sure Lin Su doesn't approve of her own residence, but she has to live tight and she has pride. I think there's probably a solution in Thunder Point. Let's start by getting her committed to letting Charlie go to school here. Then we can look around for something affordable. It won't be fancy but I don't think she's looking for fancy. One step at a time, okay? Can you try to be patient?"

"I can try," Grace said. "I didn't sleep well last night. Could you maybe loan her a baseball bat or something?"

"She's a survivor, Grace. She knows it's a bad neighborhood. She's raised a sick kid on a nurse's salary without any family support. She's had to be a survivor and she can take care of herself. Don't offend her. Let's just see if we can throw some better options her way. But you have to go slowly."

"Right. Slow. Not my favorite speed."

"I know, honey."

Charlie waited on the stairs near the beach, backpack beside him. Frank finally came into sight. He hadn't seen Frank in three days. When he got close, Charlie stood. He pushed his glasses up on his nose and Frank mimicked the gesture with a grin. Frank wore his glasses instead of his contacts on the beach because of the wind and sand. Except that when Frank did it, he didn't look like a little nerd. He looked more like Clark Kent.

"Where've you been, man?" Charlie asked.

"Mostly hanging out with Ashley, bud. Gals before pals, pardner. What's up?"

"I've been waiting to tell you. I'm going to Thunder Point High this year. At least while my mom works for Winnie, which I hope will be a long time, but it's not supposed to be."

"Fantastic. I think. Did your mom make that happen?"

"Nah. My mom would never ask for anything. Winnie suggested it, since I come over with her every day. And Troy said it wouldn't be a problem because of her job. I've been dying to tell you. I didn't want to freak out my mom but I'm really glad to get out of that other school."

"Charlie, you've got my number. If you want to hang out just call me. Or text me. Don't sit around waiting."

"I figured you were busy," he said shyly.

"I was. But not too busy for a call or a text. Let's establish something, Charlie. You have any questions or run into any trouble at school, get in touch with me right away."

"What good will that do? You'll be at college!"

"I still know people," he said confidently. "I still have a brother at Thunder Point. He's a good guy. When it comes to problems at school, especially if you're picked on, you gotta let someone know."

"I know people, too," Charlie said.

"Good. Troy and Spencer are both good to know. And there are tricks, like making yourself indispensable as a tutor. But whatever you do, don't try to outrun it or fix it alone. I speak from experience."

Charlie gulped. "Was it bad?"

"When I was about your age and the smallest kid in the class, it wasn't great. I had to depend on my big brother, the football star. I always resented him, except when I was getting backed into a corner. But then the strangest thing happened… I grew. I used to paddleboard a lot in the summer and I grew shoulders. I woke up one morning and I didn't have to look around to see where my brother was to keep from getting knocked around." He grinned. "I'll loan you my younger brother, Lee, yet another athlete. Before I head back east, I'll make sure he knows to introduce himself."

"As my bodyguard?"

"If you need one, let me know," Frank said. "I have a few markers to call in."

CHAPTER NINETEEN

It was only seven in the evening when Matt tapped lightly on Ginger's back door. She filled his arms at once.

"This is what I like," he said. "I love to feel you against me." He looked over her shoulder and saw a take-out bag on her little table. "Oh, honey, you cooked," he joked.

"You made very good time," she said with a laugh. "We could have gone out but I get so little of you these days. I didn't want to share you." She gave his shirt a sniff. "You're clean," she said.

"I had time for a quick shower before I left the farm. But if you feel like a shower, I can get cleaner."

"You like that shower business, don't you? Would you like to eat?"

He nodded. "In the bedroom." She grabbed the sack. He grabbed her wrist. "We won't need that."

"I thought you were hungry," she said.

"Oh, I am." He led her to the bed and got her out of her clothes quickly. He discarded his own and pulled her down on the bed. He began kissing and before long he was making a feast of her entire body, from her lips to her knees. There wasn't a spot he missed—the inside of her elbows, her earlobes, her thighs, her belly and breasts. He finally opened her legs, burying himself in her until she was begging for him to stop. But by that time, he'd become famished for more and he fumbled for the condom so he could get inside her. Once there, he remained still and luxuriated in the feel of her. His eyes were closed and there was a smile on his lips.

"Matt?" she whispered. "Are you going to fall asleep on me like this?"

"I might," he said. "I could stay here forever. This is like home for me."

She moved her hips a little. "Forever would be too long. It would make walking difficult. Take care of business."

He opened his eyes. "You do have a bossy side."

"And a needy side," she said.

"My aim is to please you, my lovely girl."

As he began to move in a way that had become familiar to them, he thought about the great comfort it was to have this kind of love—dependable, trusting, fulfilling, holding such promise for a lifetime of the same. He tasted her on his tongue, filled his head with that special scent of her, a combination of flowers and a musk that intoxicated him and belonged only to this woman, this soft, consuming, perfect woman. He moved rhythmically, deeply, searching for that crazy erotic place deep inside her that awaited him. When he felt that she was getting close, reaching, pushing back, gasping a little in anticipation, he smiled to himself. He knew her body as well as she did, as well as she knew his. And she came, the spasms so hot and tight his vision briefly clouded. And then, giving in to the ache of need, he let go and throbbed with the greatest pleasure he'd ever known.

When he could unclench his jaw, he covered her mouth in a deep and passionate kiss, licking her lips, sucking on her earlobe, kissing her neck and then her breast.

He was made for this, secure in the love of one woman, a woman who knew him and would let him know her completely.

He had a strong libido so there had been women, but they'd been so briefly satisfying. What he had with Ginger was different. He was not just in love with her, he was eager to commit his life to her. It felt like the perfect union, like it was meant to be. He'd never had anything like this even when he'd been married.

Love, he was learning, was deeper and more complex than chemistry, than friendship. It was about the melding of souls. Of trusting someone with your dreams and learning you were safe to do so.

They would talk about this again someday—he and Ginger. This was stuff Ginger already knew and had been trying to explain to him. Ginger had learned this in the same tough, painful way he had. She had learned that she knew everything about Mick, knew and understood his dreams, his strengths and weaknesses. But Mick had known nothing about her.

"I did something," he whispered to her. "I got out of that apartment."

"In one day?" she asked, wide-eyed.

"A little more than that but not much. I made a lot of phone calls, went over there and stuffed my clothes in two big duffels, had everything that wasn't nailed down put in a storage locker. I thought that was logical, in case we want that stuff in our house. But it didn't take me long to change my mind about that. I don't want any of it. When there's time maybe we'll run an ad and sell it. More likely, though, my brothers or sisters will hear I'm not using that sectional or bedroom furniture and borrow it. From that point on we can visit it at one of their houses because I'll never get it back. So it goes in a big family."

She laughed. "How does it feel?"

"It feels good. It feels really good. I didn't think it would matter so I'm a little surprised—the second that truck unloaded into the storage locker and drove off, I felt so much better. I only did it because you wanted me to. I wasn't convinced it had anything to do with anything. I'm appreciative of the things women do to make their houses comfortable, but I don't care about that shit. I think I could live in a cave."

"But not that cave," she said, playing with his hair.

"Not that cave," he said. "But why not?" he asked her. "Memories?"

"I'm sure there were some," she said. "But mostly you didn't really live there. It was even less personal to you than a motel room. You just needed a place to bring the flavor of the week that wasn't under your mother's roof."

"Huh," he said. "By the way, you do know there hasn't been a single flavor since you coldcocked me at my sister's wedding."

"Shoved," she corrected. "I assumed there hadn't been anyone but thanks for telling me that. So, I guess that means we're either staying with my parents when I come up to the farm or we're bedding down in the back of your truck."

"I rented us a little something. It's not much. I'm not going to tell you anything about it. I want your first reaction to be honest. It's adequate—better than being in your old bedroom or the truck bed. It's convenient. And private."

"Is it nice?" she asked eagerly.

"Well, I think so, but you've already seen how wrong I can be about that…"

"It wasn't that apartment that was wrong, Matt. It was you while you were in it that didn't seem right. If you'd liked it there, it would've shown somehow. I'm not sure how, but somehow. I can't wait to see what you came up with for us."

"There is an us, right? Because you're all I think about."

She gave him a kiss. "There's an us, sweetheart. We're just tying up loose ends so our future isn't cluttered with our pasts."

Matt had done something about that, too. He just wasn't sure whether it had worked. He had called Dr. Weymouth, the head of the biology department where he occasionally taught. He told him that he'd commit to three plant biology labs after the harvest if they needed him. And he also said, "Don't wait too long to get your teaching schedule together because I'm getting married. Before Christmas, I hope."

Matt hoped that news might filter through the biology department. If he knew Natalie at all, it would send up her radar. If that didn't happen, Matt would get in touch with her when he had the time.

He left Ginger at four in the morning to drive back to Uncle Sal's vineyard for one more weekend with the grapes. He was planning to come back to her Saturday night. When all the uncles and cousins were celebrating and drinking too much wine, dancing and toasting a successful grape harvest, Matt would drive to Ginger. He'd spend Saturday night and most of Sunday before heading back to the farm to get started on the pears. They were ready.

Matt had five seasonal hands who worked for him during the pear and potato harvest. First they would bring in the pears, which finished ripening in their shipping crates and gift boxes. They handled them carefully, delivering pristine, smooth and clean fruit to the retailers, from grocers to Harry & David.

Then came the potatoes, which were less labor intensive; they were tougher and didn't require gentle handling. Plus, the harvester could dig them and the farm hands would help to separate and bag them.

There were two Dysart semi trailers parked on the property behind the barn and house. Richard Dysart had driven them over himself, one at a time. Matt, Paco and Richard took cups of coffee on the porch. Richard asked after Ginger. "I spent Sunday with her in Thunder Point, a good day. The weather was excellent and she's in happy spirits," Matt said. "She's planning to come up on Saturday. The rest of the family will be here tomorrow sometime and she's anxious to witness this harvest business that will take every second of my time for weeks. And she's more than a little anxious to experience the food the women will put together." What he didn't share with Richard was that it had been three nights without Ginger beside him and it felt like an eternity.

"You make a good argument for the Dysart clan to show up to pick pears," Richard said.

"You are always welcome," Paco said. "I warn you, you might never be the same."

"Nah," Matt said. "The pears won't take too much of a toll on you, but if you really want an experience, come up in the spring for the sheep shearing and lambing. It's exhausting. And not just a little dirty."

Also parked on the property, on the north side of the house, was an RV. From that spot Matt could see the mountains to the north, the orchard to the east and the plot he'd chosen for his house. After the harvest was complete, he'd work with the architect to finalize the plans. At the first blush of spring, they could pour a slab, grade a road for construction access that would be followed by a better road for his personal access to his new home. His and Ginger's home, he prayed.

He'd gone to an RV lot in Portland to look at a couple of rentals, picked the best one and had it driven here. The owners made it available through Thanksgiving. If this worked out, he thought it might be time to buy one of his own. Half the Lacoumette clan had some form of trailer—fifth wheel, camper shell, RV or toy hauler. They moved around to each other's properties for family events, from weddings to funerals, planting or harvesting, reunions, whatever the call. Paco, not one to spend a dime that hadn't been pried out of his tight fingers, had a fifth wheel that could sleep six, on top of each other at that. It was not comfortable, showering and cooking very limited, but it got them to the vineyard, other family farms or the coast where cousins' fishing boats docked. Corinne was not fond of it, to say the least.

Before noon tomorrow the trucks, RVs and other vehicles would begin to arrive.

He was at the far north end of the orchard, checking trees and fruit for the hundredth time when his phone, turned to walkie-talkie mode, sounded off. He heard his mother's voice. "Matt. Natalie is here to see you."

Ah! So she's heard. He had begun to think he was going to have to seek her out. "On my way," he said. He jumped in the Rhino and headed for the house.

His mother had left Natalie alone in the yard to wait for him. She had not been happy about the way things had gone with his ex-wife.

Natalie had a new car and new hair. *A BMW?* It was a few years old, but still. Things must be going well in the secretarial trade. Or maybe some modeling had kicked in for her. He found himself hoping it had. The new hair was no surprise—it was her signature diversity—always different. Dark auburn this time— that had been one of his favorites. Very sexy, very classy look on her. But what was very new for her, she wore jeans, rolled up at the ankle, and tennis shoes. Usually when she wore jeans they were very tight with boots or heels. She also wore a light windbreaker. This was Natalie at her most practical and casual. He couldn't help but be intrigued. She'd never bothered to dress for the farm before.

He approached her and it was instantly apparent that her eyes were glassy.

"Can we talk?" she asked softly.

"Yes," he said. And he noted her surprise. He hadn't been mean or sarcastic or threatened to call security. "Come with me."

He reached out and took her hand and led her around the house to the RV. He pulled a couple of canvas lawn chairs from where they were stored beneath the RV and opened them. "Have a seat."

"What's this?" she asked.

"This is where I live now," he said.

"You weren't at the apartment," she said.

"How did you know to find me here?" he asked.

"Are you kidding me? It's the harvest! Tomorrow the rest of the family will be here."

"You were smart to come today," he said, chuckling. "What did you want to talk about?"

"I heard you're getting married."

"Yes," he said.

"When?" she asked.

"No date yet, but I'm hoping we can do it before Christmas."

"A nice Basque girl?" she asked.

He grinned and it was wholly genuine. "No, a pale, freckly, green-eyed girl. I suspect some Irish lingering back there."

Natalie looked down into her lap. "I wish you the best," she said.

"Thank you. What did you want to talk about?"

"I wanted to talk about…it." She paused and took a deep breath. "I'm sorry. I didn't do it to hurt you."

"Why did you?" he asked. He'd asked a hundred times. Well, at least ten.

"I was afraid. Terrified."

"Of having a baby?"

"Of having a life I wasn't right for! Of eventually being held captive on a farm with a bunch of kids, shunned by the Basque women because I can't cook or sew or grow anything! Of never having any fun again because your idea of fun and mine were completely opposite and it just felt…" She lifted her chin a notch. "It felt like the end. To me it felt like the end. But since I did it I've felt nothing but grief and regret and I don't know how to fix it."

"I told you not living on the farm was okay," he said. "We decided not having a bunch of kids was okay. I said that was my work but didn't have to be yours."

"You *said*, but you didn't mean it," she said. "You didn't have time for me, for our life. And we were always at the farm for family things, family things all the time. And the family, they made me feel stupid and out of place and awkward. They never liked me. Your words were all about, 'It's okay, honey, whatever you want,' unless I wanted to go dancing or out to dinner or to a party my friends were throwing or to brunch at the Monaco or to a concert at Roy's. Does this woman you want to marry by Christmas fit in? Because if she doesn't, you should warn her before she does something that hurts so much."

She started to cry.

She's right, he thought. He'd always talked a good game but his life was the farm and the family and he secretly, deep down, thought she'd come around. If she never fell in love with his work she'd at least fully understand *his* love of it.

He reached over and gave her chair a tug, pulling her closer to him. "Come here," he said. "Tell me what hurts so much," he asked softly.

"God," she said. "You think I didn't want us to live happily ever after? You think I wanted to have an abortion? I couldn't keep spending Sunday at the farm in my best clothes, my *best*, the clothes that all the girls on campus envy, only to have your mother and family speak Spanish or whatever that is in the kitchen and laugh, your brothers and their wives shake their heads like I was some stupid child, to have you put me in a fireman's carry to get me across the barnyard..." She sniffed and wiped at her tears. "I thought maybe I'd be able to figure it out someday, that maybe it would grow on me and I'd start to enjoy the same things, though it wasn't looking good for that. And then what happens? Married less than a year and I get pregnant!"

He felt his mouth go dry. "You couldn't talk to me?" he asked.

She laughed through her tears. "Matt, you always said, 'okay, fine.' Then you did what you wanted. I said those family dinners were awful for me and you said, fine, we won't do so many.

And we went just as often. I said I didn't want to be a farm wife and you said, fine, you don't have to be—but you were at the farm twelve hours a day, sometimes seven days a week. And if you had a day off, which you hardly ever did, we never did what I wanted to do."

"Never?" he asked.

"Hardly," she said. "But that's not the point. I couldn't talk to you because I already knew what you'd say. You'd say, that's great! And tell your family and everyone and then disappear into the trees again. And I'd be alone. Then I'd be alone with a child I wasn't ready to have. I knew eventually you'd get me on this damn farm! Turn me into a drudge."

"Wait," he said. "George's wife isn't a farm wife—she's a physical therapist and has a career."

"And she wasn't at all the family dinners, either. She was busy. She made her own life, but George stayed on the farm. I wasn't sure I could do what Lori did—Lori's so smart and independent and no one ever rolled their eyes at her." She wiped her cheeks. "But I loved you. So much."

He smiled sympathetically. He was guilty as charged. He had ignored her complaints and hoped she'd get over them. He'd married a prissy model and his mother had thought he'd lost his mind. He kept bringing her back to the farm even though she didn't like the landscape, the people or the food. The truth was—he didn't want to go dancing. He didn't give a shit about brunch at the Monaco and thought modeling was shallow and a waste of time.

"I'm sorry," he said. "I think I wasn't a very good husband."

"But…did you ever love me?" she asked.

"Oh-ho," he said, laughing. "I loved you like a freight train! You knocked me out. And I didn't want you to be any different, either. I wanted you to be just exactly the way you are. But I think you're right about me—my expectations were unfair. You couldn't be the way you are with me or with my family. I'm sorry. I thought I was ready to be a good husband. And maybe you thought so, too."

"Are you ready now?" she asked. "Because if you're ready now…"

"Natalie, we made a mistake. We had some good chemistry but that was the beginning and end of it. Everything else we faced as a couple? We couldn't handle it. We were too different. We'll always be too different."

"But now that we know…"

"Now that we know, we have a chance to be smarter the next time around, but I'm afraid not with each other. I'm in love with someone else now." He gestured over his shoulder. "See this RV? I think we're going to live in it while I build a house right over there. An RV, just like all those gypsies in the Lacoumette family." He shook his head. "You don't want me or my life. And, for what it's worth, I still think you're the most beautiful girl in the world. But that won't make it work."

"What about her?" she asked. "Isn't she beautiful?"

"She's beautiful," he said. *Beautiful inside and out.* "You have nothing in common with her, though. I'm not going to keep marrying beautiful women until I find one who does things my way. This woman I'm going to marry—she loves me and my life." He wiped a tear from her cheek. "I'm sorry, Natalie. It wasn't all your fault it didn't work. You picked the wrong guy."

"I loved you," she said with a hiccup.

"I loved you. We have to move on. You're going to find the right guy." He grinned at her. "And have brunch at the Monaco every Sunday!"

"I can't move on until you forgive me. I didn't do it to hurt you, I swear to God. I did it to save myself."

Despite all his effort, he felt that ache in his throat that signaled the threat of choking sobs. "I know," he said in a breath.

"Please tell me you understand."

"I think I do," he said. And then he borrowed Ginger's words.

"I think I see how I was complicit. I do forgive you. Can you forgive me? I guess I wasn't easy."

"Oh, yes, I forgive you, of course." She wiped at her eyes. "If we could run away somewhere, away from farms and modeling jobs and everything, we could be happy, I know we could."

He shook his head. "Nah, it wouldn't work. Neither one of us should try to be someone else."

"I guess that's right," she said. "Will we be friends?" she asked.

He smiled. "What would we do as friends, Natalie? Maybe go out dancing some night?" He shook his head. "Tell you what, kiddo. I'll be in the biology department now and then. If the coffeepot is on, we'll visit for a few minutes. Catch up. But you don't have to invite me to your wedding."

"Because you're not inviting me to yours," she said. It was not a question.

"I don't think we're inviting anyone," he said with a laugh. "We've both had first marriages that didn't work very well. It'll be small and efficient. Then, with luck and experience, we'll work on what it means to be partners. But you? You'll be fine. You'll find the kind of guy exactly right for the kind of girl you are."

"So you really forgive me?"

"Sure. Yes. Doesn't mean I'm not sad about it, but I share responsibility. We married the wrong people, Natalie."

"Okay," she said. "Okay. At least you're not threatening to call the police or anything."

He laughed at her. "I was still mad. I'm not mad anymore."

She put a hand on his chest. "I wish we had a second chance," she whispered.

She really was a sweet girl. So pretty. He kissed her forehead. "No, you don't. Go on now. Start over. You deserve something that really works for you."

She smiled. She stood and walked away alone.

Matt sat in the canvas chair for a long time. He heard her car start. A minute or two later he saw her white BMW turn at the road. He sat another minute. Then he folded the canvas chairs, attached them to the storage device that slid neatly under the RV and went inside.

He hoped Ginger would like this RV. The living room was comfortable with a soft leather sectional and recliner. The kitchen was compact but completely functional, the bathroom large, the master bedroom with queen-size bed was spacious. This one had a deep closet rather than narrow wall units. He wanted her to be okay with this, he really did. But if she didn't love it he would find whatever it took because this time he was going to listen.

He sat down on the sofa and leaned back. They never would have made it, he and Natalie. Now, a couple of years later and a little wiser, he wondered how he ever thought they could. After all this time blaming Natalie, he wondered if the whole thing had been his fault.

But there had been a child. Maybe it had been a little girl with Natalie's puffy, pouty lips and large eyes who would beg him to read one more story. Or a son who would ride on his shoulders and try to smuggle newborn lambs out of the lambing pens. A child of his own, a child who'd love him no matter how narrow-minded or difficult he was, just the way he loved Paco.

He felt the tears well up. Then he felt the waterworks turn on, a gulley washer, flowing down his cheeks. His nose followed suit and he wiped a shirtsleeve across it several times. All illusions about his relationship with Natalie were gone.

But there'd been a baby. A child of his own.

And for the first time since it had happened, Matt grieved.

CHAPTER TWENTY

It was mid-August, school was starting in a couple of weeks and the night air had already chilled in Thunder Point. The flower shop was cool and Ginger wore a sweater. Grace had gone with Troy for some lunch. Soon Troy would be teaching again and his days would be spent at the high school.

Her cell phone rang. She looked at the display and saw it was Matt. She smiled broadly as she answered. "Well now, I hardly ever hear from you at this time of day!"

"I wanted to hear your voice," he said. "I wanted to thank you for being the wonderful, thoughtful, sensitive woman you are."

"Thank you, sweetheart. Are you coming down with a cold?"

"No, just a little sinus thing, I guess. Ginger, you were right. I had a conversation with Natalie. She heard I was getting married and she came to the farm. I...uh...made sure she would hear the news. I phoned the head of the biology department and told him I was getting married. I thought it might get her attention."

Ginger was quiet for a moment. "And? Is she all right? Are you?"

"I made some terrible mistakes, I think. I know I did. I thought the life I chose for myself should have nothing to do

with her. I never really listened to her. I treated her like a mal-
content. A bitchy wife. It was like trying to fit a square peg in a
round hole. She was driven to such desperate measures."

"Oh, Matt…"

"I was so busy being angry I never tried to understand what
really went wrong. I swear to God, I won't let that happen to
us, Ginger."

"You must be devastated," she said.

"She wanted another chance. Can you even imagine what a
mistake that would be?"

"I know," she said softly. And she did know. It had been the
same with Mick. If she had never wanted a traditional marriage
and family, they could have been happy together for a long time.
Of course, Mick needed someone who could be happy helping him achieve success in the music industry and there weren't
many women out there who could sacrifice all their own desires
for someone else's. How was that any different from women who
married doctors or businessmen who single-mindedly concentrated on their own success and ignored their families? "I guess
no one needs a marriage that leaves them lonely."

"Lonely and disappointed," Matt said. "No matter how many
times she told me she just couldn't be happy married to a farm,
I didn't listen to her."

"Farmer," Ginger said. "You mean, married to a farmer."

"No, I meant farm. She needed my commitment and attention. I gave it to the farm instead. And then…and then there was
a child who was lost." His voice became thick again. "I think I
would have liked being a father."

It wasn't some sinus thing, she realized. He was crying. Grieving. He tried to mask it but the revelation had taken an emotional toll. He regretted his mistakes in the marriage but he
grieved the loss of his child. If she knew anything about Matt,
and she thought she knew him pretty well, he hadn't allowed
himself to grieve before now.

"You *will* be a father," she said. "You'll be a wonderful father."

"I think you knew a few things I never would have guessed," he said. "I needed to face that loss. I was doing it alone and it just wasn't working. I've never told anyone but you about that loss. I thought it just pissed me off. I didn't know how deep it cut," he said softly. His voice cracked.

"Where are you, Matt?" she asked.

"Oh, I'm alone. Of course. Hiding out in the little place I rented for us. Trying to get my shit together before anyone catches on that underneath it all, I'm just a regular human being."

She let out a little laugh but there were tears on her cheeks. "A very remarkable human being," she said. "That must have been so hard to do. I love you."

"I wish you were here," he said. "I'd hold on to you. You're the ballast in my life."

"Did you tell her she was forgiven?" Ginger asked.

"Yes, and I meant it. And I said I was sorry. And I meant that, too, because my God, what if I drove her to it? And just like you said would happen, I feel a little bit lighter. That was a load I didn't need."

And it opened the door to his grief, which was real and powerful, she thought. Holding that back must have been so tiring. Another heavy load that he didn't need.

"Natalie probably did the best she could," Matt said. "I'm not sure I did my best but we'll never know…"

"Matt, we all do the best we can at the time. I know you—you've never in your life set out to do your worst."

"Well, you might be wrong about that," he said. "When I found out about the abortion I didn't want anything but to punish her. I didn't listen to her, comfort her, try to understand her or forgive her. I wanted to crush her."

"And now you've both made amends," Ginger said. "You were kind. You can let go of her and the anger now. Whenever you're ready."

"Did you, Ginger? Let go of the anger with Mick?"

"Sure," she said. Then she gave a little laugh. "Mick is such a comical, one-dimensional character that complete annoyance with his shallowness hangs on, but mostly I feel sorry for him. He's missing out on a lot."

"We're not going to do that—miss a lot," he said. "I think we have an excellent shot at being ridiculously happy."

"I think you're right."

"I miss you."

"I'll be there Saturday. I might even drive up tomorrow night after the shop closes, if that's all right."

"Damn harvest," he muttered. "If it weren't for that, I'd take a leave of absence." He sighed. "I'm going to stick my head under the hose, shake this off and go check my pears."

She laughed. "Call me later. We can whisper in each other's ears until we fall asleep."

When they disconnected and she had slipped the phone in her pocket, she put her head down on the worktable and cried. Matt was such a big, strong man's man it was heartbreaking to think of him crying over the loss of his baby. But it took a big man to admit to real emotions. She wanted to hold him, rock him in her arms, cover his bristly cheeks with kisses, close his eyes and hold him safe against her breast.

Her tears came from the knowledge that they could move on now. They'd really dealt with the past and could forge a future cast in love, trust and hope.

"Hey, hey, hey," Grace said, coming into the workroom. Troy stood behind her.

Ginger lifted her head. "How did you get in without ringing the bell?"

"I think it tinkled, Ginger," Grace said. "You're crying your little eyes out! What's the matter?"

"Oh, dear. Listen, may I have a few minutes to collect myself? Then I can tell you all about it. It's not bad, really. I just need…"

"Sure," Grace said. "I'll be right here."

Ginger made an attempt at a smile and fled up the back stairs to that little loft she'd come to love. She washed her face, patted it dry and went back into the tiny living room.

Where she nearly ran into Grace.

"You should lock the door if you want to be alone," Grace said.

"Oh, man, what are you doing?"

"Butting in," Grace said. "Look, sometimes we need to cry alone, sometimes we need a good friend to bear witness. Can you talk about it?"

Ginger sank onto the sofa. "It's really not as dramatic as it looks. I somehow convinced Matt he had to make peace with his ex-wife before we could move on together. It was a little more emotional for him than he expected but he told me he's glad he did it. In fact, he thanked me for pushing him to do that." She shook her head. "Grace, he was so angry and from what Peyton has told me, Matt's not like that. And I know, having been divorced after a short and unhappy marriage, how feeling like a failure can just piss you off. I wanted Matt to be free of that before we try to make our way together. I just miss him. And God, how lovely for him to say he feels so much better and it was thanks to me. That's all. I got a little sentimental and weepy." She gave a helpless shrug. "I've never been with a man who said I made his life better."

Grace smiled. "I'm with one. It's very nice."

"I know. Troy is perfect for you. He's wonderful."

"Why are you here?" Grace asked.

"Here?" Ginger repeated. "I just thought I'd wash my face and—"

"No, Ginger. Here in Thunder Point. Pack a bag. Drive north." She looked at her watch. "You'll get there before dinner. You can watch the sunset together tonight. You can hold on to each other and talk about the new life you'll have together. Starting now."

"Grace, I can't leave you," she said. "I promised! You're pregnant and your mother is sick!"

Grace laughed. "Oh, I'm going to have to replace you so I hope it works out for you on Matt's big old farm because if it doesn't, I might not have a job for you!" She pulled Ginger's hands into hers. "Listen, my friend, you stepped into my shop and made it possible for me to finish building a house, get my mother transplanted, get her fixed up with a nurse she adores, helped me get married and move! I even made a trip to San Francisco to do a little work on managing that cumbersome estate while you held down the fort for me and even though you were paid a little, you did it all out of the generosity of that great big heart of yours. Now, don't waste any more time. Pack a bag. Quickly. You can come back next week to get the rest of your things."

"How can I leave you that fast?" she whispered. "What if you need me?"

Grace laughed. "First of all, I have Iris and Troy for a while longer before school starts. I have a delivery boy and he's great. I have Waylan, Al, even Seth sometimes helps me cart my stuff inside, though I don't need them—I'm completely capable. Besides, from the second I first saw you with Matt I knew I wasn't going to be able to keep you. Now, are you going to argue with me or are you going to run to him? Run to him so you can wrap him in your arms and tell him how much you love him and how proud you are of him?"

Fresh tears wet her cheeks. "I'm so proud of him," she whispered.

"It's a brand-new life, Ginger. You've waited long enough. Don't waste another minute."

Matt turned on the faucet in the deep sink behind the house, the sink used to wash the mud off vegetables from his mother's garden. He stuck his head under the cold water. He squeezed liquid detergent right onto his head, his curling black hair, and plunged his hands into the lather. He watched the brown dirt flow down the drain with the soap and water. It wasn't a proper shampoo but it would be good enough for now. He lifted his head and shook off the water like a dog would, then he took the bar of soap and the brush and began scrubbing his filthy hands while water from his head dripped on his shirt, leaving his collar wet. He rinsed his hands, scrubbed, rinsed, scrubbed, rinsed and finally turned off the faucet and grabbed the towel. He wiped it down his face and left it streaked with dirt. Drying his hands, he turned. And he saw her again.

He'd been seeing her all day. In exactly those clothes, too—that long, lace skirt, denim jacket and brown boots. He'd finally decided he at least had superior hallucinations when the breeze caught her skirt and lifted it. Some of her soft honey-blond hair blew across her face and she raised a hand to push it back over her ear.

God! She was real!

He threw down the towel and ran to her. She opened her arms and for just a split second he thought, *If I'm dying it's all right because this is the way I choose to go.* Before he could complete the thought, he filled his arms with her. His lips were buried in the soft fragrance of her neck.

"Sweetheart," he said in a breath, holding on for dear life. It took a moment for him to think straight. He should talk to her. Instead, he covered her mouth in a steamy and deep kiss, squeezing her so hard he hoped he wouldn't break her in two. It was the sound of her soft laughter that made him finally let go of her lips.

"You made me all wet," she said. "Fancy bath you have there."

"What are you doing here?" he asked, breathless.

"I needed you," she said. "You needed me."

He pushed a little hair out of her eyes. "When do you have to go back?"

"I don't have to. Well, yes, I do. I left some things behind and I haven't said a proper goodbye to Ray Anne or my friends, but there's no hurry. Next week, maybe. For one night. Or maybe I'll do it in one day."

"What about Grace?" he asked.

"She said she's going to have to replace me." She ran her fingertips through his black, curling hair. "She said the second she saw us together she knew she'd have to replace me. She told me to stop wasting time."

Cradling her head in one big hand, he gave her a tender kiss. "I've always admired Grace. Have I mentioned that?"

"Actually, no," she said, laughing. "I hope I'm not imposing."

He grinned. "Come with me," he said.

He led her around the back of the house to the RV.

"I saw that from the road. Has the family started to arrive already? I thought I had time before—"

He cut her off by lifting her into his arms. "Your castle, my love. If you approve of it, we can get one of our own and live in it while we build."

"It's yours?"

"Ours. It's rented but if it works for you, I'll buy one." He grinned devilishly. "I could come home for lunch."

"I've always been impressed by how enterprising you are."

He turned her so he could open the door to the RV and then they both laughed. It wasn't big enough for him to carry her over the threshold and inside without doing some damage. He put her down carefully.

"Oh! Matt! You did this all by yourself?"

"What do you think?"

"I think it's wonderful," she said. "It might be bigger than that little loft."

"They're getting very fancy," he said. "It has a two-person shower and a whirlpool tub."

"What a wonderful idea, I would have never—"

He grabbed her hand and pulled her into his arms again. "Thank you for making me face the ghosts. I would've fought the past forever and damn, it feels so much better to realize that I can leave some things behind and look at the future with you. I don't know how you know these things…"

"I was only guessing," she said. "But I wanted you so much and I knew I couldn't have you until you were free."

"We're ready now, honey. We have to be ready now because I'm so in love with you, I'm starting to hallucinate."

"You did have a dazed look for a second. Will your parents approve of you living in sin right on their property?"

"I don't know. I don't care. But for your information, we're not going to live in sin for long. At the first opportunity we'll get married. I need you to be my wife. You're already my heart and my breath. Tell me you'll marry me, that we'll belong to each other."

"I think we already do belong to each other, Matt. The rest is a formality. A very sweet formality."

George Lacoumette stood just outside the barn, watching the back of the house where the vegetable sink was. As Paco came out, George put out an arm, blocking him. They stood together, George leaning on a shovel handle and Paco wiping his brow with a kerchief. They watched as Matt rinsed his head, scrubbed his hands and then spotted his girl. They observed as he kissed her brainless, then lifted her into his arms to carry her to that fancy new RV he'd parked at the side of the house. After a little more kissing and whispering, they disappeared inside.

"I don't think Matt's coming to dinner," George said.

"Just as well," Paco said. "We should maybe leave a little nourishment on the step for them."

"They'd have to open the door to find it," George said.

"Let's wash up," Paco said. "Now that the coast is clear."

"Ginger is a nice girl," George said. "She makes a lot more sense for him."

"We'll get a lot more work out of him now," Paco said. "Married men are more reliable."

"You sure he's going to marry her?" George asked.

"Didn't you see?" Paco asked. "He might marry her before dinner!"

★ ★ ★ ★ ★